Carol Margar

Out of Practice

Fiction

Editions Dedicaces

OUT OF PRACTICE
Cover Design: Alerrandre Zeto

Published by:
     Editions Dedicaces LLC
     12759 NE Whitaker Way, Suite D833
     Portland, Oregon, 97230
     www.dedicaces.us

Library of Congress Cataloging-in-Publication Data
     Tetlow, Carol Margaret.
     Out of Practice / by Carol Margaret Tetlow.
     p. cm.
     ISBN-13: 978-1-77076-379-1 (alk. paper)
     ISBN-10: 1-77076-379-1 (alk. paper)

Carol Margaret Tetlow

Out of Practice

Chapter One

'Which do you think would look best?'

Slightly puffed, Clare emerged from the depths of the walk-in wardrobe with an armful of clothes. There was no reply, David, her husband, was reading a journal in bed and lost in its contents.

'Please... I need your advice. This is important.'

There were the beginnings of exasperation in her voice.

'Choose whatever you feel comfortable in,' he suggested, still reading and turning over a page. 'You always look nice' he added as an afterthought, reaching out for his mug of coffee on the bedside table. The sound of coat hangers clattering to the ground made him look up.

'David,' Clare's voice had risen several tones.

With an exaggerated sigh, he threw the British Journal of Psychiatry to the other side of the bed, smoothed the duvet over the lower half of his body and gazed intently at his wife. Clare smiled back at him, mouthing thank you. Now that she had claimed his full attention, she stood at the end of the bed and held one garment after another up for his perusal, balancing one hanger under her chin, so that she could keep her hands free to wave two more about.

'I'd wondered about this black suit. I just love the tiny pleats at the back of the skirt and jacket and it fits brilliantly, but is it a bit funereal? Chunky jewellery would brighten it up though. Or there are the camel coloured trousers that I like and you don't but they look smart and go well with the fawn cashmere V neck jumper you bought me- that's more a casual look. Then there's this blouse but it is a bit see through but I could wear a camisole under it- no I couldn't as it's in the wash-oh damn, so how about the polo neck jumper with the check skirt. No, that's a bit too school-teacherish and too hot. Oh this is so difficult. David, what do you think?'

'I think you'll look great in anything'.

'But which do you like best?'

'I like the blue trousers and pink jumper.'

Clare looked at him and then at the clothes and pulled a face.

'Mmmmm, maybe. Actually, I've just thought of those dark grey trousers and the light blue top – casual and smart at the same time and I feel good wearing them both.'

Her mind made up, she retreated into the wardrobe to hang up the unwanted articles and David watched her with a mixture of mild annoyance and amusement.

'You seem really nervous, Clare, calm down a bit. Come back to bed for a while and have your coffee- you've got loads of time.'

'David, I'd love to but I've got to get a move on, I wanted to get a load of paperwork done before she arrives.'

'But you were working at the surgery until nine o'clock last night.'

'I know- there's always so much to do when a new registrar starts.'

'What's her name again? Where's she from?'

'Emma Morris and she's just finished doing a paediatric job in Manchester.'

'So what brings her to the Yorkshire Dales to do general practice?'

'Her parents are in Harrogate, she thought it would be nice to be nearer home, plus she thinks she'd like to work somewhere rural when she's finished her training. I think she's going to be a really good registrar. When she came to look round, she seemed amazingly self-confident and enthusiastic. All the partners liked her immediately, so it should be an excellent six months while she's with us.'

'And does she know how lucky she is to have you as her trainer?'

Clare, who had been busy dressing and putting on her make-up, stopped what she was doing and went and sat on the edge of the bed next to her husband. She leant over and kissed him.

'Thanks for that, I needed it. You're right, I am nervous. I just want everything to go smoothly, for her and me to get on well and for her to enjoy being a registrar with us. I've been so lucky with all my previous registrars but I still get anxious when a new one starts.'

David hugged her and for a moment he felt her relax. Hoping that this might be a good sign, he tried to pull her down onto the bed. She laughed, wriggled out of his grip and went over to comb her hair and put little gold earrings into each of her earlobes.

Blowing him a kiss from the bedroom door, she left shouting goodbye as she ran downstairs.

'What about breakfast?' David called.

'No time' was the reply and then he heard the sound of the front door closing, followed by the car reversing down the drive.

'Good luck, see you later,' David shook his head as he looked at the clock; it was only half past six. For a moment he looked at his discarded journal and wondered whether to return to the article on personality disorders but decided against it, preferring to curl up under the bed clothes hoping for another hour's sleep before he needed to get up.

Clare and David met at medical school. He was one year ahead of her and he had showed her around when she had come for her interview. She remembered being slightly in awe of this tall, interesting-looking and quite serious young man who seemed so much more mature and wise than she felt. Having done a degree in philosophy, he had then decided to study medicine, much to his parents delight as they had never thought that his first degree would lead to a well paid job. For his part, David remembered Clare as a shy, but stunningly pretty girl, who seemed almost afraid to ask any questions but when she did he felt a completely unfamiliar but overpowering desire to look after her and protect her from the evils of the world. Despite their brief initial meeting, he never quite forgot about her and hoped fervently that she would appear in the autumn with the new intake of students. With over two hundred in that year, it took him some time to find her but then within no time at all they became inseparable.

With top grades in all her exams, Clare was an intense worker, a perfectionist. Her relationship with David came as something of a shock to her, having never experienced anything quite like it before. Academically, she slumped badly, fearful that if she did not devote all of her time to David then she would lose him. Separated from him over the Christmas holidays, she battled with emotions varying from joy, because she loved him so much, guilt, because her work had suffered so badly and pain because she could see the worry in her parents' eyes when they looked at her.

It took her the whole of her first year to achieve a balance between her work and personal life, the results of her end of year examinations catapulted her from the bottom to the top ten per cent of her year and just when she thought things couldn't get any better, David proposed to her. She was the first girl in her year to get engaged. Her friends secretly thought that she was rather foolish, committing herself to one man so early in her life, while they partied, got drunk, slept with different men and generally lived up to the archetypal life of medical students. They could not deny, however, that when they saw Clare and David together, it was completely obvious to even the most insensitive of them, that here was a match that was meant to be.

Wedding bells chimed in the village church to celebrate their union two weeks after Clare qualified and there was time for a brief but passionate honeymoon in Southern Ireland. Having known since attachment as a student to a local surgery that she wanted to be a General Practitioner, she was lucky enough to get a place on the local vocational training scheme, following her pre-registration year. Whilst she worked her way through each of the six month jobs, David resolutely pursued his psychiatry training. Working in different hospitals, in jobs that required long and often unsociable hours meant that frequently weeks would pass when they only seemed to catch fleeting glimpses of one another. Rare weekends off that coincided were usually sabotaged by the need to revise for exams, do research or complete written submissions. In the exquisitely precious moments that they did find time to relax together, they would reinforce each other's belief that, when their training years were behind them, quality of life would be re-established, they would find their perfect house and start a family.

Their delight was palpable when David was offered a consultant post in psychiatry, specialising in alcohol and drug addiction. His was a new post, bringing the number of consultants in the department to three and it was through these colleagues that he heard about the partnership vacancy coming up at the Teviotdale Medical Centre in the nearby town of Lambdale He rang Clare from work and she immediately contacted the practice manager, who sounded welcoming, cheerful and very relieved to hear from a female general practitioner who wanted to work full time. After a meeting with the four partners and a more formal interview, Clare was ecstatic when they offered her the job and rushed home, stopping only to buy champagne on the way for a fitting celebration.

She loved the job. This was what she had always wanted. She admired and respected her partners, feelings that were quickly reciprocated as she asked for their advice and heeded their replies. The practice staff loved Clare because she was courteous and happy. The patients adored her for her empathy and the amount of time she bestowed on them. Despite her regularly running late, they would sit and wait to see her, refusing appointments with one of the other doctors instead. They quickly realised that if they asked Dr Clare for a house call then she would visit, even if it was on her way home in the evening.

Life seemed to be on the verge of being perfect. Now both settled in good jobs, in all probability jobs they would stay in for the rest of their working lives, the time could not have been more ideal to start a family. Three, maybe four, children, they'd always dreamed of, though admittedly Clare wondered if maybe two might be better after a particularly difficult delivery she had to attend during her obstetric job. As the first few months of trying passed, they laughed when Clare did not become pregnant, looking forward to more sex, thinking of different ways to excite and surprise each other. Both reasonably healthy, they knew that they were probably working too hard, but felt happily tired rather than stressed and so they pinned their hopes on a two week holiday on the Greek island of Kos. When they set off for this trip, Clare was secretly, nervously optimistic, her period being two days late. The fortnight was sublime, they felt more relaxed that they had for years and Clare could not have been happier when she vomited profusely the day before they were due to return and noticed that her breasts were so tender she could hardly bear David to come near her. As soon as they got back, she rushed to the bathroom to do a pregnancy test only to find the unmistakable evidence that told her she was not pregnant after all. Their hopes dashed yet again, the beginnings of tension started to germinate and for the first time ever, they imperceptibly grew a little apart rather than closer together.

Trying a new approach, they decided that it was time to have some professional advice and consult an expert in fertility. Many tests later, some of which Clare found embarrassing and slightly humiliating it transpired that theirs was another case of unexplained infertility, that there was no apparent reason why they should not have a child. Faced with the next step of assisted conception, they prevaricated about whether to go ahead and decided that they were both still young enough to wait for another few years before having to make that decision.

So it was at this point that Clare decided she needed to do something to take her mind off her worries about getting pregnant, worries that, she had to admit had become over-invasive. Her senior partner at work, John Britton, had called her in to see him at the end of morning surgery and suggested to her that she might like to take over as the trainer in the practice from him. Initially rather taken aback, as this was not something she had ever really considered, Clare had gone home to discuss the idea with David, who had been encouraging and thought that it might be just what she needed. Flattered by the proposal and the support from her husband, she had agreed, gone on the necessary training courses and had had no problems with the interview. The practice was an extremely well thought of training practice, of many years standing and everyone agreed that she was just the person to continue the tradition.

Clare was rejuvenated by her new role. She loved the challenge of teaching, supervising and mentoring, working with new and different personalities as they spent their six months at the practice, learning from her, seeing her as their role model. Inspired by the feedback she got from them, she devoted increasingly more time to the preparation of their education, working late at the practice or shutting herself in the study at home, leaving David to cook the evening meal, which she would then take on a tray back to the computer so that she could continue uninterrupted.

To start with David was glad to see her so taken with training. He had seen the strain of longing for a pregnancy age her, subdue her and sap her of her normal vibrant energy and it hurt him to see her so changed but pretending to carry on as normal. As time passed he began to feel rather left out. He did not particularly enjoy spending evening after evening alone in the house, only being approached for conversation when Clare was planning a tutorial on some aspect of psychiatry. Summer evening walks, ending up at the local pub, trips to the theatre, the occasional dinner with friends no longer seemed part of Clare's agenda and he found himself looking forward to his nights on call, willing the

10

telephone to ring and summon him to the hospital or the police station where he could immerse himself in work and pretend to forget his worries.

He kept trying to re-create some of the warmth and closeness he missed so much. Once, he'd come home early from work, buying flowers and all the ingredients for Clare's favourite meal. He loved to cook and lasagne with a green salad and warmed ciabatta followed by sticky toffee pudding and ice cream, whilst not the epitome of nutritional excellence would always be what Clare chose when they went to their favourite pub. The table was set, the candles lit, the wine opened and chilling in the fridge when Clare rang to say that she was working late at the practice and would grab a sandwich from the café down the road. When she did return home, all traces of David's surprise had disappeared, he was in bed with the lights out and Clare did not even seem to notice when he rolled away from her as she climbed in beside him.

Yet there were some times, like this morning when she seemed so alive, so excited, so like the Clare he loved so dearly and as he lay under the duvet, wishing he could go back to sleep and escape for a little bit longer, he longed to turn back the clock. Maybe they should have tried assisted conception. The local infertility unit had an excellent record of success. They'd never even discussed adoption- perhaps he would try to get her to talk some more at the weekend.

David looked at the time. It was half past seven. Knowing any more sleep was an impossible hope; he switched off the alarm before it rang, got up and went to shower. Choosing his clothes far more quickly than his wife had done he went downstairs, made himself some cereal which he ate while finishing the article he had been reading, grabbed an apple and a banana for coffee time and let himself out of the front door.

Chapter Two

By the time the first of the receptionists arrived at the surgery Clare had completed two folders of paperwork, signed all the prescriptions that were waiting for her, written a difficult referral letter to the rheumatology department about a man with multiple joint pains and a plethora of social problems and drunk two cups of instant coffee which had done nothing to assuage her rather considerable hunger. She rooted through the her desk drawers and found the file containing the information pack for Emma, which included details of her timetable and photos of all the practice staff, with a short biography of each one, to help her settle in as quickly as possible. Grimacing at her own photo, Clare closed the folder and, hearing the unmistakable sound of Joan and Elizabeth talking, went out into the large airy waiting area that was common to all the consulting rooms.

When she had first started at the practice, the premises consisted of a large old house, architecturally intriguing as it was a listed building but geographically a nightmare for patients to find their way round. Clare's office had been on the first floor but she frequently had to come downstairs to consult with some of her more elderly patients who could not manage the stairs and the prospect of putting a lift into the building was an anathema to the local town planning department. So when the opportunity came to have a new health centre built, a few hundred yards down the road, the partners agreed unanimously that much as they loved their original building, it was far from practical and that a move was obligatory. They were not disappointed. The large, specially designed surgery gave all the partners an office on the ground floor, each one having a separate examination room (which was another bonus) but still enough space to accommodate the practice nurses and the health visitors. Upstairs, there were larger rooms for administrative workers and the practice manager, plus the staff coffee room and also an enormous meeting room.

The Teviotdale Medical centre was opened a suitably ceremonious way on a windy Saturday, with John Britton's wife Faye, cutting the gold and red ribbon that arched across the front door to the cheers of almost a hundred patients who had turned up to watch.

'Good morning Dr Jennings. Do you ever sleep?'

Clare smiled at Joan's usual greeting.

'Good morning to you. Have you a moment – I'd just like to check that everything is in place for Dr Morris starting today.'

'Certainly. I can hardly believe it's the beginning of another six months. It goes so quickly, doesn't it? We just get used to the little ways of one registrar and then it's time to start again with the next. Everyone just loved Dr Briggs who left last week. She'll be a hard act to follow.'

As they moved to the back of the reception area the telephone rang, signalling the start of another day at the medical centre.

'Right, here we are. I've put you down to start surgery this morning at eleven, which will give you a couple of hours to do your introductory tutorial with Dr Morris and have a coffee. Then, she'll sit in with you during your surgery- let her see how it's done, eh! I'll organise some sandwiches for the two of you at lunchtime and try to deflect any patients who want you to visit to either Dr Britton or Dr Diamond. This reminds me that they both said that Dr Morris could sit in with them this afternoon, if you felt in need of a bit of time to yourself.'

'That's kind of them but I think I'll let Emma stay with me all day. It'll give us a chance to get to know each other nice and quickly. I know consultations tend to take a bit longer but it's usually worth it. As for visits, I can always do them on my way home tonight.'

Joan gave her a slightly concerned look.

'By the end of today, you'll be exhausted Dr Jennings. You don't want to be doing visits then; you should just be getting off home to that lovely husband of yours and relaxing a bit. I'm sure there'll be nothing that can't wait until tomorrow and if there's something thought to be urgent for today, I'm sure the patients would be happy to see anyone.'

'Okay, but I really don't mind popping in..'

'Enough, 'interrupted Joan,' now as I was saying, I've started booking appointments for Dr Morris for next week. I'm doing it as usual, allowing her 20minutes for each patient until you tell me to change it.'

'Joan, that's brilliant. Thank you for all your work, I know it takes up a bit of your time. Will you be happy to show Emma round reception and let her sit with you for an hour or so tomorrow?'

'My pleasure. I think it helps them to see what life's like in the front line, as it were. Now, I think that's about it, so why don't you go up to the staff room, have a coffee and make yourself a piece of toast and sit down for a bit. Dr Morris isn't due for another 20 minutes or so and I'll put money on the fact that you haven't had any breakfast.'

Clare laughed. 'You know me too well, but, as usual I'll take your advice. I am starving.'

'Off you go; I'll bring her up when she arrives.'

Thus dismissed, Clare dutifully went upstairs and a few minutes later thankfully bit into the first of two slices of toast, smothered with butter and marmalade.

The door to the staff room opened and in bounded Edward Diamond, ever-cheerful, infectiously enthusiastic about all he did, the newest addition to the partnership having joined two years earlier. He had been one of Clare's best registrars, impressed everyone during his time there and was their first choice for a replacement partner when someone left to go and work abroad.

Immediately behind him came John Britton, avuncular, the traditional country GP with his corduroy trousers and tweed jacket, topped off somewhat eccentrically with a red and blue spotted bow tie. He was accompanied by Eleanor Bonnington, auburn-haired and glamorous, who, with her sunglasses perched on top of her head would not have looked out of place in a glossy magazine. Clare looked up and smiled in welcome at them, waving what was left of her piece of toast as her mouth was full.

'Mmmm, toast,' salivated Eleanor, but then shook her head vigorously when Edward offered to make her a piece. 'No thanks. Do you know I put on three pounds last week when we were away on holiday, so now I'm on a strict diet until it's gone again.'

'Ellie, you look just gorgeous as usual,' Edward laughed and handed her a mug of tea instead.

'New registrar here yet Clare?' asked John, sitting down beside her and looking at his watch.

'Should be, any minute now' replied Clare, 'oh and thanks for offering to have her sitting in with you this afternoon – you too Ed-but I'd like to spend the whole day with her.'

'She could have come with me, but it's my half day today,' apologised Ellie.

'No, honestly, it's fine' Clare stressed.

'Just don't forget, this is a training practice. You don't have to do everything yourself' warned John.

The telephone rang.

'That'll be her,' volunteered Ed, 'I'll put the kettle on again for her.'

Clare picked up the receiver.

'Hello, Dr Jennings....... Yes Joan......... really?............ is he on the line now?..... Right, I'll go to my room to take the call. Just give me a minute to run downstairs.'

The others were listening expectantly. Clare shrugged her shoulders.

'It's Matthew Smillie, the Course Organiser. He wants to speak to me. Apparently Emma Morris isn't coming to work with us at all. I'm going to ring him back and find out a bit more. Watch this space...'

'That's odd, it's not often a registrar pulls out at the last minute and it's not exactly good manners. It'll seem strange, not having one for the next six months. Anyway, time for the rest of us to start surgery. We'll catch up with you later Clare and you can fill us in on the gossip then.' John picked up his stethoscope and left the room, followed by the other two, Ed spilling tea as he went.

Back in her surgery, Clare was put through to Matthew.

'Clare, Hi, how are you?'

'Fine thanks, Matt but a bit bewildered at this sudden news.'

'And David? I've not seen him for ages.'

'He's fine but very busy. I don't seem to see a lot of him myself these days.'

'We must all get together soon.'

'That would be lovely. But, Matt, what's happened to Emma Morris?'

'I came into the postgrad centre this morning and there was a letter for me, from her. She's asking to defer her post for a year as she's off to the Far East and Australia with her fiancé. Reading

16

between the lines, I think the boyfriend gave her something of an ultimatum –you know, come with me or it's all off. So that's it – no warning, no apology, no registrar! I'm bloody furious with her.'

'Maybe we've had a lucky escape if she's that sort of person. It'll be interesting to see if she does come back in year, or if you simply get another letter from her saying she's decided to make yet other plans. I'm sorry for you, Matt. You put so much work into arranging the registrar's training schemes and this must mess up your schedules. Don't worry about us, though as John's just said, it will seem odd. Did you know that this will be the first time since the practice started training that we haven't had a registrar?'

There was a short but meaningful pause.

'Actually Clare, that brings me on to the next thing I wanted to talk to you about. Doug Smedley from Market Place surgery in Ravendale has just been approved as a trainer. He was due to have his first registrar start today but he, Doug that is, fell last week on a walking holiday and has fractured his ankle. He's non-weight bearing for at least a month and off sick. So, guess what, that leaves me with a bit of a problem but a rather obvious solution…'

Laughing, Clare responded on cue.

'I can't guess what's coming next Matt. But let me try. Yes, of course, I'll take his registrar. We're all set up here, so it would be ridiculous to try and find anywhere else for them. Tell me more- do I already know him or her?'

'Clare, you are a life saver. He's called Sam Curtis. New to the area, he's transferring up here from somewhere in the southeast. Very experienced, this will be the final six months of his training. I'll fax through his CV to you immediately and give him a call as he's waiting at home to hear what's happening.'

'That's all fine, Matt. Tell him to come to the surgery at about ten o'clock and we'll take it from there.'

'Excellent. Speak to you later and I can't thank you enough for helping out. Bye.'

Clare sat back in her chair and then logged on to her computer and composed a message which she emailed to everyone at the practice about the change of arrangements. Realising then that she had over an hour before Sam Curtis would be arriving, she clicked onto the house call screen and scrolled through the five already booked for that day. It came as no surprise to see that there was one for Prudence Kerfoot, one of Clare's frequent attenders.

There was a tap on the door and Gary, another of the receptionists entered carrying a pile of post.

'Sorry to disturb you, Dr Jennings but we've had Prudence Kerfoot ringing up. In fact she's rung twice, asking for you to visit straight away. She says she's got chest pain and it's terribly severe, far worse than she's ever had before. I suggested when she rang the second time that perhaps she should ring for an ambulance but she won't. What do you think we should do? Shall I dial 999 anyway?'

'Oh dear. It is so difficult to assess what's going on when she calls, she's always in such a panic and rarely talks coherently. Leave that visit to me. I've got time to go and do it now.'

Prudence Kerfoot lived two hundred yards from the surgery in a small, dark, stone cottage. In her late fifties, she had divorced her husband many years ago and was married in all but name to her two cats Minnie and Millie, both of whom were overweight and ginger and seemed to spend most of their time asleep, either in front of the fire, which was always on regardless of the weather, or on top of a teetering pile of clothes and blankets in a moth-eaten ironing basket, propped up against a wall. As they were virtually indistinguishable from one another Clare would repeatedly misidentify them, much to the disgust of their owner who would roll her eyes and heave her enormous bosom, across which her fat, sausage like fingers were clasped together. She liked to see Clare as often as possible, daily if she had her way. Ever the soft touch, Clare tended to acquiesce to her requests for visits, telephone calls or surgery appointments despite her partners' repeated attempts to dissuade her from becoming so involved on a personal level. Once, trying to cut down the number of face to face encounters she had with Prudence, Clare had given her her home telephone number on the strict understanding that she should only ring if it was vital. Prudence had promised that, of course, she would never dream of disturbing Clare at home and had oozed gratitude while she folded up the piece of paper with the number on and wedged it between her breasts. Inevitably, the number of times she rang slowly increased. To start with she would just ring because Minnie or Millie had done something cute or amusing and she could not think of anyone else to share this with but after a few weeks she had adopted the habit of getting in touch at least two or three times every weekend, just ' ringing for a chat, dear' she would claim. David regularly offered thanks to the inventor of the telephone which displayed the number of the incoming caller as he totally disagreed with this arrangement Clare had allowed to grow out of all proportion and repeatedly reminded her of how horrified her partners would be if they knew.

Knocking on Prudence's front door, Clare let herself in. The door was rarely locked, allowing access for meals on wheels and the home help. She stepped with care across a grubby rug with holes in, skirted past the cat litter tray, which needed emptying badly and made her way into the back room, which was where Prudence always was. The tiny window was filthy, making the room seem even darker than it was and there was little benefit to be had from the small angle-poise lamp on the table. A huge dresser took up all of one wall and was groaning under the weight of mis-matched plates, jugs, biscuit barrels and miscellaneous cat ornaments. Cards- some from Christmases or Easters long past decorated every available surface. Mugs of half-drunk tea were lined up on a small table near the fire, next to some scraped out aluminium cartons signifying yesterday's dinner and an ashtray overflowing with stubbed out cigarettes. True to form, Minnie (or Millie) was snoring in front of the gas fire and Millie (or Minnie) was curled up on what looked like an old curtain. On the television, two people were discussing the future escapades in a well known soap opera.

Prudence was in her chair, sitting back against the cushions, one hand clutching the left side of her chest, the other gripping the edge of the table. Her eyes were closed, her lips moving slightly as if muttering a prayer. Her obese body more than filled the chair and her legs, swathed in the bandages that were treating her chronic leg ulcers stuck out in front of her and rested on a footstool.

'Prudence? It's me, Dr Jennings.'

There was no response.

For a moment Clare's heart started to race as she neared her patient, fearing the worst.

'Prudence?' she repeated, reaching out to touch her arm.

One eye opened, as if to check who was calling. A small, watery voice, answered hesitantly.

'Dr Jennings, thank goodness it's you, I feel so ill. Help me please.'

'Tell me what's been happening' encouraged Clare.

Slowly and theatrically Prudence opened both her eyes, with much fluttering of her lids.

'Talk to me Prudence, try, please,' urged Clare, 'when did the pain start? Do you still have pain now? Have you used your heart spray?'

A rather clammy hand landed on Clare's like a tepid jellyfish and squeezed it gently.

'It's so good of you to come, doctor. I know how busy you are with your other patients.' Prudence managed a weak smile. 'The pain came on this morning, just after I'd made my darling Millie and Minnie their breakfast. They do miaow so until they're fed. All of a sudden my chest was gripped by this searing pain, as if I was in a vice or an elephant was sitting on me. I couldn't breathe, I'm quite sure I went a funny colour and the sweat- well it was pouring off me. It was all I could do to get back to my chair here and telephone you.'

Clare could not help but notice that as Prudence gave her history, she became progressively more animated and much more like her usual self.

'So how do you feel now?' asked Clare, shuffling her position as she realised that she was kneeling in something damp.

'Oh a lot, lot better, thank you, now that you're here. I could probably make you a cup of tea –I'm sure we'd both like one.'

'Thank you, but no. Let's concentrate on you. Do you have any pain at all now?'

Prudence massaged her chest thoughtfully.

'No, none whatsoever. It's completely cleared up. You are such a wonderful doctor, helping me like that. How's that beloved husband of yours?'

Clare ignored her.

'I think I'd better examine you, Prudence. I'd like to check your pulse, blood pressure and have a listen to your chest.'

'I'm sure there's no need for that now, dear,' Prudence tried to reassure her, lifting her legs off the footstool, heaving herself to the edge of her chair and lurching forward in a rather uncontrolled fashion to stroke the cat at her feet.

Clare was insistent, thorough as ever and went through her routine checks which revealed nothing amiss. It came as no surprise when Prudence emphatically refused to go either to the surgery or to the hospital for an ecg or blood tests, as she had done on several almost identical occasions over recent weeks.

Wondering whether to broach the subject of inappropriate emergency call outs with her patient, Clare looked at Prudence, who gazed back adoringly at her, eyes now wide open with child-like innocence and her bottom lip on the verge of trembling, anticipating what might be coming. Fully aware that she was taking the easy option, Clare decided to save that discussion for another day, sure in her own mind that there would be one, all too soon.

She spent another ten minutes or so listening to Prudence as she, in manner of many a lonely person who suddenly finds themselves with a captive audience, happily gabbled on about the cats, her leg ulcers, the matrimonial problems of her carer who came in on Tuesdays and Thursdays and the positively disgraceful state of the vegetables in her pre-cooked dinners. When she then returned to her favourite tack of heaping praise and exaltation on Clare, the latter decided it was time to make her exit. Refusing offers of an old box of chocolates (which had been opened at one end) or a bottle of sherry (that Prudence assured her she had only had a couple of sips of), she made her way back into the sunlight, gulping in the fresh summer morning air which tasted as sweet as nectar after the foetid atmosphere of the little cottage.

Chapter Three

It was such a beautiful summer's day that Clare was almost reluctant to return to the surgery. It would have been wonderfully relaxing to be at home, in the garden perhaps, with a cool drink, or doing some gentle gardening. The market square was busy with both locals and tourists visiting the shops or sitting out under the trees in the central pedestrian area. Dogs lay panting by their owners and shorts and tee-shirts seemed to be the order of the day making Clare feel awkwardly overdressed in her trousers and top. She also felt far too hot and wished that she had considered the weather forecast when she had been making her choice that morning.

At the surgery the front doors had been propped open to allow a breeze to permeate the building and patients were sitting fanning themselves in the waiting area. Joan, Elizabeth and the third receptionist, Gary were behind the reception desk, chatting and laughing with a young man, in his late twenties, who was leaning nonchalantly over the counter, oblivious of the queue of patients that was forming behind him. He was tall and blond, with quite a muscular physique suggesting that he liked to keep fit. He gesticulated wildly while he entertained the three of them, confident in their undivided attention. They were all hooting with laughter as Clare approached Joan was actually wiping tears of mirth from her eyes.

Annoyed, Clare joined the four of them, concerned that this did not look very professional and was upsetting other people. She cleared her throat in a rather obvious and irritated way and waited expectantly.

'Ooh, Dr Jennings,' giggled Elizabeth when she spotted her. Gary turned away sheepishly. 'This is Dr Curtis. He's been waiting for you to come back from your visit. He's just been telling us the funniest stories about the last practice he was at.'

'I'm sure he has. Now, there are patients here waiting- please would you see to them.' Thinking that this was far from the good

23

start she had hoped for, Clare turned to the young man. He held out his hand, made confident eye contact with her and smiled broadly.

'Dr Jennings, I am delighted to meet you. Please forgive me for holding up your receptionists. I cannot tell you how relieved I am to hear that my training is not going to be interrupted. Thank you so much for offering to have me for six months.'

Momentarily taken aback, Clare stammered.

'Hello and welcome. Please call me Clare,' she started, adding, unnecessarily,' you must be Sam.'

They shook hands warmly.

'By the looks of it, you've already met these three, so let's go upstairs and I'll tell you all about the practice. We've got about three quarters of an hour before my surgery starts. Would you like a drink? There's tea or coffee but cold drinks as well if you'd prefer. I think it's going to be a scorcher of a day.'

Deciding she was babbling on in an off-putting way, she led the way up to the staff room and they sat down with their drinks.

Sam was, without a doubt, she decided, one of the most remarkably handsome men she had ever seen and she felt rather vulnerable as he continued to stare into her eyes and smile disarmingly at her as though fully aware of his own good looks. Embarrassed, she forced herself to look away and started on her introductory talk that she gave to all her new registrars, hoping she would feel safer and more in control if she could return to familiar territory.

'So, Sam, tell me about yourself. Dr Smillie has faxed through your CV but before I had a chance to read it, I had to rush out on an urgent call. Still, it's better if it comes from you. I often think that one CV looks much like another. Everyone always sounds brilliant!'

'OK, here goes.' Sam took a drink from his mug.' Obviously, I'm Sam. When I first went to university, I read biochemistry, but after graduating, I realised that I wanted to go to medical school. I think maybe with hindsight, that's when I realised that one of my strong points was communication with people and since then I've always known that I wanted to do General Practice. I qualified in Birmingham, did one of my house jobs there and the other one in Solihull –Christ- that was such a dreadful job,' he shuddered, 'and then I went down to the south coast and joined the vocational

24

training scheme there in Brighton. I did six months each of paediatrics, A&E, medicine for the elderly and psychiatry and of course, my first six months in general practice.'

'Tell me about the practice' suggested Clare.

'I suspect very different from this one. Big, eleven partners, eighteen thousand patients, a lot from quite a deprived area, based on three sites, so that was interesting. This practice here sounds as if it will be ideal for me to see how things work in a very different set-up. There are just four partners here, is that right?'

Clare nodded.

'You'll meet them all today, I'm sure. We make a good team, we're lucky enough to have these lovely premises, as you can see. I'll show you round in a moment or two. We only have six thousand patients but they are spread over a large practice area. About a third of them live out of town. We're lucky though; most people manage to come to surgery, so house calls are usually quite light.'

'I just love house calls,' volunteered Sam. 'I believe that to be a good GP, you have to be inherently nosy. There is no substitute for seeing a patient in their own environment. How else can you adopt a truly holistic approach? In hospital, everyone wears pyjamas – the patients that is – and instantly they all look the same.'

Clare beamed at him. He was beginning to sound like a confident and dedicated registrar and unknowingly had echoed her some of her own beliefs.

'I couldn't agree more. But just to go back to the jobs you've done, I don't think you mentioned a gynaecology post?'

Sam shook his head.

'Not, as such, I haven't done a six month post in gynae. My surgical house job involved covering for the gynaecology ward and I also feel that I got a reasonable amount of experience in A&E. When I joined the scheme in Brighton, I had to choose either an obstetrics and gynaecology post or medicine for the elderly. I knew the latter would be more use to me as I have a particular interest in pharmacology and the elderly. In fact I also did a project on falls and how to prevent them.'

Clare was impressed but still concerned.

'Do you feel confident in dealing with antenatal problems or gynae problems that come into your surgery? What about family planning?'

'Well, I think I'm ok. I did not feel it was a problem in my first GP post. I've done my theoretical family planning course as well.'

He could see that Clare looked worried.

'But perhaps we could start off with some tutorials on these subjects, then hopefully you'll feel reassured.'

'That's an excellent idea Sam. I was going to ask you to make a list of your learning needs so that we could sit down together and plan a timetable to take us through the first few weeks.'

'What about my day to day timetable?'

'I've done a printout of it for you. Everything is in an introduction pack- your timetable, details about the practice, helpful telephone numbers, a list of local consultants. It's downstairs in my surgery, but in a nutshell you'll have one or two surgeries each day, house calls four out of five days and your protected teaching time will be on Tuesday, Wednesday and Thursday mornings. Two of those will be with me –I usually plan one tutorial when we both prepare a topic, for example, common gynaecological problems and in the other we do random case analysis –picking at random patients that you have seen and exploring their issues in a wide-ranging fashion. The third tutorial is with either one of the other partners, the practice nurse, the practice manager or we send you out with the district nurse, social worker or to visit the local pharmacy, In other words a chance to experience different members of the primary health care team.'

'Great,' acknowledged Sam, 'I'm looking forward to working here more and more.'

Clare glanced at her watch. 'Time to make a move, I'm afraid. Let's have a quick look around the practice and then you can sit in with me while I do my surgery. I know you've done general practice before but I'd like you to have a couple of days settling in.'

On their way downstairs, they bumped into Elliot Douglas, the practice manager, who gave Sam a welcoming handshake and promised to spend some time with him the next day, sorting out administrative matters. Elliot was a small, intense man in his fifties, hair greying at the temples, half moon glasses balanced on the end of his nose. He ran the practice with army-like precision, rightly proud of his achievements.

'Elliot's married to Gwen, our head nurse. We've a team of four practice nurses in total but the other three work part-time,' explained Clare as she walked with Sam around the building, showing him consulting rooms, the nurse treatment rooms and the small area at the end of the corridor that was the province of alternately a community physiotherapist or chiropodist.

'These premises are just fantastic. Like I said, the last practice I was at was on three sites, one of those was a converted church hall. This is just perfect.' Sam was appropriately impressed as Clare showed him into a consulting room and announced that this was for his sole use during his time with them.

'And this is my surgery. Would you like to bring in a chair from the waiting area and put it over there, next to mine?'

As he brought in the chair, Sam looked around the room. It was very soothing. The walls were a pale peach colour and the curtains at the window a more vibrant ochre and yellow. There was a notice board adorned with posters, one recommending smoking cessation, one depicting ideal heights and weights, one advising on healthy foods and one showing women how to examine their own breasts.

On the opposite wall there were a set of five prints, watercolours, serene and peaceful countryside views. Clare's desk was very tidy, as were the bookshelves full of journals and her favourite text books. Clare saw him taking everything in.

'Feel free to put up some of your own things in your room. You'll be spending a lot of time in there so you should feel at home in there.'

She sat down and logged back into her computer and started to show Sam various things. Glancing at her surgery list, she noticed that the first patient had arrived, so promising to continue later, she rose, went to the door and called him in.

Sam sat quietly, watching her work, greeting all her patients with warmth and respect, listening to them while they told her their problems. He admired the way she coped with the middle-aged lady who brought in a list of seven different problems. He envied the seamless way she leant across for the box of tissues without disrupting the flow of the consultation when a recently bereaved patient burst into tears and had to be comforted. Clare really makes this look easy, he thought. She makes each patient feel special and as if they've been given all the time in the world. It was a pleasure to watch. He dutifully took some notes when some interesting clinical issues arose and answered Clare's questions in an intelligent and thoughtful manner.

'Just one more,' announced Clare, 'then it's lunchtime. I don't know about you but I feel ready for something to eat. I've arranged some sandwiches for us, so we can carry on where we left off.'

Sam, who had been hoping to go off for a while and perhaps even go back home to the house he was renting on the outskirts of the town, managed to cover up his disappointment.

'I'll just get the last patient. It's a new lady, just registered with the practice, by the looks of things. Let's hope she wants something fairly straightforward.'

At the door, she called out a name that Sam did not quite catch and returned into the room followed by a youngish, exquisitely pretty woman, with a vampish, obviously very expensive haircut, long, shapely legs which a denim mini skirt made no attempt to hide and a cropped off top with lacy straps.

'Please come in and sit down. May I introduce myself, I'm Dr Jennings and this is Dr Curtis. Dr Curtis is a doctor who is with the practice for six months while he is training to be a GP. It's his first day today, so he's sitting in, getting to know the ropes. Do you have any objections to him staying? Dr Curtis, this is Rebecca Howarth.'

Sam stood up and reached out his hand. 'How do you do? I'm pleased to meet you.'

'I wasn't really expecting you to have anyone with you. But I guess it's ok.'

Rebecca sat down and crossed one leg over the other in a rather languorous way.

Sam gave her a radiant smile, which Rebecca clearly relished; Clare noticed and made a mental note to keep an eye on this sort of behaviour.

'So, how can we help you today?'

'I just need a repeat prescription for my pill, please.'

'Fine, which one are you on?'

Rebecca laughed, 'I'm hopeless with names but it's in a green and white pack –I knew I'd forget so I've brought a pack with me.'

Clare made a note of the brand.

'How long have you been on this?' she asked

'About three years. It suits me really well, I've had no problems with it at all.'

'Good. I'll need to check your blood pressure please. Are you up to date with your smears?'

'Yes, I had one a year ago, which was normal.'

Whilst she inflated the sphygmomanometer, Clare turned to Sam and asked if he had any other questions he might like to ask Rebecca.

Sam looked a little embarrassed and Rebecca grinned encouragingly at him.

'Er, do you smoke?' suggested Sam.

'I used to, but I stopped 4 months ago when I started going out with my current boyfriend. He's very anti-smoking, so he did me a big favour, persuading me to give up.'

There was a lull.

'Anything else, Dr Curtis?' prompted Clare.

'Of course, I'd like to know a little more about any important part of Miss Howarth's past medical history, whether she is on any other medication at the moment and if she has any allergies at all.'

'Very good,' nodded Clare approvingly. 'Your blood pressure is fine.'

'I wonder if you'd have a look at a mole on my leg please. It's sometimes a little bit itchy, so I thought I'd better get it checked.'

'Of course, 'replied Clare,' how sensible of you to ask. 'It's always better to be on the safe side. Could you show us please?'

Slowly and almost seductively, Rebecca raised the hem of her skirt, revealing yet more of her bronzed limb. Sam gulped and Clare felt uncomfortable but quickly moved round to examine the lesion which was in fact, minute and had no suspicious features at all, so she was delighted to be able to reassure her patient.

'It's absolutely fine. Do you mind if Dr Curtis has a quick look also?'

'Not at all, it'd be my pleasure.'

Clare was relieved to see Sam maintain a very professional air as he examined the mole. She decided it was probably best to try and wind this consultation up in the next few minutes, so taking some details of Rebecca's previous notable illness, which were very few; she printed out her prescription on the computer, signed it and handed it over.

'Thank you so much, Dr Jennings. And thank you Dr Curtis. I do hope you enjoy your time at the practice.'

Clare showed her to the door.

'Good-bye Rebecca.'

'See you later,' was the response and Sam was treated to a little wave and a slightly longer gaze than was necessary before she walked off.

'Wow,' began Sam, but a disapproving look from Clare made him decide not to say anything further. Sensing a slight tension in the air, he started to ask salient questions about some of the patients they had seen together and Clare soon relaxed back into her normal demeanour.

'I've just a couple of referral letters to do now. How about I meet you upstairs in ten minutes? The sandwiches should be up there if you want to start.'

Clare felt she needed some time on her own. When Sam had left, she wrote her letters and then tried ringing David, needing to hear his voice but he was not at home and his secretary at the hospital said he was on a ward round. Knowing that these could take hours, she sighed and went upstairs to find Sam chatting to Ellie and John.

'Hi Clare,' said Ellie, rummaging in her handbag for something. 'I'm just about to go off on my half day but wanted to tell you that I saw that Mrs Wilton with the anaemia and I've referred her to see the haematologist privately. She'd already made her own appointment to see him, so the letter's done. One less thing for you to do, eh?'

'Thanks, Ellie. I see you've met Sam. Are you doing anything nice this afternoon? It's just a perfect day.'

'Picking up Ian and the girls and then taking a picnic up into the Dales and forgetting all about work for a few hours.'

'Sounds ideal,' John contributed, 'wish I could join you but God willing, I'll get my turn tomorrow. Tell you what Clare, why don't you and I and Sam go and sit outside with our sandwiches. It's far too nice to stay indoors and so hot in this room that if I stay here much longer I'll be fast asleep.'

They all left together, Ellie jumping into her little convertible sports car, reversing in a reckless way and screeching off up the road. Leisurely the other three strolled down towards the centre of the market place, found an unoccupied table and spent a companionable hour, swapping ideas and suggestions.

The afternoon went smoothly. Sam spent some time with the practice nurses and then returned to sit in with Clare for the final hour of her surgery.

'It's been a really good day, thank you Clare,' he announced as they were packing up to leave. 'I'm looking forward to tomorrow already.'

Clare was appreciative.

'I'm sure it's going to be a good six months for you. I know it's all a bit of a whirlwind when you start but you'll soon get into your routine and get to know some of the patients. I expect before you know it, you'll have some regulars who want to see you each time.' Hopefully, thought Clare, not Rebecca Howarth.

'Are we done?' Sam was poised to leave.

'Just about. Tomorrow, Elliot wants to spend time with you first thing, then I thought you could sit in with Joan, the receptionist until coffee time and after that, you can come with me on some visits and I'll show you a bit more of the practice area.'

'Excellent. What time shall I come in?'

'Nine o'clock. But remember that's just tomorrow. Once you start doing your own surgery, your first appointment will be half past eight. See you tomorrow, Sam.'

Chapter Four

The warm evening air began to relax Sam as he drove home. Like Ellie, he had a soft top convertible, but unlike her, he afforded it considerably more respect and drove carefully. He was very relieved that his first day was over and felt mentally exhausted. It seemed far longer that just ten hours since he had left home that morning and his brain ached from the constant pressure of trying to make a good impression on everyone, plus remember their names. Looking forward to the evening ahead, he could almost taste the ice-cold beer that he knew was waiting for him in the fridge. With any luck, his girlfriend would have made supper, even if it was just salad, but he knew this was in reality a forlorn thought. Gorgeous as she was in many ways, culinary skills did not even feature on her list of life's priorities.

It was a glorious evening, still sunny and hot, defying anyone to remain stressed and he felt infinitely more contented as he drew up and parked outside his house.

They had been lucky to get this house, he reflected as he got out of the car and looked up. At short notice and in the height of summer, Sam had been afraid that most rental properties would be let out to holiday makers but the third estate agents he had visited had offered him this small, but double fronted detached house on the outskirts of Lambdale. Built in typical local Yorkshire stone it had a small gravelled over front garden and a slightly larger but deliciously secluded walled area at the back. The house itself was partly furnished which left them some scope to put their own stamp on it and his girlfriend had wasted no time at all in rushing out to buy standard bay trees, one for either side of the front door.

Entering the hallway, he scooped up some letters from the mat and called out a welcome. Music was wafting through the house from the back garden, so pulling off and depositing his tie on the newel post at the bottom of the stairs, Sam walked through the kitchen and went outside, grabbing his beer as he passed the fridge.

Wearing even less than she had been earlier, Becca was sprawled out on an inflatable mattress, making the most of the last sun of the day. She rolled over, looked at him over the top of her sunglasses which were half way down her nose and burst out laughing.

'That was just soooooo funny,' she began.

Sam sat down beside her and kissed her shoulder.

'Becca, it was all I could do not to burst out laughing when you walked in the room. And when you asked us to look at your mole – bloody hell, what were you thinking of?'

Becca pouted, trying to look innocent.

'I needed a prescription. I went into the surgery, which I must say is rather nicer than the one you used to be at, asked if I could register and have an appointment fairly soon. Apparently there'd just been a cancellation and I was offered one straight away. I'd no idea that you'd be in there! Did you let on that you knew me when I'd gone?'

'No,' Sam shook his head. 'I was going to and then I thought maybe this isn't the right time. I'll tell Clare later.'

'She seems nice. Better than that old chap you sent me to see in Brighton. What did you think of her?'

'As a GP, I think she's pretty impressive. As a trainer, I think six months of hard work is looming ahead. She's very intense, very patient oriented, totally dedicated to her job. I didn't even get a lunch break.'

'I hung about for a bit after my appointment, thinking you might be around to give me a lift home but I saw you walking off with Clare and an older man, so I did some shopping and then got a taxi.'

'Does that mean there's something for supper?' asked Sam.

Becca pulled a face.

'No, not really. It's way too hot to cook.'

Taking a gulp of his beer, Sam shook his head.

'Now why doesn't that surprise me?'

Becca stroked his arm and then pulled him down beside her, starting to undo the buttons on his shirt. She took off her bikini top and Sam sighed with pleasure as she began to caress his body, his last thought before he surrendered himself completely to her was that tonight was as good a time as any to try the food at the pub down the road.

Clare arrived home before David. She went round the house, flinging windows and the garden door wide open, willing a breeze to come in and cool down the house. Casting off her trousers and top, she slipped into a cotton summer dress which felt cool and refreshing against her skin. Like Sam, she too was worn out. Whilst she loved her job and loved teaching, she always found that having someone sitting in with her, watching her at work, was particularly challenging, as if it were an examination. She still hadn't quite forgotten the flirtatious atmosphere between Sam and that last patient and his rather over-relaxed manner with the receptionists. Surely Sam had enough sense and experience to remain professional but she could see that his good looks and easy-going nature would be very attractive to women of all ages. And hadn't he proffered his communication skills as one of his strengths? For reasons that she could not really fathom, Clare could not get rid of a rather uneasy feeling that she had had since lunchtime and that refused to go away, even as she sliced tomatoes, washed lettuce and threw together a salad dressing.

David was home by eight. She gave him a big hug which rather took him by surprise and he reciprocated warmly.

'Hello, my darling. How's things? Can I help with supper?'

'It's all done thanks. I've so much to tell you. Let's eat outside shall we?'

David opened a bottle of wine and poured them both a glass. He carried them outside to the patio and sat himself down at the table and drank appreciatively before helping himself to salad, quiche and garlic bread.

''This looks good. I'm starving. My ward round went on and on. The poor senior house officer who was on last night has three acute admissions, two who were acutely psychotic and one manic depressive who has stopped taking her medication because she thought she was better.'

They ate in silence, Clare realised that she too was very hungry. She could feel the wine gently oozing round her body, mellowing her thoughts and dissipating her tension.

'So, how's Emma?' David began.

'Emma?' asked Clare, perplexed.

David laughed. 'Your new registrar. You've not forgotten about her already have you? She' obviously not made much of an impact or did she upset you by not admiring your trousers?'

'Very funny,' Clare glared at him. 'As it happens, my registrar is not called Emma, he's called Sam.'

She explained what had happened and went on to describe Sam.

'He's very good looking, Joan and Elizabeth are already madly in love with him and I'm worried that some of the patients might do the same.'

'Aah,' nodded David, 'you mean you're about to have the first case of de Clarambault's syndrome at Teviotdale Medical Centre?'

Clare looked at him.

'That rings a bell but I can't remember for the life of me what it is.'

'It's when a woman develops a delusion that a man is in love with her. The man is usually someone of a higher social standing. Hence it can happen between a patient and her doctor.'

'Then what happens?' Clare began to look worried.

'Oh it's an all-encompassing passion, the patient dogs the doctor with letters, invitations, turns up for appointments wearing all their best clothes, stalks him, you know, that sort of thing.'

'What?'

Clare looked horrified.

'It's incredibly rare. Don't worry. I'm sure this guy will be fine. Does he have a wife and family? Why's he moved up here?'

'Are you sure it's rare?'

'I'm sure. I've never seen a case myself.'

Looking somewhat mollified, Clare allowed herself to smile.

'Do you know, I don't know anything about his home circumstances? We've talked so much today about work and his previous jobs that I've never got round to it. But I'll find out tomorrow.'

'What are your first impressions Clare, you've always been pretty intuitive.'

'He seems a nice guy. He's always wanted to be a GP; he made some insightful comments today in surgery. He's impressed by the surgery and seems genuinely to be looking forward to his time here.'

Briefly Clare wondered about telling David about her uneasy feeling, but after three glasses of wine and a good meal, it seemed of such little importance that she decided to try to forget about it. David was right when he commented,

'You can't get a much better start than that then. You'll have to invite him over one evening. Is there any pudding?'

'Ice cream?'

'Perfect.'

Clare went back into the house, feeling light-headed when she stood up and wished she hadn't had quite so much to drink.

'Chocolate chip, vanilla or raspberry cheesecake?' she called out, knowing what the answer would be before it came.

'I think I'll have a bit of each please.'

They ate their dessert in companionable silence. David cleared the table, washed up and brought coffee into the lounge where Clare was sitting in a chair with her legs curled up under her, feeling increasingly soporific.

'No coffee for me, thanks. It'll only keep me awake and I'm absolutely shattered.'

David poured himself a cup and sat down, studying his wife and contemplating his next move.

'You look it. Why don't you go to bed? The dishes are done and you're way too tired to do any work in what's left of the evening.'

'It's very tempting but seems rather decadent.' Clare closed her eyes, resting her head back.

'Clare,' began David.

She looked at him.

'Yes?'

'How would you like to go away this weekend? I thought we could go to the sea. The forecast is great and it would do us both so much good to get away from work for forty eight hours.'

'Go away?' echoed Clare.

'Why not?' David seized the opportunity. 'I've been thinking about this for a while. I've booked us into that little hotel just down the coast from Seahouses. We've got the room at the front that looks out over the sea. We can walk, sunbathe – I might even swim if it's this hot.'

Clare was sitting upright by now.

'David, I'd love to but I can't. I've so much I have to do. I've to plan Sam's curriculum of learning and his first tutorial and then there's a presentation I've promised to do for Elliott for the next practice meeting.'

David was exasperated.

'Clare, all of that can wait. Don't you think we deserve some time off? What about us? Tell me when the last time was that we went out together and had fun? This evening has been wonderful, just us, sitting and eating together, relaxing and talking. I can't honestly remember the last time we did that. I miss doing that. This evening has made me realise how much. I want to laugh, but even more, I want to hear you laugh. I want to walk barefoot in the sand with you, splash in the waves, hold you –stupid stuff like that, I know it sounds corny but what's wrong with that? Please come with me this weekend. I love you Clare, so much, but I miss you. Please..'

Clare was shocked by his impassioned speech.

'And I love you too, David. I'm sorry I'm busy but you've been busy too, so it's not just my fault. But, and I'm sorry about this as well, I cannot get away this weekend. I have to do these things. You should understand. You know how I like to do things properly.'

'It would do no harm to have some time off. You'd easily catch up on Monday, or, if you like, we could come home earlier on the Sunday. How about that?'

Pleased with his compromise, he looked imploringly at her but she shook her head.

'No, I'm sorry. Look, we've got two weeks off towards the end of September, so that's less than two months away. We've booked to go to New England to see the Fall, so there's that to look forward to.'

David refused to be comforted by this.

'We need to get away Clare. I'm not sure what's happening to us and I don't like it.'

'Nothing's happening to us. We're fine. We're just busy with our jobs, like we always are.'

She got up from her chair and came and sat beside him and put her arms around him.

'If that's the case, why haven't we made love for months?'

Clare stiffened.

'Oh dear, I knew we'd get round to that subject. We're just going through one of those phases I think. Work has been hectic for both of us and time has just flown by.'

David put his head in his hands, scraped his fingers through his hair, making it stand up on end and then lifted his head to face Clare.

'I thought if we went away this weekend we could talk about trying again for a family. Perhaps go back to the assisted conception unit and take things further. Or perhaps even talk about adoption.'

Clare hugged him briefly.

'It's a lovely thought. I don't know if I'm ready for all that again. And as for adoption, that's an entirely new subject I've never even really contemplated. The last thing I want to do is talk about this right now. I'm so tired; I can hardly speak, let alone think. Please don't be cross with me but this weekend is not possible. I promise I'll think about the other stuff. Perhaps we could discuss it when we're away in September. How would that be?'

David, too upset to speak just looked at her. He was trying desperately to find the right words to explain how he felt and what he wanted when the silence was shattered by the telephone ringing.

'Oh, shit,' he said, startling Clare as he rarely swore. She got up and crossed the room.

'Hello' she said, 'yes, of course, I'll just get him. It's for you, David, the police station.'

Groaning, David took the call and replaced the receiver.

'I have to go out. There's a guy at the police station they think may need sectioning. He's apparently been found walking through town totally naked apart from a straw hat.'

He gathered up his briefcase and car keys. Kissing Clare gently on the lips, he held her face in his hands and silently pleaded with her, gazing into her eyes.

'You go off to bed. I might be a while. Just promise me you'll think about what we've started talking about. Promise me.'

'I promise David. Drive carefully. I do love you, you know.'

Sam and Becca never actually made it to the pub. After making love in the garden, they had had a cool shower and then tumbled onto the bed, which was where they spent the rest of the evening, lying naked, alternately watching TV, eating takeaway pizza and trying out some virtually impossible positions to make love in which Becca had read about in a magazine.

Mentally totally relaxed but now physically exhausted, Sam was just nodding off to sleep when Becca turned to him and stroked his shoulder.

'We will be alright here, won't we lover?'

Sam rolled over, kissed her and rolled back, pulling the sheet with him.

'Sure, we will, Becs, don't worry about it.'

Chapter Five

Clare was having a difficult surgery. It was another perfect summer's day, the sun shining in a cloudless sky and the temperature heading confidently for the upper seventies. Foolishly, she'd hoped that the faultless weather would have a knock-on effect on the patients that they would be cheerful, their problems short and to the point as they would all be in a hurry to get back outside and enjoy themselves.

She'd had a disturbed night, fluctuating from wakefulness to restless sleep, pervaded by brilliant and unpleasant dreams. David had come back in the early hours. Clare had heard him let himself in and make himself a cup of tea but then, rather than coming upstairs to her, he'd stayed in the lounge listening to music which wafted up the stairs and haunted her in her loneliness. When she woke a hour or so later, he was beside her in bed, a tactful distance from her that spoke volumes, facing away from her. She was unsure whether he was asleep or not, suspecting that the rhythmical movements of his chest were designed to fool her and dissuade her from trying to communicate with him. Finally, waking from some deep ravine of sleep she realised that the alarm had not been set and that they had overslept. Horrified by the fact that there were only twenty minutes before surgery began, she felt woolly headed and achey from lack of sleep. With only time to shower and dress in a long skirt, sleeveless blouse and sandals, she left for work, driving with the car windows open to help her hair dry. Monosyllables only were exchanged with David and the briefest of kisses as she left, the air still being full of tension as yet unexplored, the thought of which filled her full of dread.

'Good morning, Dr J,' Gary greeted her as she rushed past the reception desk towards her surgery. He turned to Joan. 'What does she look like?'

Joan nudged Elizabeth.

'She looks dreadful today. Not like her not to have her hair done and her make up on.'

41

'Poor soul,' Elizabeth shook her head,' She looks shattered. I wonder what's happened. When was the last time we were here before her? I certainly can't remember, can you?'

'I was just about to telephone her house to see if she was ill,' agreed Joan. 'Gary, pop upstairs and make her a coffee and take it into her. We can manage on the desk for a couple of minutes.'

Thankfully, Clare closed her surgery door behind her. She put her doctor's bag behind her desk and walked over to the washbasin and glared at herself in the mirror above. Appalled by what she saw, she covered her face with her hands and took several deep breaths before reaching for her handbag and rapidly applying some mascara and lipstick in the hopes that this would achieve the dual purpose of making her look more human and instilling her with some self-confidence. Neither effect was achieved and combing her shoulder length light brown hair into something resembling her normal style made only a smidgeon of improvement. On the verge of ringing David, hoping to catch him before he left for the hospital, she was distracted by a light knock on the door and the appearance of Gary bearing a large cup of coffee and a plate of digestive biscuits. She smiled gratefully and felt like bursting into tears because someone had been nice to her. She nibbled at the edge of a biscuit unenthusiastically, her mouth felt dry and hostile to the sweetness of the crumbs.

There was no reply when she rang home.

The computer screen informed her that the first two patients were waiting. Scanning quickly through, she spotted several familiar names among the twenty that made up her morning surgery. Feeling as she did, it seemed like some Herculean task lay ahead and then of course there were visits with Sam. Clare promised herself that she would try David at the hospital after surgery finished. She knew he had clinic that morning and then would be back in his office doing letters and writing up notes. Having made a plan in her own mind, she felt minutely better, as if she was getting back some control of the situation and so she allowed herself a couple of minutes to do justice to her coffee before calling the first patient in.

A large, ruddy complexioned lady came bustling in with a number of bags.

'How can I help you today?' Clare began, wishing fervently that it would be a simple request for a repeat prescription of hay fever tablets.

Mrs Arrowsmith settled herself on the chair like a mother hen getting comfortable on her eggs.

'I've made a list, she announced. 'I don't come to the doctors very often. I don't like to trouble you, so I save them up so that I can make my visit worthwhile.'

Clare's heart sank. This was not a good start.

'Now where is it?'

Mrs Arrowsmith opened up her handbag which was the size of an overnight bag and plumbed its depths.

'Ah, here it is.'

She duly unfolded a piece of paper on which Clare could read three items. For a brief moment, Clare felt better, thinking that maybe after all this wasn't going to be as bad as she feared.

Mrs Arrowsmith did some further rummaging in her bag and conjured up a pair of glasses which she swapped with the ones she was already wearing and took a moment to adjust her vision.

'Ooops, no, my mistake. This is my shopping list.'

She turned the paper over.

'Ah, this is it. Sorry doctor.'

Aghast, Clare was confronted with a list of some twelve or more subjects and she instantly knew that, far from being better that she'd feared, it was going to be infinitely worse.

Some twenty minutes later, Mrs Arrowsmith left the room, cheerfully brandishing her prescriptions and looking forward to receiving appointments to the appliance clinic about her orthopaedic footwear and the surgical clinic about her piles.

Fate smiled kindly on Clare and her next three appointments were indeed straightforward and she dealt with them swiftly but efficiently.

Mrs Wilberforce however was another lengthy consultation. A small, angst-ridden lady with prune-like skin that bore witness to the ravages of many years smoking announced defiantly that her depression was no better. No, the new tablets had not helped; in fact she'd had to stop them after only two days because they'd made her veins throb and her skin dry. They'd been no more of a success than the previous ones she'd tried or the two other types she'd been given before that. A well choreographed dance ensued.

For every suggestion that Clare made, Mrs Wilberforce had some cast iron excuse why it would not be possible in her case and no amount of persuasion could convince her otherwise. This went on for over ten minutes before a mutually agreed conclusion was attained with the promise of a repeat performance in a month's time.

By two thirds of the way through her surgery, Clare was feeling more at ease with herself, pacified but the familiarity of her routine and the satisfaction she never failed to get from the interfaces with different personalities.

'Alexa Thetford,' Clare called into the waiting area. 'Hello, how nice to see you, come on in and have a seat.'

'Hello Dr Jennings,' responded Alexa, a fresh, freckle-faced woman in her mid-twenties, looking cool in a smock-like sundress and a floppy straw hat,' I'm pregnant! We're so thrilled!'

Far too professional to let her façade drop, Clare wished for once that it was another patient with a list rather than this particular topic which was so emotive to her this morning.

'Congratulations Alexa. That's wonderful news. How long have you known?'

My last period was five weeks ago. I've done a pregnancy test every day since I was late. I couldn't believe it at first. Will is so excited at the thought of being a dad. What happens now?'

'Have you been taking folic acid every day, like I suggested?' inquired Clare.

'Yes, right from when we first started trying in the early summer. How amazing is it that it has happened so quickly?'

'It's brilliant news. Keep on taking the folic acid until you are twelve weeks pregnant, which will be the end of September. Now we'll run through a few things about diet, alcohol, smoking and pets and I've got a really good booklet you have had to read at your leisure. Then, when we're done here today, I'll arrange for the midwife to contact you and meet up with you and then please come back to see me in five weeks.'

It was impossible not to be infected by Alexa's happiness as they discussed pertinent issues before Clare answered more questions. Alexa seemed positively to bounce out of the room, longing to share her joy with everyone else.

Clare sat at her desk and took a couple of minutes to write up some notes. For a second she allowed herself to imagine what it would be like to have news like Alexa's to share with David. Perhaps he was right and she should consider IVF. If she was honest the thought of the process scared her. Having seen some of her patients go through it Clare secretly doubted that she could cope with the emotional and physical demands that it would place on her.

Shaking herself back to reality she saw the next patients, ironically enough a couple with a newborn baby and a rather recalcitrant toddler, all four of them full of cold. The latter promptly vomited but, a well-timed reflex action by the father at the first warning burp resulted in the child being whisked over to the sink, thus saving the carpet from any insult.

With a sigh of relief, Clare finally saw the last patient leave and closed the door firmly behind them, relishing the peace and quiet, however brief. She sat with her eyes closed, took some deep, controlled breaths and then started to write her customary list of things to be done. The telephone rang.

'Dr Jennings?' It was Joan. 'Two messages. Could you ring your husband at the hospital when you have a moment? The other message is Prudence Kerfoot. She's rung the surgery three times already this morning, asking for you to call her. She's got chest pain again, going down her left arm but she won't let us ring 999 and she refuses to speak to any of the other doctors.'

'Leave it to me, Joan. Thank you.'

Clare dialled David's number and his secretary transferred the call to him.

'Hi,' she started, guardedly.

'Hi yourself. How's surgery been?'

'Oh you know, usual stuff. How was clinic?'

'Good, thanks. Just doing my letters now. How do you fancy eating out tonight? We could go up the dale to the Bull and Dog and sit out by the river.'

'I'd love that David.'

'Fine, I'll book for eight o'clock. See you at home this evening.'

'Great- see you then'

With some relief, she felt as if at least part of a small bridge had been built in an attempt to span the chasm that had developed between them.

A quick call to Prudence established that she would visit her. It would be a good educational experience for Sam; she was sure that he would have many encounters with her in the forthcoming six months.

Upstairs in the coffee room, the other three partners were sitting with Sam, comparing notes and swapping anecdotes from their early surgeries and waiting for Clare to join them.

'Come and sit here,' cried Ellie, shifting a pile of paperwork of the chair next to her. 'Sam, make her a drink. You look shattered. Bad surgery?'

'No, not really. I'm just a bit tired. I didn't sleep well last night. It was so hot and David was called out to the police station.'

'You need some time off. We had just the best ever picnic yesterday afternoon. The girls absolutely loved it and you will just never guess what Ian has promised to get them for their birthday later this month.' Ellie and Ian had twin girls, soon to be nine years old, Virginia and Lydia. 'I think he must have had too much sun!'

'Don't tell me,' Clare said. 'I know. Riding lessons. They've been after those for years.'

Ellie nodded, barely able to control her excitement.

'But not just riding lessons. A pony as well!'

'They must be over the moon, Ellie.'

'It's quite incredible. They've promised to be good for ever more and so far they're keeping to it! Ian's taken them off today to make enquiries at the equestrian centre out towards Dunnington Hill.'

'I bet you wish you were with them,' Clare sympathised.

'Of course I do. But I'll see them at lunchtime and hear all about it and then again this evening! Ian's so enjoying spending time with them, he goes to Milan for a month soon, so he's really making the most of every minute. The plan, such that it is, is that they learn to ride and how to look after a pony and then, if they're still keen, they'll get their own pony later. Hopefully that way, we'll be able to tell if they're really committed to this.'

Clare shot her a look of disbelief.

'Oh I know what you're thinking. Ian's so impulsive all the time that he'll buy the first pony that looks at them, but I really think I've managed to establish some ground rules this time, for once.'

They looked at each other then simultaneously burst out laughing and Clare realised how much better she was feeling. Her head had cleared considerably. Sam was arguing amiably with Edward about the use of statins in the elderly and John was trying to concentrate on a life insurance medical report but struggling because of the noise.

A mobile phone beeped and Ellie reached into her bag to read a text message. She grimaced, still laughing.

'It says, "First lesson this afternoon. Can we have Smudge kiss kiss kiss." '

'Ground rules, eh?' grunted John, looking up.

'Keep us posted, Ellie. It sounds so exciting. Sam, let's go on some visits. Are there many today?' Clare got up and went to wash her mug.

Edward and Sam broke off from their conversation.

'Only four visits so far.' Edward informed them and clicked on the computer screen for Clare to see. 'One of them is for George Clarke, who's my patient with heart failure, so I'll take that one. There are two calls at Bellevue nursing home and then one for a three year old, Abigail Woods.'

'I'll do the nursing home,' volunteered John.

'Then Sam and I will go and see Abigail. I've also promised to look in on Prudence Kerfoot and Betty Aylward, my terminal care patient.'

The others, apart from Sam, groaned.

'Not Prudence again.'

'I don't know how you put up with her Clare.'

'We ought to put her off the list.'

Clare rallied to her defence.

'I know she calls a lot but she has got a lot of problems plus she's lonely and easily gets frightened.'

'We know that, but she really does have you twisted round her little finger, Clare.' Edward knew that saying this would make no difference.

'Maybe so, but she has chest pain this morning. We know she has angina and diabetes, so there may be something serious wrong.'

The others shook their heads.

Putting her mug back in the cupboard, she picked up her things and summoned Sam.

'OK, Sam, let's go.'

'Be right with you,' was the reply as Sam jumped to his feet and bounced past her to open the door for her.

Deciding to visit Prudence first, as this visit sounded potentially the most serious; Clare led the way down the road, turning off the market square to the mid-terrace cottage with the paint peeling off the front door. As they walked, she gave Sam a resume of Prudence's past history, both medical and social. Inside the house, it came as no surprise and some relief to find the patient in her kitchen, buttering some bread while she waited for the kettle to boil. Millie and Minnie, oblivious to their arrival, snored robotically in their usual places. Sam took in his surroundings with some incredulity before fixing all his attentions on Prudence when he was introduced. Clearly delighted to have not one, but two doctors to listen to her tale of woe, Prudence lurched back into her living room and threw herself into her armchair with a dramatic wheeze.

Her chest pain, it transpired, had settled and she now felt back to normal, hence her being in the kitchen.

'I was just going to ring the surgery and tell you not to bother coming round,' Prudence gushed.

Clare, however, took some time to check her over, noticing, while she was leaning over to listen to the back of her chest, two plates of cat food on the floor behind the chair that were besieged by flies. Sam listened attentively to Prudence's version of her past medical history, which was far more verbose than Clare's. He nodded encouragingly, empathised appropriately and even mana-ged to make one or two perfectly timed amusing remarks which Prudence found hilarious and she became noticeably coquettish in her manner towards him.

Starting to feel like a gooseberry, Clare decided to take control over the consultation and so, while packing up her bag, reassured Prudence that everything seemed to be fine and she should try not to worry so much.

Prudence looked after them longingly as they left and Clare felt a twinge of guilt that she had not stayed as long as she normally would have. Pushing this to one side, she quizzed Sam about the problems of patients who contact their doctors too frequently. As usual, Sam relished the discussion and had plenty of points to make, most of which were excellent and Clare rewarded with due credit.

They drove off in Sam's car. It would have made more sense to go in Clare's, so that she could drive, knowing the route but able to take detours to show him points of interest in the practice area such as the local hospice, a residential home for adolescents with learning difficulties and the Bellevue nursing home. However, as Sam pointed out, if they went in his car, they could have the top down and keep cool and Clare saw little point in putting up any sort of protest. It was therefore a rather disjointed conversation that continued as it had to be punctuated by directions to turn right or left at various junctions.

'Abigail Woods, aged three,' read Clare from the printout of visits she had brought. 'Hot, not eating, very drowsy. Ok Sam, what thoughts are going through your head as we drive to see her?'

Sam provided Clare with a more than satisfactory list of differential diagnoses and seemed very pleased when Clare suggested that he should do the consultation and she would simply observe.

Abigail was lying on the sofa, hugging a pink rabbit that was approximately half her size. She looked flushed and wary. Having taken a history from her mother, Sam sat down on the edge of the sofa and started talking to her. Initially quiet and unresponsive, she began to brighten up as Sam directed questions to her and listened very seriously to the answers. She watched while he solemnly examined her rabbit and then allowed him to do the same to her.

'She has an otitis media,' he diagnosed to Clare and then turned to Abigail and her mother,' an ear infection.'

He went on to discuss the pros and cons of antibiotic treatment and Clare was impressed by the rapport he built up with the little girl and her mother.

'That was excellent, Sam,' she congratulated him as they drove off, glad to be back outside in the fresh air.

'Thanks,' acknowledged Sam. 'I just love talking to kids. They see everything in such a simple way. Adults seem to make everything so complicated sometimes.'

Clare agreed whole-heartedly.

'We're off to something completely different now. Betty Aylward is only fifty seven and has terminal ovarian cancer. Like so many other women, she presented with her first symptoms only to find out that the disease was widespread and incurable. She tried some chemotherapy but hated the side effects, so chose to stop. She lives at home with her sister, Doreen. They used to have a dance school. Turn left at the end here and then park anywhere you can. It's that big house over there.'

They walked up the drive together, feet crunching on the gravel and saw the front door open in anticipation. Doreen was waiting for them; she looked tired and thin but welcomed them warmly and offered them tea, which they declined politely. Betty was in bed in her room at the top of a magnificent staircase with a banister made of elegantly twisted spindles, polished and gleaming. Clare tapped on the door and they went into a big, airy room. Two large windows allowed the sun to stream in and the pristine white net curtains billowed in the breeze created by their entrance. The furniture was almost exclusively mahogany. A large wardrobe, a dressing table and a hefty chest of drawers helped to fill the room but were still eclipsed by a magnificent four poster bed. A quilted bedspread of the richest reds was half tumbling off the bed on which there lay a large golden Labrador who raised a lazy eyelid to look at them and then closed it again. Beside the dog and seeming tiny in comparison there was Betty, sleeping, her pale features peaceful in repose but emaciated by her malignant disease. Only the sound of the clockwork mechanism of the syringe driver broke the silence. Motioning Sam to stay where he was, Clare tiptoed over to the side of the bed, patted the dog gently and then stroked Betty's hand.

'Hello Betty,' she whispered.

'Mmmm?' Betty, roused from her slumbers took a moment or two to realise who it was and then smiled and took hold of Clare's hand.

'Don't talk, if you haven't the energy, Betty. Just squeeze my hand or nod your head. Have you any pain?'

'No.' Betty patted her syringe driver. 'No pain, just sleepy. Where's Max?'

'He's here, right beside you, as always.' Clare put Betty's hand on her dog's head and Betty smiled and closed her eyes again. The dog snuggled a little bit closer to his mistress intuitively.

'She's asleep again, doctor,' murmured Doreen. 'I don't think it will be long now, do you?'

Clare agreed and they left the room, closing the door quietly behind them, before talking further.

'I'll be back in tomorrow, Doreen. Ring me anytime if you want me.'

'Thank you doctor. We're doing fine here. So long as she's peaceful like this, I can cope. Of course, Max is the best nurse of all for her.'

Clare and Sam said their goodbyes and walked without speaking to the car. Sam started up the engine, turned to look at Clare and noticed she was surreptitiously wiping a tear from one eye.

'Terminal care is emotionally exhausting isn't it?'

Clare nodded and sighed.

Not having any directions of where to go next, Sam drove off and started to head back for the surgery but then pulled in to the side of the road.

'Hey,' he said, 'it's a beautiful day. Why don't we go and find a pub somewhere and have lunch? We need to chill out a bit.'

Clare glanced at him, surprised, but agreed and he turned the car around and drove out of town.

Chapter Six

Clare directed Sam to a small pub, off the beaten track, more popular with locals than tourists, who rarely discovered it. Whilst looking unremarkable from the front, there was a positively delightful garden at the back, mostly paved over but awash with a huge variety of flowering plants which wove their way up trellises or exploded from tubs, bowls and a variety of less conventional containers such as watering cans, old saucepans and decorative chimneys pots. The tables, shaded by colourful and cheerful umbrellas were mostly occupied but, spotting an empty one, Sam sent Clare to stake her claim while he ventured inside to buy drinks and sandwiches. Clare sat down and put her feet up on the next chair, closed her eyes and leant back, letting the sun soak into her face and bare limbs, cajoling her to relax. She realised how very tired she was. Last night seemed like a lifetime away.

Before she could actually fall asleep, which she could have done very easily, the sound of ice cubes chattering in the glass that was put on the table in front of her made her open her eyes and watch Sam as he sat down. He opened a packet of crisps and offered them to her but she shook her head.

'Thanks, how much do I owe you?'

Sam shrugged.

'Nothing, this one's on me. The sandwiches are on their way. Egg and cress, as requested for you, rare beef and horseradish for me.'

They sat for a while silently, basking in the fine weather, Sam respecting her need not to be disturbed. While Clare was lost in her own thoughts, which he presumed were mostly centred around Betty Aylward, he thought of Becca and what she might be doing. She had promised him that she would go out today and start looking for a job, but he knew that the lure of the sun would have proved too much for her and she would be lying in the back garden again, wearing all or, more likely, part of that impossibly small bikini. He allowed himself to luxuriate in visions of her incredible body until the sandwiches arrived and Clare started talking.

'We shouldn't really be here,' she began. 'We should be back at the surgery, writing up our notes, checking on messages and then having the next part of your introductory talk.'

'Let's do that here. This is a perfectly good spot for a tutorial. In Brighton my trainer used to take me out for walks. Once we went to an art gallery and another time to a museum.'

Clare expressed interest and admitted that she had never done a tutorial away from the practice.

'I've thought about it,' she admitted, ' and I've read that it can be a good way of seeing things from different perspectives, but I've never tried it. Certainly not in a pub at lunchtime!'

She picked at some shredded salad that garnished her lunch. Sam was tucking in , hungrily.

'So, how was Elliot this morning?' she asked.

Washing down his mouthful with a gulp of orange juice and lemonade Sam replied, 'great. Very helpful, just like everyone else has been. We went through my contract, sorted out some details about my pay – all of that sort of stuff. Best of all, he's promised to plan some tutorials with me on practice management. That's a huge area that I know very little about, so I really need to make it one of my main learning points and work on it before I start looking for a full time job when I finish my training..'

'Elliot's amazing,' Clare agreed. 'He lets the doctors get on with the clinical work – the real reason why we're there, looking after patients, safe in the knowledge that the administrative details are being dealt with in the most efficient manner possible. After that, did you sit in reception with Joan?'

'I most certainly did. They were quite busy with telephone calls and patients arriving at the desk but she still found time to make me feel welcome and explain how they all work. The three of them make a good team, don't they?'

Clare put her feet back up on the next chair.

'They're much valued members of staff. We couldn't function without reliable people on the front line.'

'I was surprised to see you had a male receptionist,' Sam commented.

'Yes,' Clare replied,' initially we thought it might be a gamble that didn't pay off, but he's great and the patients think so too. He's really good with them – the young ones think it's cool to be greeted by a bloke, the older ones appreciate his courtesy and the time he takes with them.'

It's only my second day here, but already I feel I know everyone. I feel much more at home in a smaller practice. I think this is definitely going to turn out to be a good move.'

Seeing an opening, Clare asked why he had moved. Sam looked away for a minute, seemingly distracted by two children who were fighting over a sausage. He finished the last mouthful of his sandwich, tilted the crisp packet and poured the final few crumbs into his mouth. He scrunched the empty packet up into a small ball, which he tossed onto his plate and watched while it slowly uncurled.

'It's quite a complicated story,' he began. 'When it came to discussing my second six months attachment in general practice the course organiser offered me three choices. One was to go back to the practice I had been at and the other two were practices of a similar size. I just knew that I wanted to experience a more different type of practice. I mean, how am I to chose the sort of practice I'd like to end up in for the rest of my working life, if I don't take the opportunity of my training jobs to see some alternatives?'

Clare nodded in agreement and offered him her plate of sandwiches

'So, I started to look around for jobs, but as you know, it can be hard to transfer mid-scheme. I wasn't sure which part of the country I wanted to be in and then my brother – Jed- announced that he and his wife were going to New Zealand for a year. He asked me if I would like to house-sit for him and as I knew how nice his house was and the area, I found out who the course organiser was up here and rang him. I was preparing myself for a long daily commute, so I couldn't believe my luck when he told me about the vacancy he had. Then of course I thought things had all gone pear-shaped when I heard that my trainer-to-be had fractured his leg. But it seems that someone up above was smiling on me for once and… here I am.'

He took two sandwiches and ate them without stopping. Clare who, to start with thought that she might feel better for some food, realised that she wasn't hungry at all and motioned to him to finish the others off as well. He looked at her questioningly and in confirmation she pushed the plate even further towards him.

'Not hungry?'

'I think I'm too hot to eat. But I'm thirsty. I'll just get another drink. Would you like one?'

On her return with the drinks, Sam asked her how long she had been at the practice.

'About ten years now,' she answered. 'My husband, David, is a consultant psychiatrist. When he started, some of his colleagues told him that there was a vacancy at Teviotdale and I was lucky to be in the right place and the right time.'

'And what about the others?'

'John, obviously is the senior partner. I suppose he'll be coming up to retirement in the next seven years or so. He sometimes makes threats about going part-time, but that's usually only after he's had a run of bad days. Then when things go smoothly again, he calms down.

'Ellie had already been a partner for a couple of years when I joined and quite soon after that she was off on maternity leave with the twins. She was quite ill with high blood pressure and had the hugest swollen ankles you've ever seen so had to take some sick leave as well. Fortunately after the twins arrived she improved rapidly and then came back to work part-time at first but then full-time once they started school.

'Ed was a registrar, an extremely good one and he joined two years ago when Dylan Morgan went off to work in Africa.'

'You seem a very closely knit bunch of partners,' remarked Sam.

'We are, thank goodness. Oh, we have our minor tiffs and fall outs but nothing that we can't put right over a meal out and a bottle of wine. I think four or five is a good number to have in a partnership. Any more and you start to lose the feeling of camaraderie and it gets a bit impersonal..'

'You're really lucky, Clare. I hope I find somewhere as contented.'

'I'm sure you will Sam. You seem to have made your mark already and that consultation you did just now with that little girl was excellent. And, while we're on that topic, don't forget that you start seeing patients on your own from tomorrow. We'll give you lots of time for each one to start with so that you don't feel under too much pressure for the first week or so. It's familiarising yourself with the computer system that takes the time as much as anything and then gradually increase the number of patients you see until you're running at the same rate as us, ten minutes for each one. If you have any problems, ring me. Don't worry about interrupting me or any of the others. We're all there to help. If it can wait then we can discuss it in the debrief we'll have after surgery is over. Is that ok?'

'That sounds fine. Thanks again Clare.' Sam finished his drink and noticed that Clare was checking her watch. 'Time to make a move?'

Clare stood up.

'Yes, I've got you down to spend this afternoon with the practice nurses. I'll be in surgery, but if you finish before me, which is highly likely, then get off home a bit early and I'll see you in the morning.'

They strolled back to the car and, with Clare's help, Sam navigated his way back to the main road and then into town.

Back at the surgery, Clare had time to write up the notes from her visits and make some telephone calls before her afternoon session began. She was secretly quite pleased that Sam was busy with the nurses as she was only too aware that her mind kept wandering off to consider the forthcoming evening and what she might say to David. She had more or less decided that honesty was the best policy and she would voice her fears and let him know exactly how she felt. Part of her hoped that she might be kept so late at work that going out would become unrealistic but she know that this would only be postponing things rather than dealing with them. She found it amusing how, repeatedly, she could give sound and commonsense advice to patients with anxieties and worries, being eaten up by their indecision but when it came to facing comparable dilemmas in her own life, she was incapable of listening to her own mind. Whilst she knew exactly what she should do, putting it into practice was an entirely different matter. But David was right. Her approach of the ostrich with its head in the sand was totally unproductive, so she must start to be open with him.

Surgery progressed in fits and starts, much as the morning had done. She was pleased to find a gentleman, who had been very depressed when last seen, much improved for his antidepressant medication. A middle aged lady, recently returned from Australia had to be sent to the hospital to either confirm or exclude a thrombosis in her very swollen calf. A child had chickenpox and the grandmother needed a prescription review. Two temporary residents did not impress her when they showed Clare their painful sunburnt shoulders, acquired out walking in the Dales the previous day with no thought of sunblock at all.

Her final patient of the day was an extra patient, squeezed in at the last moment after she had burst into tears at the reception desk, saying it was really urgent and thus melting the heart of Gary. Clare steeled herself for a difficult consultation but it turned out to be a request for the morning after pill and although other aspect of sexual health had to be discussed, it was at least straightforward and not overly long.

Before leaving, she checked with the nurses that Sam had had a useful afternoon. Predictably, their feedback was unanimously positive, he'd won them over with his personality and charm, asking all the right questions and showing interest in their replies. He had gone home about thirty minutes earlier, as had the other partners. Clare tidied her desk, finished her own paperwork and then made her own way home.

David's car was in the drive and he was mowing the front lawn.

'You're in good time,' he shouted, above the noise of the mower, delighted to see her, having worried that she would be late. 'I've nearly finished this, then I'll be in to shower and we can get off.'

Clare acknowledged this with a wave and went indoors, setting her bag down by the study door as usual. Calculating that he would be at least another ten or fifteen minutes, she went upstairs and showered, glad to wash away the stickiness of the day and washed her hair again. At least this time, she would have time to blow dry it into its customary style as opposed to the lopsided mop effect that she'd tried to ignore all day. She chose a dark pink sundress to wear and teamed it with a string of tiny pearls and matching earrings, before sitting on the bed to paint her toenails a brighter, more shocking pink. She still felt exhausted, but at least in some ways refreshed. David bounced upstairs and busied himself around the bedroom, as if trying to infect her with his energy and enthusiasm for the evening ahead. He was desperate for it to go well and for them to agree on the conclusion that he yearned for. Knowing him of old, Clare could see this in his eyes and felt consumed by guilt, her stomach churning with what she hoped was hunger but suspected was something entirely different – fear.

Leaving him to shower she went downstairs and uncharacteristically poured herself a glass of wine, never a good idea on an empty stomach, but hoping that it would calm her down. Briefly she toyed with the idea of a diazepam tablet from her bag but sternly told herself not to be so stupid, that this was just an evening out with her husband who loved her and who would understand. She took a large gulp of her wine, opened the French windows and stepped out onto the patio, breathing in the warm evening air. She listened to the water from David's shower gurgling down the pipes. Neighbours were arguing over a barbecue while children squealed with delight as they played with giant water pistols.

The wine began to have its effect. Her stomach stopped churning, her mind began to relax and calm and she began to feel the rekindling of some self-esteem and self-confidence.

'Ready? You look lovely.' David's eyes surveyed her appreciatively. He too, had made an effort – light beige cotton trousers with a dark blue short sleeved shirt which showed off his tanned arms. As they walked through the lounge the telephone rand and David who was nearest cursed and snatched it up. Clare heard him making one or two very forced pleasantries and then he handed the phone to her.

'It's Prudence Kerfoot. Please, for once, tell her you're about to go out. I'll be starting the car.'

So saying he left noisily and Clare heard the front door bang followed by the car door slamming shut.

Prudence wanted a chat, to tell Clare how nice that young man was who had come with her that morning and to reassure her that she was feeling a lot better. Clare listened patiently but then explained firmly that she did have to go out as she had an appointment to keep. Apparently understanding completely and apologising for bothering her, Prudence promised to be ever so quick but she did just have to tell her what Minnie and Millie were doing at that moment as it was so funny.

Clare heard the car horn beeping impatiently. She thanked Prudence for ringing and managed to bring the conversation to a close but not before Prudence had promised to ring again soon for a longer chat when she wasn't so busy.

David started the engine as Clare emerged from the front door.

Not wishing to say anything that might jeopardise the evening ahead, he wisely chatted about uncontentious matters as they drove to the Dog and Bull, telling Clare about his day, asking her advice about a patient, even passing on one or two snippets of hospital gossip.

The pub was busy and they had to fight their way to the bar to announce their arrival and order food before fighting their way back out to their table by the river. Delicious smells drifted up to them from other diners' plates and the happy chatter around them plus the regular chink of glasses made for a continental atmosphere. They sat down with their drinks, more wine for Clare and a pint of beer for David. Home-made bread, still warm was placed in front of them in a linen-lined wicker basket, together with mats and cutlery. They continued to make small talk while they did justice to the bread until their meal arrived. Clare's appetite, enlivened by her alcohol, looked forward to her salmon with lemon and lime mayonnaise and she helped herself generously to chips.

They both ate well, David announcing that his steak was melt in the mouth. They debated over desserts, both putting up a token protest before opting for the fresh raspberry cheesecake, with ice cream for David and cream for Clare.

Well satisfied with their meal, they say languorously with their cups of coffee watching the river ooze silently past. David was the first to speak.

'I'm sorry about last night, Clare.'

'I know, it's ok, it's as much my fault.'

'I had to say it. I've been bottling it up for so long. We need to talk about things openly. We always used to, didn't we?'

Clare nodded, hands clasped round her cup, gazing into its muddy contents.

'I've cancelled this weekend,' David continued. 'It was stupid of me not to ask you first. But I thought you'd be thrilled.'

'We can go another time maybe. It's never an easy time when a new registrar starts. There's always so much to do. You know that, because you have new junior staff at the same time.'

'I know, I should have thought.'

He reached for her hand. There was a silence and then he spoke again.

'Clare?'

'Yes?'

'What about IVF?'

'What about it?' she replied, knowing that she sounded ridiculously childish.

David took her cup from her and put it back in its saucer. He held both her hands and stroked them with his thumbs.

'I'd like us to have a go, Clare. We have to do this sooner rather than later because of our ages. We can't keep putting it off. You know that there's nothing I would love more than to have a family with you. I accept the IVF might not work but if we don't try I have this awful feeling that we'll spend the rest of our lives regretting it and wondering what if and if only. Can you understand that?'

Clare looked at him intently.

'Of course I can. But David, I'm scared of all that this involves. I'm scare of all those hormones I'd have to take, of their side-effects both short and long term. I'm worried that they'll make me sick and emotionally all over the place and a pain in the neck to live and work with. I'm terrified of the egg retrieval procedure and even more terrified of the horrendous let down if it doesn't work the first time. And I know that if that happens, we'll try again and again –where do we stop? It's easy to promise myself that I'd be calm and laid back, que sera sera, but I know, I just know,' she repeatedly banged their combined hands emphatically on the table, 'that if I actually go through with it, it will take over my life and I may never be the same again.'

'It's natural you should be scared, Clare. I am too –for you and for us. If there was a way I could take all the hormones for you, I would. I don't care if you become dreadful to live with –and I'm sure you wouldn't- but I can cope. I'll look after you and be there with you every step of the way so that you'll never need to be frightened. We'd cope with everything together, just as we always have done.'

'I'm not sure if I can do this David,' Clare pleaded.

'You can, you can – we can. Clare, I want this so much for us. If you'd only agree, I thought that we could get an appointment to see the gynaecologist pretty quickly and aim to start the treatment as soon as possible. It could be perfect. What do you think?'

Clare had watched his face while he had talked to her; she'd watched his passion, his longing, his desperation and pain. She had to look away.

'I'm not sure.....' she repeated.

'Clare, please, let's do this, for us.'

She turned back to him, their eyes locked and this time she saw love, desire and hope, knowing, as she did, that her resolve could never compete with such compelling emotion.

After a long pause she whispered, 'David, all right, we'll try.'

He leapt from his chair and enveloped her in his arms, but even cocooned therein, she still felt doubt and dismay along with an increasingly growing self-accusation.

Chapter Seven

It was half past six in the morning and Clare was sitting at her desk in the surgery, cradling a mug of coffee in her hands and staring at nothing in particular. The Bank Holiday weekend was over, September loomed, bringing with it longer nights and autumnal weather.

Clare was replaying the last three weeks over and over again in her head, trying to make some sense of it but failing. She'd tried looking at things in various different ways but none seemed any more successful than the previous ones. If, as her professional training would advise, she focussed on the positive first, then that was definitely the easy part. Sam, had continued to be an excellent addition to the practice and was now confidently coping with ten minute appointments and house calls. He rarely interrupted Clare in surgery for advice but when he did, it was wholly appropriate. Reviewing his work, it was clear that he had a sound knowledge base and made reliable decisions with regard to his patient management. Several patients had already asked to see him specifically, according to Joan, who also had kept a record of complimentary remarks that had been passed about him. If she had one criticism then Clare would have had to admit that she wished he would prepare more fully for his tutorials. He always seemed to arrive a little late for these but, once they got settled into them, his spontaneous input never failed to result in some lively discussions, peppered with good humour and lots of laughing. His lively, inquisitive approach kept Clare on her toes and ,not wanting to fail him as his trainer, she had spent a number of evenings working late into the night, trying to anticipate his queries and find new ways to challenge him. She was slightly concerned that her own preoccupation with her own worries might interfere with his training, but Sam gave no sign that he was in anyway dissatisfied and seemed genuinely to be enjoying himself thoroughly.

Clare's thoughts moved reluctantly to herself and David. He had continued to be attentive, openly adoring and transparently so excited about the prospect of IVF. The Monday following their dinner at the Dog and Bull he had rung her at work. He had made them an appointment to see Professor Corbett at the assisted conception unit the following day, which was Clare's half day. Clare had been taken aback by the speed with which this had been arranged but could not bring herself to suggest that they should wait a little bit longer.

The meeting had gone quite well. Professor Corbett, an erudite and compassionate man had been delighted to see them again and had talked them through the process step by step before letting them spend some time with the counsellor. Clare had been quiet throughout but this had hardly been noticeable as David's demeanour and constant flow of questions had more than compensated. She had found herself looking at him and smiling. She had not seen him so excited and animated since they had got married.

As they left, Professor Corbett had warned them that the waiting list was quite long but that hopefully they should be called early in the New Year. Inwardly Clare's heart had heaved a sigh of relief and she had cuddled David's arm affectionately as they returned to the car. They had driven home, David chattering continuously, still giddy with happiness, Clare monosyllabic, afraid but more than a little relieved.

Life had continued after that in its normal routine, David busy but buoyant at the hospital, Clare at the surgery. Betty Aylward had died shortly after their joint visit, very peacefully with her dog beside her on one side and her sister on the other. Clare had managed to go to the funeral and was comforted to find the church full of more than a hundred people who had known her mainly through her dancing and had come to pay their last respects. In the days that followed, she occasionally saw Doreen out walking the dog, both of them looking sad, their heads drooping, united by their grief.

Prudence had continued to call on a regular basis. There had been a further five home visits because she had intolerable chest pain which had mysteriously vanished by the time Clare had arrived.

Just before the Bank Holiday weekend there had been much excitement when Ellie's twins celebrated their birthday. Ian, true to form, had either totally forgotten or chosen to ignore the original plan and when the girls had run outside after their breakfast, there was Smudge, grazing contentedly in the small paddock at the side of the house. Ellie, who had tried briefly to be disapproving had melted immediately as her two daughters smothered first Smudge, then Ian and then her with kisses and hugs.

Ellie had recounted the birthday with maternal pride and then had persuaded Clare and Sam to come round to the house after work the next day. Virginia and Lydia were over the moon to see them and dragged them off to fetch brushes, the saddle and bridle. Virginia had taught Clare how to brush Smudge's tail and Lydia had tried in vain to get Sam to pick out Smudge's hooves. They had then watched as each child in turn had given an exhibition, persuading the little piebald pony to trot round the field in a purposeful manner while Ian puffed along protectively beside them. Apples and carrots that Clare and Sam had brought were crunched noisily and rhythmically by the grateful pony afterwards.

Driving home from Ellie's, Clare had kept smiling to herself, visualising the girls' ecstatic faces and those of their proud parents. She had still been grinning to herself when she had let herself into the house and had been amazed to find the hall full of fresh flowers. A track from her favourite CD was wafting its way from the lounge and, if she was not mistaken, that was lasagne and garlic bread she could smell coming from the kitchen. Curious, she had gone into the lounge, only to be startled by the unmistakable sound of a champagne cork popping and before she knew it she had accepted a glass full of the effervescent liquid. David had given her a big kiss and told her to sit down and put her feet up. He'd then proceeded to top up her glass at regular intervals and then serve her a delicious supper. As they'd been eating, she'd regaled him with a description of Smudge, Virginia, Lydia, Ellie and Ian, adding that it was hard to tell who was the most excited out of all of them, which had made him laugh.

When the washing up had been done, they'd sat together on the settee and David had produced a small jeweller's box. Opening it had revealed the most exquisite pair of solitaire diamond earrings. Overwhelmed, Clare had hugged him tight before trying them on and admiring the effect in the mirror, examining herself from every angle.

David had watched her and told her that the earrings were just to tell her how much he loved her. And then he'd dropped the bombshell. He'd started by saying how he'd noticed how quiet she'd been recently, particularly when they had been driving home from seeing Professor Corbett. He'd gone on to say that he realised that she was upset that that they had to wait until the New Year. So, as a surprise, he'd rung the Professor and asked if it would make a difference if they paid for their treatment. Apparently it would, considerably. Clare had wheeled round from the mirror as soon as he'd said that and he'd gone over to her and put his arms around her, playing for time before he announced that he had arranged for their treatment to start at the beginning of October, just after they returned from New England. Blind to Clare's look of horror and mistaking it for one of speechless joy, David had hugged and kissed her before holding her at arms' length at which point she had seen the tears of joy trickling down his cheeks and burst into tears herself.

Since then, Clare had barely slept. This morning was yet another when she had woken early and known that there was not the remotest chance of any further sleep. She'd got up quietly, taking care not to wake David, dressed and slipped unnoticed out of the house and come to the sanctuary of her own room at the surgery. Her coffee was cold by this time and undrinkable but this was no bad thing as she knew that she was drinking far too much, to keep her awake and as a substitute for food. Pushing the mug away from her, she rested her head on her arms, folded on her desk and closed her eyes, trying to block out her thoughts.

An hour later she was suddenly recalled from a bottomless pit of sleep by the sound of laughing and chattering signalling the arrival of Joan and Gary and thus the start of another day. Wondering if this was how one felt if a rhinoceros had just rolled over on you, Clare lurched to the sink and washed her face. She applied a basic layer of make up and combed her hair, ignoring the haunted face that gazed back at her in the mirror.

Taking a deep breath she went out to greet her staff. They'd spotted her car in the car park.

'Not again,' Joan had said.

They looked up as she came towards her, welcoming as always, but hiding their concern.

'Did you have a good weekend?' Clare asked them.

They replied in the affirmative and politely asked after Clare's.

'Fine,' she responded, flatly.

'I'm just putting the kettle on, Dr J,' Gary called from the bottom of the stairs, 'I'll bring you a drink, shall I?'

Clare sat down on one of their chairs and Joan, after a quick thought came and sat beside her.

'Clare?' she rarely used her Christian name,' are you ok?'

Clare sat herself more upright and tried to put on a cheery face.

'Of course I am.'

'It's just that you look so tired. You've lost weight and you always look preoccupied. I know it's none of my business but it really worries me to see you like this. It can't be Dr Curtis, because he's no trouble to anyone. Don't feel you have to say anything at all now, but, if you ever want to talk to someone, away from all this, you've got my number at home. Give me a ring whenever and come round for a natter. It'll go no further than you and I, I promise.'

With that, Joan got up, patted Clare lightly on her shoulder and set about her first jobs of the day. Clare felt torn, angry with herself that anyone had noticed her angst but tearful that someone had been sensitive and kind. Trying hard to pull herself together, collected up some notes and ran upstairs to the coffee room, logged on to the computer and did some searches that she had promised Sam she would do.

John arrived shortly afterwards and surreptitiously gave her a long hard look, having been taken to one side by Joan as he walked through the front door.

'Good morning!' he said, brightly and received a similarly bright reply from Clare although she did not look up from the computer. He went over and stood behind her while she explained what she was doing and made some helpful suggestions which she tried as he watched.

Sam and Ed burst in simultaneously, followed by Ellie, who still managed to look absolutely stunning despite the fact that she had been up for some time, mucked out Smudge's stable and taken him for a walk with the girls. They all quickly swapped details about their respective weekends until, with ten minutes to go before their first patients, Clare went with Sam to his room and together they glanced through his appointments so that Clare could fill him in on any background that might turn out to be relevant. She warned him that there may be extras tagged on to the end, if demand was high, as it often was after a public holiday. She left him then, walked across the waiting area and watched from her door as he called in a stressed-looking woman with a recalcitrant teenager, holding out his hand to greet them and introduce himself.

Clare motioned to Mrs Benjamin to follow her in. A chunky, thickset woman with hair that badly needed cutting and dressed in shapeless clothes, nearly all of which were black sat down. They exchanged some pleasantries about the prevailing good weather while Clare got her notes up on the computer screen and then turned to her.

'How can I help you today?' asked Clare.

Mrs Benjamin's shoulders sagged, her greasy-skinned face which had been devoid of expression, crumpled as she began to cry.

'I'm just so tired all the time.'

Clare deftly passed her the box of tissues and then carefully mirrored her posture, so as to invite more confidences and build rapport. But Mrs Benjamin needed little persuasion to talk and for the next ten minutes Clare listened to how she had a husband who didn't understand and went to the pub every night, coming back drunk, a fourteen year old daughter who she was sure was having sex with an older boy and how it was left to her to bring money in which meant her having to have two jobs, one at a supermarket during the day and then the other cleaning in the evening. All Clare could do was let her talk and make some suggestions, which all sounded hopelessly inadequate but never the less Mrs Benjamin seemed to appreciate. She invited her to come back the next week to talk again and to ask for an appointment at the end of the surgery, so that there would be plenty of time for her to talk. Mrs Benjamin seemed covered with confusion at that point by the thought that someone was doing something just for her but agreed to come as she mopped her nose and eyes.

As she showed her out, Clare was met by a line of patients all waiting to see her, each one looking at her in the hopes that they would be next. Clare slowly worked her way through them all.

That morning, even the straightforward seemed difficult and three interruptions by phone calls did not help.

With the biggest sigh of relief, she finished forty five minutes late and spent a few minutes more writing her to do list and making sure she had completed everyone's notes. The house call list looked reasonable. The sunny weather was obviously continuing to work its spell and less people were feeling that they needed the doctor. Scanning through the requests for visits, Clare was surprised to see one for Alexa Thetford and instantly hoped that there was nothing wrong with her pregnancy. She uttered a groan when she saw there was a visit for Prudence Kerfoot.

As usual, Clare was the last to reach the coffee room and Ed nobly sprang to his feet, told her to sit down while he made her a drink. He offered her a delicious looking oaty biscuit from a tin that one of his patients had brought for him.

'Where's Sam? She asked, spotting his absence. 'Surely he must have finished surgery. He'd have rung me if he was having problems.'

John looked up from his papers.

'He's fine, Clare. He finished bang on time. Apparently his patients were mostly quick things like upper respiratory infections or cystitis. He came up here and was reading when Elizabeth came running up to say that there was an urgent visit for that girl Alexa Thetford and that she'd sounded very upset when she rang. So Sam immediately offered to go straightaway. He didn't need any prompting. He's a good lad Clare, we're lucky to have him.'

'Thanks John. Yes, everyone thinks he's wonderful – so do I. What was the problem with Alexa?'

'Abdominal pain and feeling dizzy. She's pregnant isn't she?

Clare nodded. 'She must be about eight weeks by now. I hope everything's fine. How long ago did he go? Perhaps I'll just sit here and wait for him to come back and make sure he managed.'

John sighed.

'Clare, you've just agreed that he's one of the best registrars we've ever had. He's certainly not put a foot wrong so far, so have faith. He's only five months off completing his training. Go on your visits, finish off and then go home for your half day. You look dreadful, if you don't mind me saying. If there's something wrong, you know that you can always come to me and talk.'

'I'm fine, just tired. I've not been sleeping well. It's good job that it's my holiday in a couple of weeks. I'm really ready for it.'

John looked unconvinced.

'All right, if you say so. But remember what I said. I'd hate to think you were struggling with something that you couldn't cope with on your own. I know you'd do nothing to compromise patient care but you have to look after yourself as well.'

She knew he was right. Clare decided to take his advice and went on her visits but made a mental note to telephone Sam at lunchtime and check on his morning's work. She spent a tedious half hour with Prudence, whose chest pain had mysteriously vanished yet again and had been replaced with a variety of trivial complaints which she suspected had been devised with the sole purpose of keeping her there as long as possible. Two more visits later, Clare drove home, went upstairs, lay on the bed and was asleep within seconds, still fully clothed but under the duvet. She woke just before six, stiff from having moved very little but feeling more refreshed. There was just time to ring the surgery and luckily Sam was still there.

'Hi Clare.'

Sam, hello. Sorry I've not had much opportunity to catch up with you today. I just wanted to check you'd not had any problems.'

'I've been fine. It's been a busy afternoon, but we all seem to have coped. Ed and I are just off for a beer. You should relax and enjoy your free time, I'll see you tomorrow.'

'Yes I will, I mean I am,' Clare stammered. ' How was Alexa Thetford?'

'Who?'

'You went to visit her this morning. First trimester of pregnancy and some abdominal pain and dizziness.'

'She was pretty good. Much better. The dizziness had worn off as she'd managed to eat some breakfast and I'm sure that the pain was simply due to constipation. She'd not had her bowels open for two days.'

'That's a relief,' stated Clare. 'She'd not had any bleeding then?'

'Just some very slight spotting. More discharge that anything. I promised her I'd arrange her a scan. I forgot to do it this afternoon as it's been so hectic but, never fear, I'll be on to it first thing in the morning.'

She said goodbye and wandered down to the kitchen. There was a message on the answering machine from David, who was on call that night, saying he would be late and would eat at the hospital. Armed with this knowledge, she showered, put on her nightdress and made herself a salad from an assortment of odds and ends she found lurking in the fridge. She ate curled up on the settee, watching television until fatigue overcame her again and she crawled back up to bed. Four hours later she was up again, this time in the bathroom, leaning over the toilet being violently sick repeatedly, inwardly cursing alternately the cold ham and the potato salad and feeling worse that she had done for many years. David came home to find her sitting on the bathroom floor, her hair sticking up on end, her face pale green in colour. He cleaned her up, helped her back into bed and made her a hot water bottle as she was shivering with shock. Stroking her forehead until she drifted back off to sleep, he then got ready for bed himself, climbed in beside her and lay in the dark, listening to her breathing.

Chapter Eight

A couple of days later, she woke up and realised that she was on her own. She stretched out under the duvet, enjoying having so much space and then rolled over onto her left side, hoping for some more sleep. A sudden wave of nausea had her throwing back the covers and rushing for the bathroom. She couldn't really believe that she still felt like this, having hoped that her symptoms would settle within twenty four hours. But this morning she felt as bad as ever. Wrapping a dressing gown around her, she crawled downstairs and wandered into the kitchen, switching on the kettle as she past it, more from habit than desire for a drink. Outside, the weather had changed completely. The sky was full of heavy, bulbous grey clouds and branches were being tossed in all directions by gusts of wind. She watched as people hurried past, no longer dawdling in their sleeveless shirts and shorts but now intent on reaching their destinations and back in their jumpers and coats. A few splashes of rain landed randomly on the window.

Aimlessly, she wiped the worktop and washed up a cereal bowl and mug that were lounging in the sink. The kettle boiled and after a moment or two's contemplation, she opted for tea, for some unknown reason choosing a raspberry and Echinacea variety which she usually despised as its aroma promised so much but the taste never quite delivered. Waiting for it to mash, she tidied up some papers into a pile and glanced fleetingly at the morning's post which had been left next to the fridge.

Two sips of the raspberry tea had her heaving over the sink.

Work had been told that she would not be in for the rest of the week and she felt that she was letting everyone down and wondered what was going on in her absence. Thinking that perhaps something solid might sit more comfortably in her stomach, she put a slice of brown bread into the toaster and looked out a pot of honey. As she waited she turned back to the post and opened a letter addressed to her. It turned out to be an invitation to a friend's hen night. She took this, with her toast and tea and relocated to the lounge where she sat down and picked up her diary to check the date. There seemed to be nothing planned for the night of the hen party, so she made a quick note and then idly flicked backwards and forwards through the pages.

She was actually taking a bite from her toast when she realised with some shock that it was well over a month since her last period. Coincidentally another blast of nausea besieged her and the toast threatened menacingly to return before having a change of heart and settling again.

She couldn't be. Surely not. But maybe – the signs were all there.

It simply was not possible. But as the idea propagated in her brain, she imagined that she could feel her breasts starting to become tender, plus everyone knew how tired she had been. A microscopic frisson of excitement temporarily replaced the nausea, an infinitely more preferable a feeling.

'I'm being ridiculous,' she told herself and tried to divert her attention to a magazine, which she opened randomly only to find that she was faced with an article on how to get fit for pregnancy. She cast this onto the floor, discovered the remote control behind a cushion and switched on the television. Flicking between stations, there was nothing that held her attention and reading the news headlines on ceefax failed to do so as well.

With her heart in her mouth, she went back upstairs and rummaged into the very back of the airing cupboard, unearthing an old sponge bag. Unzipping as far as it would go before the zip stuck, she found what she was looking for, a pregnancy testing kit, left from before. Time wasting, she read and re-read the box and leaflet inside. She then wandered around the landing and folded some clothes and put them away before being drawn, as if by some huge invisible magnet back to the bathroom. She urinated and then stayed sitting on the toilet, her eyes closed, her thoughts exploding like a Catherine wheel.

She counted back from ten and then again, though this time starting from twenty.

Time to look at the result, she thought.

'Pregnant.'

She shook it about a bit but it still read the same.

'I don't believe this,' she cried out loud and then burst into tears.

A further, now familiar lurch of her stomach assured her that there was no doubt.

Wiping away the tears with her hands, she went and lay on the bed, oscillating between the feelings of euphoria and despair. How could something so minute exert such an incredible and irresistible effect on her both emotionally and physically.

After a few moments, she sat up determinedly and started to get dressed.

'Okay, so if this is for real, I've got to do it properly. There's no need to tell anyone until I'm absolutely sure so I need to do what everyone else would do and that's go to the doctors.'

Feeling resolute now, she almost ran downstairs and grabbed the telephone and dialled.

'Good morning, medical centre,' answered a friendly voice.

'Hello, can I make an appointment to see a doctor please? Today if possible.'

'Of course, you're in luck. We've just had a cancellation for this afternoon at three thirty. Would that suit you?'

'That'd be perfect.'

'Can I have your name please?'

'Yes of course, it's Rebecca, Rebecca Howarth.'

'That's three thirty this afternoon then, with Dr Bonnington, one of our lady doctors.'

Clare too was still off sick, for the first time in many years. Her vomiting had abated only to be replaced by violent stomach cramps and diarrhoea. Even when these symptoms had settled, she was left feeling like a half wrung out dish cloth and was forced to admit that it would have been pointless trying to go to work. David, predictably, had proved to be a sympathetic nurse. He had rung the surgery for her, thus taking that decision out of her hands, plied her with plenty of fluids when he was not at work and then come home with flowers, paperbacks and little gifts. Too weak to do otherwise, Clare had surrendered to her illness and spent many hours asleep, either in bed or on the settee, amazed by how much rest her body needed. She was beginning to feel much more like herself by the Thursday evening and, as David had dictated that she would not be returning to work before the weekend, she had the luxury of the prospect of a day at home, on her own, with nothing specific to do.

On the Friday morning, she actually felt like putting on some proper clothes and doing her hair. Downstairs she began to make one list of what was to be done before their holiday in ten days time and a second list of what they would want to take with them. She searched out the tickets and travel details and refreshed her memory of their destination by browsing through some brochures. What would have been an exceedingly pleasant experience was marred only by the thought of what she had to face when they got back. One of the blessings of being ill was that she did not have the strength to wrestle with thoughts of the IVF but now in the convalescent phase, they were returning in a malignant fashion.

Shortly before lunchtime, Clare decided to make herself a sandwich but still felt wary enough to choose cheese over cold meat. She was buttering a bread roll when the telephone rang and she went to answer it.

'Dr Jennings?' It was Elizabeth. 'I am so sorry to bother you. How are you feeling?'

'I'm much much better, thank you. Just about back to normal.'

'Oh, I'm so pleased to hear that. We've all missed you terribly. The trouble is though; we've got a bit of a problem at the surgery. Dr Bonnington has rung in and cannot get into surgery this afternoon and we have a fully booked surgery for her. Is there any way you could help out?'

Clare automatically replied without thinking.

'Yes of course, I can. I'm sure I'll be fine, if I just come in and do that. I've got the whole weekend afterwards to take it easy in. But what's happened to Ellie?'

'I think one of the twins is ill. Her husband has gone abroad and I think she's stuck for someone to stay with her daughter.'

'Don't worry, I'll come and help. What time is her surgery starting, three?'

'Yes, Dr Jennings. We'll do our best to keep it as short as possible, so that you don't have too much to do. Dr Curtis and Dr Britton have both offered to see some extras at the end of their surgeries and Dr Diamond is starting early.'

'OK Elizabeth. I'll see you soon. I'm glad you rang.'

The cheese sandwich tasted like cardboard but she forced it down, followed by a banana and then went to tidy herself up, put on some make up and change into more suitable clothes for work.

She knew that David would not be pleased so she hoped that she would be able to finish and get back home before he did and then perhaps only even tell him about it if the subject arose.

True to their word, the receptionists had limited her surgery to fifteen patients only and, as the first two were waiting for her when she arrived, Clare went straight to her room and prepared to start. At just after three thirty she called in her next patient, whom she barely recognised from the last time she saw her. Instead of the smouldering, vividly attractive girl she had met when Sam was sitting in with her, there was a pale, exhausted woman, whose hair had obviously not come into contact with a hair brush that day and who appeared to have dressed in what ever she managed to get her hands on first. Gone was the self-confidence and cocky awareness of her sexuality. She looked much as Clare had felt the past few days and her first thought was that maybe she had a similar problem. Instantly sympathetic, Clare sat her down.

'Hello Rebecca, what's wrong?'

'I think I might be pregnant. I wonder if I could have a test. I've done one at home which was positive, but I thought it might not be reliable, or it might have been too old as I'd had it for some time.'

'What about your periods? Weren't you on the pill last time I saw you. Had you stopped it?'

Rebecca looked forlorn.

'I think I missed one or two, what with moving up here and settling in. I've been sick quite a lot over the last few days.'

Clare nodded, knowing at least, what that bit felt like.

'Of course we can do a test for you. How will you feel, if it is positive?'

'I don't know. Part of me would be thrilled. I'd have to go away and think about things.'

'What about your partner?' asked Clare. 'How would he feel? Perhaps he'd be thrilled as well,' she ventured.

Rebecca looked less convinced.

'I don't know,' she repeated.

Clare could tell that nothing more was forthcoming.

'Right, let's start at the beginning then. You go along to the nurses now and they'll do a test. If it's positive, then look on the weekend as a chance to have a think bout things. Talk to your partner, if you feel ready to do that. Then come back and see me at the beginning of next week. Make that appointment before you go and then we can talk some more.'

Rebecca, nodding in taciturn agreement, went out, leaving Clare to email the nurses and warn them that Rebecca was on her way.

Some time late, when Clare had finished seeing patients and was about to leave for home, she checked in Rebecca's notes and saw that the test was indeed positive.

Sam was unequivocally relieved when his final patient of the day left. The last two days had been very hard work, with Clare off ill and all her work to cover. As her registrar, the receptionists seemed to see fit to transfer Clare's regular patients to him and as a result he was treated to a further insight into the complex nature of some of her chronic attenders. Part of him relished the challenge, he wanted the partners to be impressed by his ability and willingness to cope, thinking ahead to when references would be required or, if he was exceptionally lucky, a partnership vacancy came up at Teviotdale. The patients at this practice were by and large middle class, well educated people with high expectations and well rehearsed lists of demands, expecting to barter and negotiate their health care, a far cry from the more working class list he'd experienced before who simply wanted the doctor to tell them what to do.

He was upstairs; doing the last of three referral letters when John came in and feigned collapse on one of the chairs.

'What a week,' he pronounced, taking time over each word. 'Fancy a pint before you go home?'

'Music to my ears,' Sam had no hesitation in replying and the two of them were soon strolling across the market place and into the pub where John bought a round of drinks.

An hour later and feeling distinctly more mellow, Sam made his way home, driving even more carefully that usual, aware that he had drunk two pints of beer. He was looking forward to a relaxing evening at home, with the prospect of a weekend ahead of him, perhaps another beer or two, some supper, television and then bed, all in the company of the lovely Becca. She'd been remarkably quiet for the last few days, he mused, with some sort of tummy bug. He'd taken care not to wake her that morning when he got up and went to work, so hopefully the rest would have been just what she needed. She appeared to be settling in well to life in Lambdale. Sunbathing had been abandoned and she'd found herself a job in a small but highly exclusive dress shop, which stocked the latest in several designer labels and attracted clientele from all over the north of the county. Becca had already become quite well respected by the owner of the shop and her daughter who also worked there and she genuinely seemed to be enjoying having regular employment. They had sounded like really pleasant people when he'd rung them to explain that she was too ill to come to work.

As he went into the house, he instantly knew, even before he saw Becca, that she was no better. Everywhere was a mess. The hallway looked positively unhygienic, the floor needed sweeping and the washing had been abandoned in a huge pile over the bottom of the stairs and appeared to be crawling down to greet him.

He called out and she answered from the lounge, where she was half lying in a chair, feet out on a stool, all enveloped in the duvet which she had brought down with her.

'Hi sweetheart,' he bent down to kiss her on the cheek, 'not feeling any better?'

'A little,' she conceded.

'Good. Fancy a drink of anything?' he asked.

'One of those instant hot chocolate drinks would be nice.'

In the kitchen he peered into a dismally empty fridge while the kettle boiled. Just as there was no food, there was no beer, but he found a bottle of red wine in the cupboard, so opened it and poured a large glass, not bothering to let it breathe.

'There you go, honey,' passing her the mug of piping hot chocolate.

'Thanks.'

'How've you been today. Still being sick?'

'I'm afraid so, though perhaps not quite as much.'

'Any other symptoms?'

'Not really.'

'Maybe you should go to the surgery on Monday if you're no better,' he suggested,' but I bet it's just a viral thing. I've seen quite a lot of people with similar symptoms this week. In fact, Clare's had it too. She's been off work. There's nothing to be done apart from rest and take plenty of drinks.'

'I've been to the surgery today, Sam,' Becca blurted out.

Sam stopped in his tracks, wine glass half way to his lips.

'Today, Becs? Why didn't you say? You must have been feeling rough.'

'I only decided to go this morning, when I woke up and knew that I still felt just as grim.'

'Good for you. I bet they said just what I've told you.'

'No they didn't actually,' Becca told him, quietly.

'What did they say then?'

'They said that I'm pregnant.' She tried desperately to say these words in as neutral a voice as she could, not knowing what the reaction would be.

Sam put down his glass.

'Bloody, bloody hell Becs. Not again!'

'I'm sorry darling. It was an accident,' Becca pleaded.

'How could it be an accident? You're on the pill.' Sam tried unsuccessfully to keep his voice calm.

Becca shrugged.

'I missed a couple of pills when we moved. I didn't think it would matter. I'm sure you told me once that it didn't.'

'Hang on now, don't you dare try to blame this on me. What pills did you miss? Where about in the packet were they?'

'Right at the end.'

'Becca, you idiot. Those last seven are some of the most important ones, ones that you shouldn't miss. Why didn't you tell me? This could have been avoided.'

Angry now and no longer afraid to show it, Sam was on his feet, pacing about, waving his fingers in an admonitory fashion at Becca.

'Oh Christ. How far are you on then?'

Becca shrugged again.

'Only a few weeks,' she replied in a small voice hoping that this might make it soften the blow.

'Well that's one blessing then,' snapped Sam. 'There's plenty of time to do something about it.'

'What do you mean, Sam?' asked Becca, knowing that she knew exactly what he meant but hoping fervently that she might be wrong.

Sam sat down beside her and held her hand.

'I'm sorry I was so angry. It was just such a shock. It was the last thing I was expecting you to say.'

Becca attempted a laugh.

'"Expecting" is a good choice of word.'

Sam ignored her.

'Let's talk about this seriously Becs. You know as well as I do that you've got to terminate this pregnancy. We've not been together that long, I'm still doing my training, you've barely settled here and for all we know, we'll be moving off somewhere in a few months time. I might not get a partnership immediately- it's worth my while hanging on for the one I really want, so I might have to locum or do out of hours sessions. It's all far too unsettled a situation to introduce something as complicated as a baby into. It wouldn't be fair on any of us, particularly the baby. You know that I hope we stay together but it is early days in our relationship, far too early to be having a baby. Surely you can see that.'

Tears welled in Becca's eyes.

'But Sam, I had a termination just a few months ago. You know how upset I was then. I can't go through that again so soon. We'd be fine with a baby. You'd love it when it arrived. Other people cope with far worse circumstances than ours and you don't need me to remind you of that as you come across it every day at work. Let's not make any hasty decisions, let's just think about it for a few days and discuss it some more.'

'You can think about it all you want Becca but I am not going to change my mind, so the sooner you come round to my way of thinking the better. On the other hand, if you want to go ahead and have this child, then you do it on your own. I do not, repeat not, want to be part of this escapade.'

Becca burst out sobbing and made a grab for Sam's arm but he pulled away roughly and marched out of the room, pausing only to grab a coat before opening the front door, leaving and slamming it behind him.

Chapter Nine

Monday morning and summer seemed to be long forgotten. It had rained steadily for most of the weekend and the skies still looked full of foreboding. Clare, now fully recovered got up at the same time as David and, unusually they ate breakfast sitting at the table together. David was due to be away for a couple of nights on a course in Nottingham, so they were enjoying some time together before he left. She waved him off from the front door and as his car disappeared around the end of the road she returned indoors to put the dishes in the sink to soak and get herself ready for work. Normally, if she'd been away from the practice for any reason she would have gone in early to read e-mails, catch up with letters and review particular patients. She felt slightly uncomfortable at not having done this today, aware that she was not starting the day fully in control, a feeling that she found unsettling and uncomfortable. She tried to reason with herself calmly that, with David away, she could quite easily spend as much time at the surgery at the end of the day as she wanted and catch up then if necessary.

The first part of the morning was taken up with tutorial time with Sam. They met upstairs and took their mugs of coffee down to Clare's consulting room where the next hour and a half was spent reviewing cases that he had seen, discussing his decision making and deviating off laterally to discuss other unrelated topics as they cropped up. Clare loved this form of teaching and excelled at it. She was naturally clever at asking the unexpected and so keeping her registrar constantly on his or her toes having to think and decide quickly. Sam was normally well up to the challenge. Well read and up to date, he could give as good as he got and for the two of them the time would pass in a flash as they happily exchanged ideas.

On that particular Monday, Sam was late for the first time. Not just by his usual few minutes, which Clare would have found slightly irritating though excusable but by nearly half an hour and she had been on the verge of ringing to check where he was. She was horrified by his appearance. His eyes were lack-lustre with dark rings beneath them, he badly needed a shave and his clothes looked as if they had been worn continuously for several days. He was clutching a bacon sandwich, half concealed in a paper bag with grease seeping through it, which he proceeded to eat and wash down with great gulps of coffee from a polystyrene cup. His performance in the tutorial was appalling. Try as she might, she could not get him to engage in any form of discussion, his answers were brief, almost curt and smacked of disinterest. Repeatedly he tried to hide his yawns.

After twenty minutes of uphill struggle, Clare admitted defeat, closed her notebook in which she kept a record of his progress, pushed her chair back from the desk slightly and switched off the computer.

'There's not much point carrying on, is there?' She confronted him.

He did not reply and had the decency to look ashamed.

'What's the problem?' she inquired.

'Sorry I was late. I – er – overslept,' he replied unconvincingly.

Clare gave him a long look and waited but nothing more was forthcoming.

'Is that it?' she went on, incredulously.

'More or less. It's just been a really bad weekend. I felt dreadful. Maybe I had something like you had. I didn't want to have to let people down by not coming in. I will be fine, don't worry. I know I look a bit of a mess. It won't happen again.'

All the time while he was talking he refused to look her in the eye.

'Are you fit to work today?' Clare voiced concern, not without, however a degree of irritation.

'Yes, I'm fine,' he repeated, emphatically.

'Well, you don't look fine and there's no way that you're to see patients in that state. You need a shave and a wash at the minimum but preferably some clean clothes as well. Go home; you've just over half an hour before your first appointment, so that should give you plenty of time. I want to see you looking presentable before you start.'

'But what about the tutorial?' he asked, rather pathetically.

'We can arrange to do that another time. Get off home – NOW.'

Sam stood up and walked towards the door. His hand was turning the handle as he turned,

'I'm really sorry Clare. I can see you're disappointed in me. I really meant it when I said it won't happen again.'

'Go home,' Clare almost snapped adding as an afterthought, 'Sam, if there's something I can help you with, you know I will. If it's something personal and you'd rather not talk about it, then I respect that but I have to step in if I feel that your work is being affected.'

He left her on her own. She did feel very disappointed in him and knew that there was more that he had been prepared to admit but also knew that she had offered her help and the rest was up to him. She hoped that none of the other partners had spotted him, John in particular being a stickler for professional smartness.

Clare went out to the waiting area and found it heaving with people. Walking across to reception, she nodded in acknowledgement to several greetings. She'd had the idea that this would be an ideal opportunity to start catching up with some of her own work but bad news was waiting for her when she asked for the morning's post.

'Could you possibly see some patients, Dr Jennings? Dr Bonnington's rung in and won't be in until lunchtime. She's just been on the phone to Dr Britton for quarter of an hour so now he's running late as well and we've all her patients to accommodate. Everyone seems miserable because it's still raining and things are generally in a state of chaos.'

The morning continued to spiral insidiously and steadily downwards. All the surgeries over-ran. Doctors were harassed. Patients were disgruntled. They grumbled about having to wait and argued with each other about who should go in to see the doctor next, regardless of their appointment times. There was a constant queue waiting at reception, shuffling their feet, coughing, trying to attract the attention of the staff who were working flat out and desperately trying to keep everyone happy. Gary was answering the phone, booking appointments for the doctors or nurses, taking repeat prescription requests and fielding general enquiries and messages, leaving Joan and Elizabeth on the front line. The intention was that they would swap round every so often but there was never a quiet enough moment to do this.

Clare had to deal with a succession of irate, damp people whose opening comments were complaints about the way the surgery was run and how shocking it was that they'd specifically booked to see one doctor and then had to see another. Her attempt to explain that Ellie was unable to be there that morning met with little sympathy. To make matters worse, some of Ellie's patients with more complicated problems had returned for follow up which unfortunately meant that Clare had to go back to square one with them which they did not appreciate and took much longer. Exasperatingly, test results were missing, hospital reports had not arrived and some of Ellie's notes were so impossibly brief that it was extremely difficult to move the patients' care on smoothly, resulting in mutual exasperation for both parties.

As Clare progressed on to her patients, hoping for an easier time, it turned out that her first appointment had been double booked and both people demanded to be seen. This was followed by a tired-looking woman with a family of four. While she addressed her own agenda, the children wreaked havoc with a box of toys that they found under the examination couch. To add insult to injury, she then asked Clare if she could just have a look at the youngest two while they were there, despite the fact that she had not made separate appointments for them. As if to compensate the next consultation went well and culminated in a request for ten items which were on repeat prescription. As Clare pressed to button for this to be printed out, a decidedly unhealthy noise emanated from the printer which stopped working, thus necessitating Clare writing out the whole thing by hand.

It was a group of depressed and demoralised doctors who finally met for a much needed coffee. The usual camaraderie was replaced by dismay and they sat concentrating on their paperwork, making telephone calls, writing messages for health visitors, looking at the day's post. Even the normally ebullient Ed was subdued, intent upon making his way diligently through his normal, plus his extra work. Sam, now tidy and far more like his usual appearance was beavering away on the computer.

John put his work to one side and asked for everyone's attention.

'We've got a bit of a problem, chaps. Can we all meet back here at lunchtime? Visits are pretty easy today, so it should be possible. Elliot's going to organise some sandwiches and Ellie is coming in. Shall we say one o'clock? Sam, I'd like you to be here as well. Okay?'

Ed, Clare and Sam nodded in assent; all wondering what this was about. They divided the few visits up between them and Clare wearily made her way round to Prudence's house and had the usual discussion about her chest pain with the usual outcome of Prudence refusing to be referred for further investigations, much preferring to continue with Clare's regular attentions. She drove then to the Bellevue nursing home. The dark red flock wallpaper on the walls of the reception hall seemed even grimier that usual. She was directed to an elderly gentleman who was sitting in an armchair, one of many that lined the periphery of the lounge, all of them occupied by residents who seemed lost in their own reveries, unaware of the constant patter bellowing out from the television in the corner. As she got back into her car after the latter visit she realised with disgust that she had left her car window open and the rain had soaked the driver's seat. Making do by putting her coat, folded up, onto the seat and then sitting precariously on top of that, trying to put as little weight as she could on it, she made her way uncomfortably back to the surgery and ran upstairs.

Ellie was deliberating over which sort of sandwich she was going to have. She looked a little tired but not in the least bit ill. The others appeared one by one and then, when they each had filled their plates, John began.

'Thank you everyone for coming at such short notice. I know that it's been a pig of a day so far and we're only half way through. A dilemma has arisen that we've not had to cope with before but I'm confident that we'll handle it appropriately. Ellie-do you want to take over at this point?'

Ellie put down her plate.

'Yes, please. I'm afraid that this dilemma is due to me and I apologise in advance and just hope that you can all both understand and help. At the weekend, Virginia fractured her femur..'

Clare gasped. Murmurs of sympathy filled the room.

'How did that happen?' asked Ed.

'She didn't fall off that pony did she?' suggested Sam.

87

Ellie shook her head, her thick auburn hair wafting across her face. She laughed a little.

'No. We were out with Smudge though. Lydia was riding and Virginia was sitting –against my advice might I add at this point – on the gate which wasn't closed properly. It got caught in a gust of wind, blew back, completely unbalancing her and she fell off.'

'That's dreadful.'

'How is she?'

'She's doing ok. In hospital at the moment still but all being well coming home soon. This is where the problem starts,' she looked round at each of them in turn. 'As you know, Ian is in Milan and cannot get out of the job he's doing there for at least a fortnight. I'm sorry to have to ask you all this, but I need some time off. I have to be there for her.'

'Of course you do,' Clare reassured her. 'Don't worry about us, we'll manage.'

Elliot cleared his throat.

'We have to think carefully about this. I can tell you all agree that Ellie must have the time she needs. But that leaves us with a big gap in the day to day work. It will be nigh on impossible to get a locum in at such short notice. And let's not forget that Clare is on vacation for two weeks as from next week, which leaves us two doctors down. Can anyone think of anybody who might be able to come and help us? Clare, do you know of any ex-registrars who are looking for work at the moment?'

Clare shook her head.

'No, sorry, I don't. I could ring Matt Smillie though and see if he knows of anyone.'

'It's worth a try.'

John and Ed looked very perturbed.

'It's a fairly horrendous prospect, trying to cope on our own,' admitted John, 'though if push comes to shove, we'll simply have to inform the patients and hope that they will understand.'

Ed grimaced.

Elliot was making notes.

'John, you and Ed will have to work your half days, I'm afraid. I'll organise some time off in lieu at some point to pay you back of course. Sam, do you think you could help out at all?'

Sam was quick to answer.

'Count me in, I'll do as much as I can.'

88

John and Ed looked appreciatively at him.

Ellie started to apologise again. Clare went and gave her a hug.

'Of course you must be with your daughter. You'd say the same if it was one of us with a problem. Look, I've been thinking. The best thing would be if I cancel my leave and take it later on when life's back on an even keel.'

'You can't do that Clare,' protested John. 'You need your holiday as much as any of us. Possibly more, at the moment, as you've been looking very tired.'

'I'm perfectly happy to go another time. It's far more important that I'm here to help out and it will make all the difference. Plus we won't have to search desperately for a locum and end up with someone who we don't know and who doesn't know us.'

'But what will David say? You're going to the States, it was all booked months ago.'

'David will understand. I'm sure we can get most of our money back and then perhaps get somewhere at short notice next month or in November.' Clare spoke with more confidence than she felt.

'I don't know about this,' worried John. 'I'm torn. It would be an ideal solution but it's asking such a tremendous amount of you Clare, and David. Do you want to talk to him first, see how he feels about it? We can hang on until tomorrow, for sure.'

'David's away for a couple of nights at a psychiatric conference in Nottingham so he's not easy to get hold of. He knows how these things crop up and I'm sure he'd want me to offer to help. Let's just settle this now, then Ellie can relax and so can the rest of you.'

Elliot looked at John, who glanced at Ed, raising one eyebrow as he did.

'Shall I ring round some locum agencies first?' offered Elliot.

'No, please, I'm happy to do it.'

'I'll ring David when he gets back,' promised John and Clare smiled.

'Clare, I am forever in your debt.' Ellie was overwhelmed.

'Ellie speaks for all of us,' agreed Ed.

'Give Virginia my love and tell her I'll come and visit her soon. How's Lydia coping with all of this?' asked Clare.

'Oh, she's brimming over with glee. Once she'd got over the initial shock, it dawned on her that she had Smudge all to herself for a while. I expect you'll get another demonstration when you come round.'

They laughed and the general atmosphere seemed to have relaxed and lightened. General chatter broke out and the remainder of the sandwiches were eaten. Clare and Sam sat together and compared notes from the morning, Clare diplomatically avoiding any reference to the tutorial. Sam seemed to have rediscovered his usual self-confidence and studiously related some of his morning's encounters. He showed her the outline of an audit he was starting and asked for her suggestions to improve it, so she had little time to ponder on the possible consequences of her actions until later in the day. The lunchtime meeting over, the afternoon surgeries beckoned, all fully booked but at least Ellie stayed to do hers before going to pick Lydia up from school and head for the hospital.

When the last patient had gone, Clare found she had a list of things to do that went on for two pages. With a big sigh, she set about trying to get as many crossed off as possible, but really longing to go home and put her feet up. Painstakingly, she did referral letters, telephoned patients, checked results and ordered further investigations. She was pleasantly surprised but the speed at which she got through her list and decided to spend a little time checking on the work that was waiting for her on account of her having been off sick. E-mails revealed nothing startling, a couple of test results would need following up and a prescription was generated as a result of some advice in a letter from a consultant. That too, proved to be far less onerous than she had anticipated. Finally she read through a screen that recorded hospital admissions and discharges. There were the usual things- a couple of maternity patients had delivered, some other patients had finally had the surgery they had been waiting for and a fifteen year old boy had had his appendix removed. Clare was just skimming through the names and on the verge of logging out when a name caught her eye –Alexa Thetford. Hoping that she had not miscarried, she opened up Alexa's notes and saw that she had been rushed into hospital with an ectopic pregnancy.

Instantly concerned, Clare clicked into Alexa's notes and saw that she had been admitted the previous Wednesday, two days after

Sam had seen her but there was no mention of her discharge. Hurriedly she dialled the hospital and having ascertained which ward Alexa was on, asked to be put through. A weary voice answered and identified itself as the senior house officer on call for gynaecology.

'Good evening, my name's Clare Jennings, I'm a GP in Lambdale. One of my patients was admitted last week when I was off, an Alexa Thetford. I was just ringing to see how she was.'

'Hang on a minute.' Clare could hear papers being shuffled whilst she hoped fervently that Alexa was fine and had not had an ectopic pregnancy.

'Yes, she was admitted as and emergency last week with a ruptured ectopic pregnancy. It's been a long time since we've seen one that ill. She was quite shocked on admission and we had to rush to theatre with her. Let me just check in her notes- ah, I thought so. She had a left salpingo-oophorectomy but there was a lot of haemorrhaging so she needed several bags of blood. She's doing remarkably well now, though she was on high dependency for twenty four hours post-theatre. She should be home this week, I would have thought.'

Clare could barely speak.

'How dreadful, poor Alexa. She was so excited about the pregnancy. Thank goodness she's doing ok now.'

'I was talking to her earlier. She told me that she'd seen one of the doctors from the surgery earlier in the week. Makes you wonder if maybe at least some of this could have been prevented. But you know what ectopics are like, buggers to diagnose sometimes.'

Clare mumbled in agreement and rang off but not before asking him to pass on her good wishes to Alexa. She sat and tried to recall her conversation with Sam, playing it over and over in her head, trying to convince herself that he had done everything right. His notes were sketchy to say the least. Thoughts in a similar vein were all pervasive as she drove home. She felt angry with Sam and furious with herself for not checking his work more thoroughly. She toyed with the idea of ringing him at home but decided that this would achieve little as a face to face discussion would be much more productive.

The relaxing evening Clare had promised herself was a nonstarter. All she could think about was what she would say to Sam the next morning. She poured herself a glass of wine and boiled some pasta while she idly chopped up some mushrooms and tomatoes to make a sauce. It really had been one of the most dreadful days she had had for many months. As she sat down in front of the television with her supper she saw the holiday tickets on the coffee table and momentarily felt uplifted as at least she had that to look forward to next week. But then she came plummeting down again, remembering that she was no longer going on holiday and would be working every day. She was just trying to imagine what David would say and debating the pros and cons of telling him when he called that evening when the telephone did ring and she guessed it would be him. However it was not David's voice she heard after she said hello.

'Good evening, is that Clare?' It was a pleasant voice; deep, melodic and she recognised it from somewhere but couldn't immediately place it.

'Yes?'

'Clare, it's Piers Corbett, from the assisted conception unit. How are you?'

Taken aback, Clare replied that she was fine, thank you.

'I'm ringing with some good news for you and David. I've sorted out and actual date for you to start your first cycle of treatment. October the second.'

Clare nearly dropped the receiver. This was the last thing she wanted to hear.

Professor Corbett erroneously took the silence to indicate that she was speechless with joy, which was the reaction he usually got when he rang his patients.

'If you could come to the unit..' he began to continue but Clare interrupted him.

'I'm afraid that won't be possible. There have been one or two problems with work and there's no way that I could be ready for this.'

'But I understood from David that you were keen to start as soon as could be.'

Clare racked her brain for what to say.

'Oh, we are of course but it's just that now is not a good time after all. Thank you for your trouble though and taking the time to ring.'

'Is there something you're not telling me, Clare? Something worrying you, that maybe we should discuss?'

'No, no, not at all. You've happened to catch me after a really busy day and I'm worn out, that's all. Look, I think the best thing is if we get back to you when life's treating us more kindly. I would imagine it will be in the New Year or perhaps next Spring.'

'Are you sure about this? It seems such a dramatic change of heart from when I saw you and then spoke to your husband.'

'Yes, I'm, I mean we're sure.'

'Well if that's the case then I can easily fill that slot that you were going to have and I'll wait to hear from you. Feel free to contact me anytime, even if it's just for a chat to go through the procedure step by step again.'

'That's so kind of you. I'm sure we'll be in touch soon.'

Returning to her chair, she curled her legs up and hugged them to her body. Amazed by what she had just done, she found she was trembling inside. The immediate feeling of relief that she had just eradicated one huge worry was extremely short lived as she then faced up to the fact that she would now have to tell David not only about the cancelled holiday but also shatter his dreams about starting the process which he hoped would lead to a family.

Chapter Ten

Sam and Becca were in bed together but only in the sense that they were lying on the same mattress. Sam, exhausted, was asleep or pretending to be asleep, flat out on his stomach with his head turned away from his girlfriend. Becca was rolled onto her side, her back towards Sam, trying to disguise the fact that she was crying. She'd managed the whole evening without crying but now tears crept silently down her cheeks and dripped off the end of her nose while she tried desperately not to sniff or do anything that might give away the fact that she was so upset.

They had had an evening that was an emotional rollercoaster. The initial consoling feature was that Sam had actually come back to the house at all and had not stormed off again at bedtime. She had wondered tentatively if this might convey the smallest flicker of hope.

He had arrived home just after seven and had clearly been to the pub after leaving the surgery. He had made no attempt to be affectionate and had just barged into the kitchen, opening and closing cupboard doors as he searched for something to eat. His quest had been fruitless and with an exasperated sigh, he had rung and ordered a takeaway. They'd sat in silence waiting for it to arrive, both pretending to be immersed in a quiz programme on the television which was normally one of Sam's favourites, in which he delighted in calling out all the answers. Becca had watched him furtively as he refused to look at her. When the doorbell had rung, she'd leapt up and gone to collect and pay for it and, despite the deliciously spicy and tomato-y aroma making her stomach perform a variety of acrobatic feats, had served it out onto plates for them both. She'd even poured him a glass of wine, in the hopes that more alcohol might mellow his mood. But he'd pushed it away, commenting scathingly that she knew that he never drank wine with Indian food and did she never think of getting any beers in.

Sam had eaten ravenously. Becca had pushed hers around the late and had chewed on a piece of naan bread. When Sam had finished by wiping his plate clean with the left over bread, he had merely stood up, picked up her plate without even inquiring if she had finished with it and taken them into the kitchen. On his return, he'd brought with him a cup of tea, a packet of chocolate digestive biscuits and a mug of hot chocolate for Becca. Taking this as possibly some sort of peace offering, she had dared to break the silence.

'How was work today?'

He'd carried on dunking his biscuit, eyes fixed firmly on the television screen.

'Bloody lousy. One of the partners has just announced she needs some time off so we've all got to step in and breach the gap.'

'I'm sorry about that. You work hard enough already.'

Sam had grunted in a non-committal way.

'Have you been to work today?' He'd noticed when he'd had to return home to shave that morning that she'd been out.

'Yes, I have. I felt a bit better, so I thought it might help if I went in. We had quite a busy day as well. I got some good sales, so that pleased Imogen, my boss.'

Another grunt. Becca had wondered what to say next.

'It's been awful weather, hasn't it? We thought we'd have a really quiet day but it turned out to be the opposite,' she had tailed off towards the end, thinking that she was sounding stilted and stupid.

Sam had refused to be drawn and had irritatingly flicked through all the channels with the remote control. Then much to Becca's surprise, he had turned the set off and turned to her.

'So have you decided what you're going to do?' he had demanded.

'About the baby?' she'd replied needlessly.

'Of course, the baby,' Sam had enjoyed the sarcastic comment.

'I want to keep the baby,' she'd announced, more emphatically than she felt, 'but I also want to keep you.'

'I told you, you cannot have both of us.'

'Sam I can't believe you're being so heartless. It's easy for you to look at things in a completely black and white way as you've not got hormones whizzing about pulling you in all directions. I can be realistic and see your point that maybe the

96

timing isn't ideal but at the same time something is telling me that there is a tiny life inside me that is so, so special. And what makes it even more special is that half of it belongs to you and that we created this minute person together.'

'I do realise that it's hard for you, Becs and that's why I'm trying to be strong for both of us, trying not to let emotion get in the way of practicality. I'm sorry I disappeared for the weekend but I needed to get my head round this and you needed time to think, too.'

'I didn't do that much thinking, I'm afraid. I thought you'd left me for good and wouldn't come back. You didn't ring me or even text me. Now you're back, telling me to get rid of my baby.'

'Your baby? A second ago it was ours!' Sam had snapped.

'You know what I mean. Oh Sam, please help me here. This is so difficult for me. I felt so ill after the last termination and so depressed I really don't want to have to go through it all again.'

'It'd be different this time. Our relationship is much stronger. We can look forward to me finding a full time job and really settling down somewhere, buying a house, being together. Becs, if it helps, we could get married.'

She had dropped the mug that she was holding, barely able to believe what she had heard. He had never before even hinted at putting their relationship on any more formal a setting such as buying a house together, let alone taking a major step like getting engaged. It was what she had wanted from within the first few days of going out with him, fully aware that she was hopelessly in love with him and would do anything for him.

'Get married?' she had echoed, cautiously.

'Yes, if you'd like to.' He had switched the television back on at this point.

Becca had got up and gone and sat on his knee and hugged him tight.

'You know there's nothing I want more.'

She had hugged him again and, unbeknown to her, he, had continued to watch his programme over her shoulder.

'That's settled then,' he had said, gently untangling himself from her arms. It had hardly been the most romantic of moments but Becca had been blinded by infatuation.

'Are you sure?' she'd asked him, fearing he would have already changed his mind.

'Of course,' matter of factly. 'Now we've settled that, what about this termination? Shall I arrange an appointment for you at a clinic?'

Defeated, she had acquiesced.

'I could go back to Dr Jennings; she did want to see me again to discuss things.'

'No need for that, we can sort things out ourselves. You didn't say anything about me when you saw her, did you?'

'No, Sam. I wanted to but didn't know if you'd told her about us yet.'

'Not yet. I'm going to, soon, of course.'

He had patted her thigh in an avuncular rather than lover-like way.

Perfunctorily, Sam had told her to leave the arrangements to him and he would get her an appointment at a private clinic that he had heard one of the partners talking about. Much to her dismay, he had then avoided all talk of engagements and weddings, claiming that he was far too tired to discuss all that. They'd gone to bed early and Sam appeared to have fallen asleep very quickly, leaving Becca watching the hands of the clock go round and round, one hand resting protectively over the lower part of her abdomen.

Clare too was awake, alternately planning the conversation she was going to have with Sam in the morning and musing guiltily what she had said to David when he had phoned her late in the evening. Or rather about what she had not said to David. He'd been chatty and vivacious, barely able to contain his excitement for what he had to tell her. After a brief description of the first day of the conference, mentioning some interesting presentations, he'd told her that he'd met up with Howard Maxwell, a mutual friend and contemporary of theirs from medical school. Laughingly he'd described to Clare how Howard had changed, knowing that she would be amused to hear that his long unruly locks and hippy like attire had been replaced by a trendy haircut and an expensively cut suit. He knew that she would be amazed to hear that Howard had finally chosen psychiatry as his career speciality. Not only that, but as they'd been chatting together in the bar after a deliciously satisfying dinner, it had transpired that, as if by some fateful coincidence, that Howard and his wife had two children, both the result of assisted conception. David, keen to hear more, had pumped him for all the details and was overjoyed when Howard had informed him that the treatment was successful first time on each occasion. Howard had been understandably enthusiastic for the technique and had infected David with his optimism, the end result of which Clare had to listen to. In a way, she'd been relieved that he had been so chatty as it had meant that she had to say very little other that utter some unintelligible but hopefully appropriate noises. He had, of course because he was David and never selfish, asked Clare about her day, which she had described sketchily, focussing largely on the weather but had seen fit to mention Virginia's broken leg. David had been very upset to hear about that and had sent all sorts of good wishes to Ellie, Ian and their daughter. Clare had then pleaded exhaustion and the prospect of another very busy day to come and David, instantly understanding had said his goodbyes, telling her how much he loved her and how he couldn't wait for their holiday and the even more exciting prospect of what was to happen in October.

When he'd rung off, Clare was literally shaking, unable to believe the hole that she had dug and put herself in and which seemed to be getting deeper and deeper. She had showered, as if hoping that the water would wash away some of her worries and then climbed into bed and attempted to read a novel. The words had refused to make sense and after three pages she had abandoned it and had tried to read another book, this time one she had read a great many times before and which she would resort to in times of great stress as it was as familiar and safe as a warm blanket and held no horrid surprises as she turned each page.

Eyelids dropping she'd turned off the light and there she still was, watching the digital display on the radio alarm and reciting alphabetical lists of towns, countries and rivers which was her own peculiar version of counting sheep.

Clare did eventually fall into a deep dream-packed sleep and woke feeling unrefreshed but glad to see that the rain had finally stopped and sun was streaming in through the window. She hoped that it would be a good omen of the day to come and found she was feeling quite cheery as she showered and then made her breakfast. Dressed in a dark blue linen skirt, teamed with a fitted T shirt with three quarter length sleeves and wedge sandals, she nodded in approval at her reflection in the mirror, twisting this way and that to examine as many angles as she could.

David rang, just before she was leaving, hoping to catch her simply to say good morning and ask if she'd slept well. She'd kept the conversation short and light and he'd wished her a better day before going off to do justice to a full English breakfast in his hotel. Clare felt far more confident that she would be able to explain to him what had been happening. Having spent what felt like most of the night rehearsing what she would say to him, she was pleased to find that her arguments sounded just as logical by the light of day and thus decided to put these thoughts to one side until tomorrow when he returned. It was her half day and she planned to spend at least some of it shopping, a pastime she thoroughly enjoyed but rarely allowed herself to indulge in.

It was funny to see how the nicer weather had brought out the kinder sides of everyone's characters at the practice. Ed's normal humour and energy had been restored, John looked ten years younger and Sam, Clare was secretly delighted to see, was clean-shaven and smartly dressed. They all greeted each other cheerily and sat, finding time for a coffee, before surgeries began.

John stopped Clare at the top of the stairs and asked her if she was definitely sure about cancelling her holiday and covering for Ellie. Clare assured him that there was no problem, omitting to say that she had not yet mentioned it to David.

Her surgery went well. She ran more or less to time. Reviewing some patients who had presented a couple of weeks earlier with a mixture of symptoms that were baffling to say the least, she was relieved to find that they had both recovered, as mysteriously as they had been smitten. There were several cervical smears to be done, some chronic disease management and finally a young schoolgirl in her early teens troubled by panic attacks. Her notes completed, Clare logged into Sam's diary and found that he too had finished. She tracked him down, already upstairs and eating biscuits and summoned him to come and join her, in her room.

He knocked and entered simultaneously, passing on the good news as he did so that there were only three requests for house calls that morning. He sat down and looked at her attentively.

'Talking of house calls, Sam, we need to talk about one that you did last week, just before I went off sick.'

'Really?' asked Sam. 'Which one was that?'

Clare got Alexa Thetford's notes up on the computer screen to share with Sam.

'Do you remember going out to see this patient?'

'Er.... Yes,' Sam started, hesitantly.

'Tell me about it, what happened.'

'I thought we'd already discussed it. Anyway, if I recall correctly, she is about 8 weeks pregnant. She was constipated and had felt a bit dizzy but that had settled by the time I got there.'

'What made you think she was constipated?' inquired Clare.

'She'd had some discomfort, or pain, low down in her abdomen, on the left and not had her bowels open for a few days. Constipation is very common in pregnancy.' He tried to justify his words.

'Had she any other symptoms? Your notes that you've written are really very brief.'

'No, I don't think so.'

'What about bleeding?'

'Oh yes, there'd been the tiniest bit of spotting. I promised her I would arrange and ultrasound for her and – oh shit- I forgot to do it.'

He looked earnestly at Clare and saw the serious expression on her face.

'What's happened, Clare? Something must have, tell me, please.'

'Sam, Alexa was admitted two days after you saw her with a ruptured ectopic pregnancy. She was haemorrhaging badly, needed emergency surgery and a blood transfusion.'

Horrified, Sam put his head in his hands.

'Oh Clare, I'm so sorry. I really just thought she was constipated. She seemed fine.'

'Sam, this is really important. Did you examine her at all? You've put nothing in her notes.'

Sam shook his head, which was still in his hands.

'She seemed so well, she said she felt better. I just listened to her and then reassured her. I didn't even consider an ectopic. Oh shit shit shit. How is she now?'

He looked at Clare through his fingers.

'She's ok; they had to remove her left ovary and tube. She should be home in the next few days.'

'Clare, I just don't know what to say. I've messed up big time here and I feel dreadful about it. I've let Alexa down and you. What should I do?'

'Sam, I appreciate your honesty. At least you've not tried to cover up your mistakes and make things worse. I don't know how this is going to pan out but the first thing you must do, or we must do, is make contact with her when she comes home.'

'Shall I telephone her?'

'I think, in the circumstances that a visit might be more appropriate. She may have questions that she wants to ask and it's preferable to do that face to face. I think we should probably go together, as I'm responsible for your work, as your trainer.'

'But it's my fault, Clare, I'm happy to go on my own.'

'Thanks for offering, I know you would, but as I said, I think we should do this together.'

'Do you think she'll put in a complaint?' Sam asked tentatively.

'I don't know. I hope not. She's a sensible lady who I know quite well. Let's just see how it goes when we visit her.'

Clare could see how devastated Sam was by his error. She was relieved that he had not tried to bluff his way out of it but she was also extremely disappointed in his poor clinical care. As gently as she could, she took him through the visit step by step, discussing each point, encouraging him to identify his mistakes and say how he would have preferred to do things differently. They spent almost half an hour talking, sharing ideas, Clare trying to be supportive but feeling far from it.

She let Sam go and sat pondering over all they had said before deciding that it would be prudent to inform John, as the senior partner. He was in his surgery, typing up some referrals and listened seriously to all Clare had to report. She found some comfort in his words and advice, as she always did and they agreed that her suggestion of a joint visit was the best one.

They went upstairs together and found that Ed had taken one visit and Sam another, leaving one which John immediately appropriated as it was one of his elderly patients. He suggested that Clare got off on her half day but she was reluctant to go before seeing Sam again.

'You go, Clare. It'll probably do you both good to have a bit of cooling off time. I'll go through Sam's visit with him in minute detail, don't you worry.'

Seeing that she was still dithering, he picked up both their bags and together they walked out to their cars, where he saw her safely into hers and waved as she drove off.

The fine weather looked set for the day and Clare found herself relaxing as she drove to Harrogate. She felt better for having spoken to John and for having made a plan of action. There was just the merest hint of autumnal colour in the trees but with the sun shining down on them, they simply looked glorious. Amazingly she found somewhere to park almost straightaway and, locking the car door, she decided to allow herself to enjoy her afternoon. Spoilt for choice, she ambled from shop to shop, trying on skirts, suits, trousers and shoes until she was so laden down with successful purchases that she had to go back to the car to leave the bags there so that she could continue. She bought David a recently published book by his favourite author and was on the verge of buying him some new shirts for his holiday, when she remembered that they would not be going. Regardless she decided to get the shirts though the thought of telling David tarnished her happier state of mind and she no longer felt like shopping. Instead she made her way to her favourite tearooms and was fortunate to get a table by the window, looking out over the gardens which were a fantastic jumble of different coloured flowers. She savoured the moments as she treated herself to tea and cakes, watching the other customers choosing their cakes from a trolley of irresistible and mouth watering delicacies, initially professing to be on diets but moments later surrendering to the temptations. She lingered over her last half cup of Earl Gray tea and chased chocolate vermicelli around her plate with a fork as she tried to postpone the moment when she would have to return home.

Chapter Eleven

David returned home the following evening, bursting with news of his conference. They opened a bottle of wine and sat out in the garden, as it was just warm enough to do so, Clare trying hard to listen to him as he described the different papers that had been presented, particularly emphasising extracts that he thought would be useful for her in general practice. When he had finally finished recounting his past three days, he sat back in his chair and inhaled deeply, enjoying the scents of the September evening.

'It's good to be home. It's been a great meeting but I never really enjoy staying in hotels on my own. How have things been here? Tell me about poor Virginia. How's work been?'

Clare laughed.

'Which one shall I answer first?'

Steering clear of the subject of Virginia as this would inevitably lead on to the holiday issue, Clare told David about Sam and the ectopic pregnancy. As always he was full of sensible, objective comments, which Clare appreciated.

'How's your patient doing anyway?' he asked.

'I rang the hospital today. She's doing really well. I spoke to the consultant too. She should be home at the weekend so Sam and I will go and visit her next week.'

The words were out of her mouth before she realised what she was saying.

'Don't be daft- we'll be in the States. Ask John, he'll go with him and then it'll all be sorted out by the time we get back.'

Clare bit her upper lip and then took a large swallow of her wine.

'Actually David, that's something we need to talk about.'

'What's that?'

Now that the moment had come, all her carefully rehearsed lines deserted her completely.

'We can't go on holiday, David. Well, I mean we can but just not this weekend.'

'What are you talking about? We leave the day after tomorrow and fly out overnight.'

'Yes, I know, but we're going to have to postpone it. I'm sure we can get some of our money back.'

'Clare, this is quite simply ridiculous. What in God's name is going on?'

'You were asking about Virginia. Ellie has asked for some time off to look after her and it was going to cause such problems at the practice if she and I were both off at the same time, that I've told them that I'll work the next two weeks and take my holiday later on.'

'This is unbelievable. Did it not occur to you that maybe it would be nice to discuss it with me first?'

'Well, you were away.' Clare cringed at how pathetic this sounded.

'Away in Nottingham, not outer space,' shouted David, 'with a mobile phone.'

'I know. I'm sorry. I should have talked to you but they needed a quick decision and I felt sure that you'd understand.'

David picked up his drink and went inside. Dejectedly, Clare followed. This was not going as well as she'd been foolish enough to hope. He was leafing through a pile of letters that had arrived in his absence. Without looking up he asked if they couldn't have got a locum.

'It's unlikely,' replied Clare.

'Did you try?'

'Er, no, I said not to bother.'

'Clare, I cannot believe you've done this. I thought you were looking forward to the holiday. If I remember correctly, it was you who wanted to go to New England in the Fall. You desperately need a holiday and, strange though it may seem as I don't seem to be part of this equation in any way, so do I. Have you forgotten that I work very hard? I do out of hours work as well, which is more than you do. When you wouldn't come away for that weekend, you promised me that this holiday would be wonderful and I, for one, have been pinning all my hopes on that. You can be so selfish at times. I know that you think you are in fact, being self-less by continually putting work first but there are other people in your life who are equally, if not more important. I'm fed up with being the understanding husband all the time and simply fitting in with your whims and fancies. Can't you see that?'

'I'm sorry,' repeated Clare, not knowing what else to say, wishing she could turn back the clock and make everything different. She didn't know if she had ever seen David quite so angry. For sure, he could be passionate and outspoken about topics he strongly believed in but anger was an emotion that rarely afflicted him. As if reading her thoughts, he turned to her.

'I'm so angry with you Clare. What's got into you?'

'There's something else, too,' Clare began.

'I'm not sure I can take much more.'

Clare took his hand and persuaded him to sit next to her on the settee. Taking a deep breath in and trying hard not to look above the level of his chin she began.

'There isn't an easy way to say this, David, because I know it will hurt you but it is something that I had to do. I love you so much that I would never want to hurt you and that's what made this decision so difficult, though making it has made me feel so relieved. While you were away, Professor Corbett rang with a date for us to start the IVF.'

She paused but David was silent, his anticipation palpable.

'I told him that it wasn't a good time for us. I had to. I'm too scared. The thought was making me ill. I'm sure that it's just that I need more time to think about it, so I've told him, promised him, that we'll contact him in the New Year.'

Gradually she raised her eyes to his but found she was unprepared for the coldness in his face that met her.

'You seem to have been very busy "postponing" things while I've been away.' He remarked, flatly.

'I had to do it, David.'

'So, here we have another example of you not bothering to consider me in a decision which is of paramount importance. Yet again we have an example of your remarkable selfishness and your total disregard for me. Well, I think that's about as much as I can take, unless of course you have any more startling revelations to tell me.'

Clare shook her head, sorrowfully.

David removed her hand from his, not unkindly, stood up and went out of the room. She heard him go into the study and shut the door. Feeling very alone, she drank her wine and poured another glass, filling it right up to the rim. Hands trembling, she sipped repeatedly at it, nervously, hating the chill in the atmosphere that was usually their cosy lounge, aware that it was entirely of her creation. She wished fervently that there was something that she could do to make amends.

After a while, Clare went into the kitchen and started to make supper. Calling David when it was ready, she sat at the table waiting for him but he simply helped himself, buttered two bread rolls and took these, with his plate and fork and retreated back to his study. Clare sat; no appetite and drank more wine, not because she had any desire to but more because it was something to do. She got up and started to walk towards the study but chickened out half way across the hall. She washed up and made a pot of tea. Taking David a cup, he indicated a place on his desk where she was to leave it without even looking up from whatever it was that he was so intent upon.

Clare tried to watch television and then tried to read, first of all a medical magazine, then the novel that she had started the night before, but it seemed to have been translated into an alien language.

Time seemed to crawl past.

Just when Clare was about to give up and go to bed, David surprised her by putting his head around the door.

'I'm off to bed. I've done a lot of thinking. I still can't come to terms with what's been going on so I've decided the best thing would be for me to go on holiday on my own. It'll give us both a break – some time apart which might be helpful, even if all it achieves is some respite from these endless rows we seem to have all the time at the moment. Maybe when I come back, we might be in a better position, have clearer heads to understand what we want from the future.'

With that, he quietly closed the door, not waiting to hear any reaction and Clare heard him run up the stairs. Totally bewildered, Clare spent the night downstairs, half lying, half sitting, dozing at times but her mind far too active to achieve any useful sleep. She wondered if David was experiencing the same insomnia upstairs in their bed but one silent foray met with a firmly closed bedroom door, something that they never usually bothered about, which clearly stated keep away.

She saw him briefly at breakfast. He came down, ready for work and helped himself to cereal and a cup of instant coffee, ignoring the pot of freshly ground that she'd made. Cursory greetings were exchanged and Clare waited in vain for some more friendly conversation. Putting his spoon down finally in his bowl, David glanced at the front page of the newspaper before getting up and, without further word, leaving the house. When Clare went up to shower and dress, she noticed that he had retrieved a large suitcase from the spare bedroom and had laid out some clothes that he obviously intended to pack. She didn't really believe that he would go without her and thought that this was just an expression of his anger which he hoped would frighten her.

Clare's day passed in a rather robotic way. She performed all her duties punctiliously but emotionlessly, though taking care to ensure that her seemingly cheerful façade was maintained at all time. She took extra time with Sam, going through all his surgery encounters, one by one, but could find no criticism with any of his decisions, or indeed with his note writing. They had a tutorial in which she kept veering the topic of conversation back to problems in early pregnancy but again, was unable to fault his intelligent responses.

Resignedly, she visited Prudence Kerfoot and listened once more to her tale of chest pain, which had been excruciating and had radiated up into her jaw, leaving her breathless for several minutes before settling completely, funnily enough, just when Clare arrived. She examined her carefully, mindful of Sam, but, other than minimally raised blood pressure, could find nothing amiss. She tried to persuade Prudence to consider going to the hospital for some diagnostic tests but was met with the usual emphatic refusal. Millie snored liked someone who needs their adenoids removing as they spoke but Minnie wound her way ingratiatingly around Clare's legs, rubbing her chin against her and purring. The air was rancid with stale cigarette smoke which Clare abhorred, knowing that it would cling to her clothes after she had left the house and haunt her for the rest of the day. Clinical matters, to her mind, dispensed with, Prudence started to regale Clare with protestations of how lonely she was, how the carers who came in barely stayed long enough to take their coats off and the lady who brought her dinners (which incidentally left a lot to be desired) never even came over the threshold. Clare suggested, not for the first time, that perhaps a day centre would be the answer, where Prudence could attend two or three times a week and meet lots of like-minded individuals who badly longed to socialise more. Prudence silenced her with a look of one who has been heinously insulted. There was no way she would go to one of 'those places.'

Back at the surgery, Clare expected that there would be a message asking her to ring David and was surprised to find none. She wondered for a fleeting moment whether to phone him but decided to leave things be for now as they would be able to talk that evening. Her afternoon appointments were almost exclusively children and women and she tolerantly she worked her way through, giving advice about head lice and threadworms, contraception and the menopause. One lady brought her a small bunch of flowers for having solved the problems that she had been having with the contraceptive pill by simply discussing the alternatives, one of which had proved to be a great success.

She had asked Sam to wait for her at the end of the day and again made him talk her through each patient that he had seen. When they finished, Sam suggested that they have a quick drink in the pub before going home as he wanted to thank her in some small way for all her support. Clare checked her watch and, realising that David would not be home for probably another hour, agreed. They sat and chatted about work and mutual acquaintances. Sam's amusing and unique view of life had Clare laughing out loud and she recognised that it felt good to be enjoying herself.

Draining her glass, she started to gather her coat up but Sam urged her to stay for just one more drink before they left.

'Well, alright then, but I'll have to be quick as David will be home soon,'

Sam fetched the drinks from the bar and placed them on the table before sitting down. Clare thanked him and took a sip of her wine.

'Don't you have to be home soon as well, Sam?' she asked casually.

'I suppose so. I had promised myself that I would do some reading this evening – you know – catch up with some journals.'

'Do you live on your own then? Sorry, I didn't mean to be rude.'

'You're not being rude. There's no one special in my life at the moment and I'm not looking for anyone. Maybe when I'm settled in a partnership I might think about it but at the moment, work's my priority.'

They continued to chat before Clare got up and said she really had to go.

'Thanks, Sam. I enjoyed that. You'll have to come round for supper one evening,' she suggested.

'That'd be great,' replied Sam.

Clare drove home exceedingly carefully, feeling slightly light headed after two glasses of wine (one of which had seemed awfully large) on an empty stomach. She really felt that she had got to know Sam a little better and had rebuilt the bridges in their relationship that had doubtless crumbled somewhat in the fallout from their discussions about Alexa Thetford.

David's car was in the drive. She parked next to it, rather crookedly and went indoors. Hearing noises from the bedroom, she followed in their direction and found David actually packing his suitcase. She went up to him and tried to kiss him but he turned his head away and made a big show of choosing the appropriate gaps between his shirts for his rolled up socks. Clare sat on the edge of the bed and watched him as he fetched his things from the bathroom and chose two or three sweaters to include. She noticed that he had left the new shirts that she had bought him in Harrogate, hanging in the wardrobe.

'Are you really going?' she asked finally as he zipped up the case, picked it up and placed it near the door.

'I am.'

'Please don't go,' she begged.

'Clare, if you were really bothered, you'd have been here waiting for me when I got home, as I hoped and prayed you would be. But no, you weren't. I could just about cope with that if it had been a medical emergency that kept you. However, there's the smell of alcohol on your breath and you reek of smoke, so I think you chose to go to the pub with your colleagues, rather than come home to me. That, Clare, at this moment in time, speaks volumes. So, yes, I am going to the States tomorrow for a fortnight.'

They continued to argue intermittently for the rest of the evening, achieving nothing other than an increasing sense of disharmony. At bedtime, David chose to sleep in the spare room, giving the excuse that he was leaving very early to go into work for a couple of hours, so that he could leave in good time to get to the airport.

Clare, left alone, curled up in a ball and sobbed. She heard David leaving the next morning and got up to watch him from the window, but he never bothered to look up and see her waving, her face swollen by all the tears that she had shed.

Quite how Clare got through that Friday at work without making any major errors, she never quite knew. She spent as much time as she could in her room, pretending to be making calls and writing notes, but really avoiding everyone. She had caught a fleeting glimpse of John, first thing but this was enough for him to spot instantly that something was very wrong. Sam, too at his de-brief after surgery had not been unable to miss her distraction and the fact that her hands trembled as she reached for the keyboard or mouse. Unheard of for her, Clare went home at midday, leaving the others to do the house calls, which they willingly agreed to, recognising that she needed some time on her own. Ruminating on reasons for her uncharacteristic behaviour, the three men wondered if she was regretting her decision to cover for Ellie but during their discussions, none of them even came close to the truth.

At home, Clare had convinced herself that she would find a suitcase in the middle of the hall and David, repentant in the kitchen, making a sandwich. But he wasn't there, nor was there a note, a message on the answering machine or event a text message on her mobile that she had mistakenly left behind that morning. The total lack of communication made Clare all the more afraid to make the first move and contact her husband. She did manage to dial the first five digits of his mobile number but then paused, thought the better of it and cancelled the call with one swift thumb movement. She sat, drinking sparkling mineral water and nibbling at some crackers and cheddar cheese, willing the phone to ring, until it was time to go back to work. Before leaving, she diverted all the incoming calls to the house through to her mobile, which then, switched on just in case, lay silently in her bag for the entire afternoon.

With hindsight, it was a good thing that her surgery proved to be challenging. She had to break the bad news to a patient that the small but craggy lump that she could feel in her breast was very likely to be a cancer, she had to convince another that the benefits

112

of taking their medication outweighed the minor side-effects, she had to excise a sizable warty lump from another patient's buttock and the last patient of all had to be admitted to hospital with probable appendicitis. Having to concentrate on all these issues, plus cope with the more routine, without a doubt, helped Clare back onto a more normal level of functioning. When she had finished, she felt pleased with the way she had handled the tricky problems and sure that she had done her best. Efficiently she completed her paperwork and then ran upstairs to find Sam and check that all was well with him before he went off for the weekend. He had, in fact gone, but had left a note saying that John had checked his patients with him and that he hoped Clare would have a good weekend and looked forward to seeing her on Monday. Relieved, Clare left the surgery, locking the door behind her as, as usual; she was the last to leave.

Trying to keep positive, she stopped at the supermarket on the way home and did her shopping, carefully buying enough for two, just in case David returned home. She allowed herself one or two treats, chose some magazines and also a CD before stacking all her purchases in the boot of her car and heading off home, trying hard not to think of how she was going to keep busy for the whole weekend.

The telephone was ringing as she opened the front door and she rushed to answer it.

'Hello,' she spluttered, breathlessly, hopefully.

'Clare, hello, it's John. Are you ok?'

Clare did her best to disguise the disappointment in her voice.

'I'm fine, just ran to get the phone, that's all.'

'I wondered if I could have a word with David,' John inquired.

'He's not here at the moment,' Clare replied.

'Oh, well I could ring back later, or could he ring me? I just wanted to apologise to him about his holiday. Faye and I wondered whether the two of you might like to come over for dinner one evening in the next fortnight. It's the very least I can do to say thank you to the two of you.'

Clare was torn. She was very fond of John, he'd always been not only a good mentor and support but also a good friend and she felt that, much as she might be tempted to, she could not lie to him.

'This is really difficult, John, but I'm afraid we won't be able to do that. The thing is, you see, I didn't tell David about my covering for Ellie until he came home from the conference. In a nutshell, he wasn't very pleased with me and we had a bit of a row and he said he was going on holiday on his own. I'd thought he might be here when I got back this evening but he isn't and, looking at the clock, the flight would be due to take off about five minutes ago.'

'Clare, I am so sorry. You should have said something. We could have found a locum or even managed ourselves. The last thing any of us would have wanted to happen was for you and David to fall out.'

Well, it's too late now, I guess,' Clare tried to sound bright. 'I'm sure it'll all be ok when he gets back.'

She wished that she felt as confident as she sounded.

John chatted on a little longer, offering his help if Clare needed a chat, urging her to try to contact David as soon as possible to put things right, rather than wait for him to get in touch with her. Clare thanked him profusely but was relieved when the call was over. She made some supper, cheese on toast with brown sauce, fresh pineapple and sat, whiling away the evening watching American comedy shows on television until after midnight. Much to her surprise, when she lay down in bed and switched off the light, she was asleep in an instant and slept refreshingly for an uninterrupted nine hours.

Chapter Twelve

Clare quite enjoyed her weekend. She gave the house a thorough clean, caught up with the washing and ironing. Ruthlessly she worked her way through piles of papers and journals, throwing out the majority of them, aware that they had either been read or would never be read. In a moment of supreme domesticity, she emptied kitchen cupboards, washed them out and then replaced everything very neatly before polishing the doors and worktops. Concentrating on keeping as busy as she could meant that she had less time to sit and think, so she then tackled the garden. She weeded vigorously, cut the lawns, trimmed the edges and dead headed the roses. Exhausted on the Saturday evening, she made herself a good meal, rewarded herself with a couple of glasses of excellent wine and watched one of her favourite DVDs. The latter turned out to be a big mistake as the opening music immediately reminded her that she and David had seen the film together, when they had first started going out.

Despite this she had another good night's rest but found that she was at rather more of a loose end on the Sunday, having achieved so much the previous day. Reluctant to leave the house, even though she had a mobile phone, she wandered from room to room, looking for things that needed to be done, rearranging ornaments, plumping up cushions and arranging CDs in alphabetical order. The house seemed huge and lonely; it felt as if David had been gone for weeks, not simply two days. By the time the afternoon arrived, Clare had run out of steam for coming up with ideas of jobs to do and ended up sitting, wading her way through the Sunday papers, drinking innumerable cups of tea and eating far too many chocolate finger biscuits. The cryptic crossword three quarters finished and the general knowledge one all done bar two clues (thanks to the help she got after searching on line), Clare dozed off for an hour and woke with a start and a stiff neck. She longed for it to be time to go to work but even more she longed for David to get in touch.

After what seemed like an interminable evening, not helped by the lack of any interesting or mind diverting programmes on television, Clare settled for an early night but found sleep impossible, unable to switch off from thoughts of David, where he was, what he might be doing and wondering if he was thinking the same thoughts about her.

Bleary eyed on the Monday morning, she got up, made her side of the bed and got ready for work, trying to take some pride in her clothes but feeling disinterested decided on a very plain pair of dark charcoal gray trousers and a black cashmere jumper with a square cut neck. Reflecting that the end result was too sombre as she looked in the mirror, Clare rummaged in her jewellery box for something to brighten up her outfit. She gulped as she saw the diamond earrings winking at her but felt too consumed by guilt to wear them. She chose a simple string of pearls and matching earrings instead.

As she drove off in her car, Clare decided that she must do her utmost not to let her home problems interfere with work. She reconciled herself to the fact that she had her mobile with her at all times and could check emails regularly both at work and at home.

Locking the car door, she took a deep breath and then marched determinedly into the medical centre, greeting Joan and Gary with what she hoped sounded like her normal cheery tones. Sam, she was impressed to see, was already there, at work on the computer in the coffee room. He turned to say good morning and was pleased to see his trainer looking much better.

'Hello Clare, how was your weekend?' he asked but then thought perhaps he should not have.

She wandered over and stood beside him to see what he was doing.

'Very useful,' answered Clare,' I managed to catch up with loads of jobs at home. How about you?'

'Yes, pretty good on the whole. Clare, I came in early to check on hospital discharges. Alexa came home on Friday evening. When do you think we should go and see her?'

'I think we should go today, don't you?'

Sam looked nervous, but nodded.

'Try not to worry. I think she'll be fine about it.'

Sam gave her a rueful grin.

'I wish I shared your confidence, Clare. I cannot get over how completely and utterly stupid I was.'

Suddenly very sorry for him, Clare put her arm around his shoulders and gave him a slight squeeze. He glanced up at her and thanked her. They agreed to meet up after morning surgery as usual and then go on their visit.

Surgery was very much like any Monday morning – busy. People clamoured to be seen, having tolerated their symptoms over the weekend, preferring to consult their own doctors rather than have to queue up and visit the out of hours clinic. Clare worked her way through her list, which included three extras at the end, only stopping very briefly four times to check her phone.

When she went upstairs, she was amazed to be greeted by a huge bunch of exotic flowers together with a card from Ellie and the twins, thanking her for agreeing to work. She was just about to make herself a coffee when she spotted the look of abject despair on Sam's face and decided that it would be better just to crack on and visit Alexa.

Sam proffered no argument when Clare offered to drive and they made their way to a small cul-de-sac of ten houses on the west side of the town. All detached, the buildings curled their way around the curvature of the road, each one fronted by a meticulously groomed garden full of symmetrically arranged plants. Clare pulled up outside one of them and switched off the engine. They exchanged looks, she nodded virtually imperceptibly and they synchronously got out of the car. Walking up the short drive, Clare patted him on the arm, trying to reassure him but his face was ashen and his brow covered with tiny beads of sweat.

Alexa opened the door and smiled at them both.

'Come in, how kind of you to come round.'

She led them into the lounge, a large, open plan room with polished floorboards and a pair of vast cream leather sofas awash with chocolate and lilac coloured cushions. A black and white photograph of Alexa and Will, her husband, caught off guard, looking relaxed and ecstatically happy was hung prominently above the modern fireplace.

She motioned to them to sit down, before doing the same, albeit rather cautiously.

'Sorry,' she explained. 'I'm still quite sore.'

'How are you?' began Clare. 'We were so sorry to hear what happened.'

'I'm fine now, well, nearly anyway. Getting better each day. My wound's healing up nicely. The district nurse came in to check it yesterday and was quite happy with it. She says there's no need for her to come in again unless I'm worried and then I can call her.'

'You are looking really well,' Clare agreed, sincerely. 'But you must feel very upset about losing the baby.'

Alexa nodded, thoughtfully.

'Of course, but I also understand that the baby could never have survived, growing in my tube, as it was. The consultant at the hospital was excellent though and said that my other tube looks fine and there's no reason why I shouldn't manage to have a normal pregnancy next time.'

'That's very good news,' nodded Clare. 'We'd arrange a scan for you as well, as soon as we knew you were pregnant.'

'Yes, that's another thing the hospital said.'

Clare continued to ask questions about her progress and what had happened while she was in hospital, trying to explore her feelings and concerns. Sam stayed very quiet, listening intently.

'So, how do you fell about all that's happened to you?'

Alexa took her time before replying.

'Most of all, I feel lucky to be here. They told me my tube had ruptured and that I had lost a lot of blood. I feel very upset about the pregnancy, because, as you know, we were so excited but it was not meant to be, this time. I've always been a positive person, so's Will, so we'll simply try again when we feel ready, which we both hope will be sooner rather than later.'

Sam cleared his throat.

'I er I,' he stuttered. 'I wanted to apologise. When I came to see you, I think I should have been more thorough. I should not have allowed myself to be mislead by the fact you said you were feeling better. I feel that I've let you down.'

But I WAS feeling better,' Alexa emphasised. 'I'd got up that morning feeling really dizzy, admittedly but I had some breakfast and by the time you got here, I felt back to normal. You gave me some advice about my constipation. I felt fine for the rest of the day and the next. If I hadn't, I'd have got back in touch with a doctor.'

'But, I promised to arrange a scan for you and I forgot, because I was busy. That's no reason to forget. I'm really sorry.'

'And I forgot about you saying anything about a scan. I went away to stay with my mother for two nights –Will was away- and it was only when he was driving me home that I got terrible pains in my stomach and almost fainted. So he drove straight to the hospital. I can just about remember getting there but not much afterwards. You mustn't feel bad, Dr Curtis. The consultant told me how difficult ectopic pregnancies can be to diagnose in the very early stages. Don't worry, I don't blame you.'

Sam looked very relieved but still concerned. Now that he had started to talk and explain to Alexa, his confidence grew and he found it easier to carry on, so Clare let them converse for some time before prompting that it was time to take their leave.

Alexa, suddenly worried because she had not offered them a drink, thanked them for coming, shook hands with them both and saw them to the door.

They climbed into Clare's car and she carefully negotiated her way out of the close and turned left at the end of the road to head back into the town centre. Sam opened the window next to him and let the air blast into his face. Clare concentrated on her driving but then steered into a parking space and stopped.

'Are you ok?' she asked.

Sam considered his reply.

'I feel very much better in some respects. She's a very understanding person. I'm glad I had the opportunity to apologise and say my piece and of course I'm very pleased that the conversation went the way it did. On the other hand, I still feel that I did not handle this situation well in the first place and that maybe things could have been different for her. I know that I didn't do a proper consultation. I keep going over and over it in my head and I wish I'd done things differently. I owe you a great deal, Clare. You've been a great support, when you must have wanted to slap me round the head and a good friend.'

'That's what I'm here for. I hear all that you say, Sam. I think you've learned a very salient lesson that will stay with you for the rest of your life. Let's now try to put this episode behind us as, as far as I am concerned, the matter is closed. Whatever you do, remember that, apart from this, your work has been of a consistently very high standard and that none of us are perfect, however hard we try to be.'

So saying, she put the car into gear and drove off back to the surgery, leaving Sam to his own devices for lunch and turned her own attentions to some outstanding telephone calls and the day's letters. John had seen her car in the carpark and searched her out, sitting down opposite her and raising his eyebrows quizzically.

'Are you coping Clare? I've been worrying about you all weekend.'

'Thanks John. I feel quite a lot calmer now. David was probably right to go away and not waste both tickets. He'd have been bored and frustrated at home for two weeks on his own with me at work.'

'How's he getting on? Did he have a good flight?'

Clare waited a little before clearing her throat.

'I haven't actually heard from him yet. I expect he'll have had difficulty working out the time difference or getting to a phone – something like that.'

John recognised her rather lame excuse but was too experienced a communicator to probe where he wasn't wanted. He was gratified at least to see that Clare looked well, better rested and seemed relaxed. She turned the subject adroitly round to the visit that she and Sam had just done and recounted events to John who congratulated her on her handling of the matter. He invited her to go home with him for lunch as Faye was cooking and he know that there would be plenty for Clare as well, but she declined politely on the grounds of work pending. After he had left, she popped out for a sandwich and some fruit which she ended up eating on one of the benches under the trees in the market place, enjoying the tranquillity of the moment on her own.

Sam had made a beeline for his car, jumped in and driven home where he knew Becca would be as it was her day off. She was reading a magazine on weddings and brides, which he noticed she hastily sat on when he surprised her by entering the room.

'I'll make us a snack,' he announced, kissing her briefly on the lips and stroking the back of her neck.

'You're in a good mood,' Becca commented, following him into the kitchen where he was already breaking eggs into a bowl and putting bread under the grill to toast.

'I am,' was the reply. 'I've been worrying a lot about a problem at work but it's all sorted now, so that's just great. Scrambled eggs all right for you? Do you want cheese in them and baked beans on the side?'

Becca, still very nauseous would have preferred not to have anything other than toast but did not want to do anything that might upset Sam.

'Just eggs please. No cheese, no beans.'

Sam looked at her and laughed.

'Feeling sick, eh?'

Becca confirmed this with and involuntary belch. She sat down at the kitchen table and allowed herself to be waited on. Sam's culinary skills were basic but what he could cook he did exceptionally well and, true to form, the eggs were mouth-wateringly light and slipped down easily. Becca managed to eat most of hers, which she had to admit did quell the nausea to a degree and then sat and watched Sam as he made inroads into a plateful of food that to most people would have constituted a meal rather than a snack.

He burrowed in the fridge and produced yoghurts for dessert and then made himself a coffee, Becca having demurred.

'Mmm, that's better,' Sam pronounced, leaning back in his chair, patting his stomach and smiling broadly at Becca. 'I was starving.'

He leant forward and started to caress her hand, then her arm and then her cheek.

'Let's go upstairs for a bit.'

Becca, not normally one to turn down the suggestion of sex and on many occasions the instigator, had found that her nausea had had a similar effect on her libido as it had on her appetite. In addition, she felt too tired to move. Nevertheless, she smiled in what she hoped was a seductive way, pushed her chair back and allowed Sam to lead her upstairs and coax her onto the bed. Sam made love to her slowly and gently, so tenderly that she felt she wanted to cry. As he held her in his arms afterwards she wished that it could always be like this, just him and her but of course it would be infinitely more perfect if their baby was there too.

Over the weekend he had not mentioned her pregnancy once. She couldn't work out if this was because he considered the matter dealt with or maybe he was perhaps having second thoughts. He had seemed preoccupied though and now that he had mentioned a problem at work, she reluctantly supposed that this would explain his behaviour.

He moved his arm from under her to check the time on his watch.

'Time to get up,' he cried, giving her a quick, last hug.

She watched him as he rushed around, preparing to go back to the surgery and decided that she would stay exactly where she was and have some more sleep.

He bent over and kissed her.

'See you later Becs.'

'Bye, lover.'

He was half way through the door when he turned.

'Oh and by the way, I'll ring the clinic from work and sort out an appointment for you. We'd best get things moving now that we've decided on the termination. Just keep reading that magazine, as once this is over, we'll be spending all our time discussing the details for our wedding.'

So much for even briefly contemplating that he might be having second thoughts, mused Becca as she listened to the sound of Sam's car disappearing down the lane. Still, at least he had mentioned the wedding, which was the other topic she'd been afraid to mention all weekend. Trying to comfort herself with that thought, she rolled over onto her side, closed her eyes and was asleep in a moment.

When Ed and Sam announced that they were off to the pub for a swift drink before going home, Clare saw no reason why not to accompany them. Not wanting to be left out, John joined them also, after a quick check with his wife that she was not on the verge of serving supper. It was quiet in the pub and they congregated around a large table in the window before sending Sam to get the drinks, trying to kid him that it was one of the duties of the registrar. Clare carefully put her flowers on a spare chair, well away from everyone.

John raised his glass.

'Cheers'.

They chatted about a variety of subjects, all refreshingly non-medical. Ed told them about his weekend. He'd been rock climbing in the Lake District with a bunch of friends and had had a fantastic time. He proudly showed off the bruises and abrasions on his hands, making Clare shudder to think how dangerous a pursuit it might be. John asked Sam about his weekend but received a very vague response, so he skilfully moved on to some outrageous event that had occurred in the political world that day which inspired them all to debate heatedly on whether the particular minister involved should resign.

Clare, holding her orange juice and lemonade was enjoying herself and realised with a start that she had not thought about David for some hours. She was in good company with friends that she both admired and trusted. Aware that an empty house was waiting for her, a thought that did nothing to enthral her, she deliberately spun her drink out for as long as possible.

Ed was the first to finish, tipping his head right back to catch the last of his drink before slapping the glass down on the table.

'I'm off folks. I've got a date! See you in the morning.'

He delighted in leaving them all agog to know more and was out of the door before the others had a chance event to stand up and put their coats on.

Going out of the pub, John pulled Clare back and asked her for supper but she thanked him and refused politely. They walked with Sam back to the surgery car park. Having waved John off, Clare was juggling her flowers and trying to locate her car keys. Sam stepped over to help and opened the back door so that she could gently place her bouquet in a safe position. He then opened the driver's door but held it almost closed.

'Thanks again for today, Clare.'

'That's what trainers are for,' Clare answered light-heartedly.

Impulsively, he enveloped her in a big hug, squeezed her tight and kissed her on the cheek but then let go just as quickly, a move that was over so rapidly that Clare almost wondered if it had ever happened.

'See you tomorrow.' He now let her into her car, closed the door for her and went over to his own vehicle.

Parking her car in the drive at home, Clare wondered if there was any post, in particular something from David. If he had sent her a card from Manchester airport then it would arrive about now, she calculated. There were, however, only three circulars, a couple of bills, a catalogue from a clothing company that Clare had once bought a shirt from and some letters for David but nothing from him. Sighing, she started making a pile of post that was to await his return. She checked the telephone but remembered that the calls were diverted and there had been nothing. She rushed into the study and checked her emails but the result was the same. Deflated, she made supper and ate it in front of the television, which was served more as company and noise rather than entertainment. She toyed with the idea of not washing up, as there was so little to do but then sternly berated herself and made a mental note that she was not to let her standards slip. After all, there was just the smidgeon of a chance that David might not have gone to the States at all and might come in at any moment with no warning.

The kitchen spotless, she rang Ellie to thank her for the spectacular flowers. They gossiped for some while and Clare heard all about the twins, how Virginia was getting on, which sounded excellent and about Ian's frequent calls from Milan. Clare felt a little envious at this point. Ellie asked about work, in particular one or two patients that she was worried about and then asked Clare to come over the next afternoon to see them all. Clare accepted with alacrity, having had no plans for her half day.

Feeling more cheerful with something to look forward to, Clare started to watch a video of Sam consulting, making notes as she did so of his strengths and weaknesses. She admired his easy going consulting style and could understand why he was already quite popular with the patients. Hopefully, he would be back on track now after their joint visit that morning. He'd had a very loud wake up call but, he seemed to have learned from the experience and would emerge a better doctor.

Later, as Clare luxuriated in the bath, filled to the brim with deliciously hot water scented with her most expensive gel, she for a moment imagined that she could still smell Sam's aftershave, spicy and exotic, distinctly different from the brand that David preferred and had been using for years.

Chapter Thirteen

Tuesday turned out to be another good day for Clare. She woke to a fine day, which held the promise of at least some sunshine and it was still warm enough to feel comfortable without a coat. She dressed in a smart cotton dress, which fitted her snugly and matched with some dark blue strappy sandals that she was very fond of, planning that she would have time to go back to the house to change into something more practical for her visit in the afternoon, which was sure to involve a trip out to the paddock to see Smudge.

Their tutorial went well. They watched the video of Sam together and discussed aspects of consultation skills in general before identifying some particular areas of Sam's techniques that came to light. Surgery, too, was straightforward. There was only one rather complicated consultation which was with an anxious gentleman who had discussed his symptoms with all three of the other partners and also Sam and had now decided that none of them had fully understood his problem and it was up to Clare to see that something was done.

They all met for coffee, eager to find out more about Ed's evening. He had had a wonderful time, he recounted and was clearly completely besotted with Hannah, a trainee solicitor and fellow rock climber, whom he'd met that previous weekend. Clare was thrilled to hear him so excited. He'd never really been in a relationship that had lasted more than a week or so since joining the practice and she knew that he would love to settle down with someone. She hoped that Hannah would live up to his high expectations and certainly, if first impressions were anything to go by, then the future looked promising. He was seeing her again the next night and taking her for dinner at the most expensive restaurant in Lambdale.

It was with some reluctance that they finally broke up and went off on their house calls. Clare visited a young man with acute low back pain which had come on, ironically, when he had bent over to help an elderly lady who had fallen in the street. This was followed by a visit to an eight year old with a rash, apparently far too ill to be brought to the surgery, who had to be called in from the garden where she was playing to have her chickenpox diagnosed.

Work over for the day, Clare walked into the town centre planning to buy some groceries and also look for some presents to take for Lydia and Virginia. Supermarket purchases in a bag, she walked around the corner, making her way to a rather nice toy and gift shop which always tended to stock items that were a little out of the ordinary. Her eye was caught by the sight of a stunning blouse in a dress shop window. Made in the most delicate of materials, it had wrist length sleeves and a low neckline and was finished with the most exquisite details of tiny pleats across the front and back and tiny frills around the edges. Captivated and unable to resist, Clare entered the shop and looked around, wondering where she might find one identical. The goods were tastefully laid out, with space between the circular rails and soft music played in the background. The only person in the shop, Clare began to slide the hangers to one side, searching for her blouse.

'Can I help you?' asked a pleasant voice, behind her.

Clare turned, instantly recognising the beautiful face.

'Hello, it's Rebecca isn't it? How are you? I didn't know you worked here.'

Becca reciprocated the greeting, feeling slightly embarrassed at who her customer was.

'Hello Dr Jennings. I've been working here for a few weeks now, since just after we moved here. Are you looking for something in particular?'

'Yes, I was. I spotted that lovely blouse in the window and wondered if you had it in my size.'

'The cream one? It's gorgeous isn't it? Let's have a look. It's also available in the palest peppermint colour which is also rather nice. What size are you, a ten?'

Clare nodded and stood back to let Becca search for her and in no time at all she triumphantly produced the green version, which Clare had to agree was very pretty.

'I can get the other one from the window for you, I know that's a ten as I put it there.' Becca squeezed past a row of clothes to access the display.

'You're very kind. I'd like to try on both please.'

'Just go through into the changing room,' Becca indicated to a small area designated by a gaily coloured curtain. 'There's only a small mirror in there, if you need a full length one, then there's one out here.'

Clare pilled the curtain across and moments later was admiring her reflection, delighted to find that the blouse fitted perfectly and looked as good as she'd hoped it would. Hearing Becca cough discretely she emerged from the cubicle.

'Here's the cream blouse. Oh, that looks really good on you. Also, I wondered if you might be interested in trying these trousers. They're new in today and I think that they'd look great with either blouse.'

Clare disappeared again, swapped blouses and decided that there was no harm in trying the trousers.

'How's it going?' Becca inquired through the curtain which was then pushed to one side to reveal Clare. 'That is nice. Do they fit ok?'

Twirling in front of the bigger mirror, Clare succumbed to temptation and told Becca that she would buy both the trousers and the pale green blouse. Back in her dress she walked across to the counter where Becca was starting to make up her bill.

'Do you work here all on your own?' asked Clare.

'No,' replied Becca, not looking up as she was removing the price tag from the blouse. 'My boss and her daughter, Imogen work here too but they've gone off to lunch, so I'm in charge. I love it here. I'm in my element amongst all these clothes and I get quite a good discount.'

Clare handed her credit card over, baulking slightly at the price. As Becca waited for the transaction to go through, she chewed on the side of her thumb.

'Dr Jennings?'

'Yes?'

'I'm sure you hate it when people ask you things when you're not in surgery but I wondered if you had heard of a place called the Greenaway Clinic.'

'Yes, I know about that. We quite often refer patients there.'

127

'Is it a good clinic?'

'It has an excellent reputation.'

'Oh.'

Becca concentrated on folding up Clare's clothes in tissue paper and then sliding the resultant parcel into a carrier. She handed it to Clare along with her card and receipt.

'I think I might make an appointment to come and see you to discuss something.'

'Of course.'

Clare took her carrier and was half way to the door before wheeling round.

'What time's your lunch? Do you want to talk now? I could meet you in that teashop across the road in, say, fifteen minutes.'

'I'd really appreciate that, but I feel awful as you're obviously not at work,' replied Becca.

'I've a little bit more shopping that I must do and then I was going to have a cup of something and a bite to eat anyway. If you'd like to join me, I'd be delighted. I can see you'd like to talk about something that's quite pressing and I think I can guess what.'

'Okay then, fifteen minutes. The others should be back anytime now.'

Clare smiled encouragingly and held the door open for a lady who was prevaricating on the doorstep.

'Do come in and have a look. They have some beautiful clothes and very helpful and persuasive staff,' encouraged Clare, before laughing and winking at Becca and leaving her to the new customer.

Around the floor of the toyshop were a collection of baskets, each one filled with a different type of little toy or puzzle. Clare was spoilt for choice as she carefully examined each one before picking a selection to take with her. Going through to the back of the shop there was a separate room, rather akin to a cave, three walls of which were lined with shelves holding glass jars of every imaginable sweet from cough candy to pear drops, aniseed balls to bullseyes. Again she chose a selection for the girls and then asked for some of the handmade chocolates for Ellie, which were arranged temptingly behind the glass counter.

More than pleased with her purchases, Clare made her way back to the little tearoom where Becca was waiting, looking out anxiously for her. Clare picked up the menu and ordered tea and a bowl of home made leek and potato soup. She asked Becca what she would like.

'Just tea, please and a toasted teacake. Not too much butter though, please.'

The waitress disappeared but returned almost instantly with cups, saucers, milk and a large pot of tea.

'So, how can I help, Rebecca?' began Clare. 'Why were you asking about the Greenaway Clinic?'

Becca took a sip of tea.

'My boyfriend,' she started to explain,' well, no, he's my fiancé I suppose now that he's proposed, he wants me to have an abortion. He came home last night and told me that he's made an appointment for me to go and see someone there at the end of the week.'

'How do you feel about that, Rebecca?'

'I don't really know. Part of me wants this baby so badly that it hurts, but then I know I have to consider his thoughts and he's dead set against it.'

'Why do you think he feels this strongly?' probed Clare, leaning to one side while the waitress put down her bowl of soup, slopping some of it onto the mat and then offered her a choice of bread rolls from a wicker basket.

Becca considered her reply.

'Maybe, because he wants us to be more settled. Buy a house, get married, that sort of thing. He never really struck me as the old fashioned type of guy but perhaps, deep down, he is.'

Clare stirred her soup.

'Regardless of what he says, you should still make up your own mind. Don't let him force you into anything you aren't sure you want. The final decision about the baby must be yours, not someone else's.'

'But I think he might leave me if I don't have an abortion,' blurted Becca, idly picking currants out of her teacake.

'I hope you don't mind me saying this, but if he did leave you, then he's not worth having and you're well rid of him.'

Becca looked afraid but then laughed it off, trying to sound convincing when she said,

'But he's asked me to marry him – well not in quite those words, but it amounts to the same thing, so he must want me.'

'Then maybe he'd accept the baby as well, given time,' suggested Clare. 'Do you feel that the two of you have talked this through properly?'

'He does.'

'That goes nowhere towards convincing me that you feel you have, Rebecca. Is there someone else you could talk to? Do you have any close friends?'

'Not here in Lambdale. My best friend, Alice, lives in Stratford.'

'Then why not ring her and ask for her opinion. Better still, could you go and stay with her for a few days?'

Becca pondered on the idea.

'I don't see why not. My boss is very kind. She's already said that she owes me for a few days when I covered for her while she went to a fashion show, buying. I might just ask her.'

Clare finished her soup and wiped her mouth.

'Please think about it,' she implored Becca. 'If I'm honest, I'm worried that you're being railroaded into a decision that you're not ready to make.'

Nodding, her head, Becca agreed.

'Thank you Dr Jennings, for being so understanding.'

Clare put her hand gently on Becca's arm.

'At this moment in time, I'm Clare. None of this is going in your notes. Promise me that you'll come and see me at the surgery and tell me what you decide.'

With that, she raised her hand to summon the waitress and ask for the bill. Becca had eaten none of her teacake which was now an artistically sculptured pile of crumbs on her plate.

They walked together back to the dress shop before parting, Clare whispering 'good luck' as Becca went inside.

Virginia and Lydia squealed with delight as they opened the bag of presents that Clare had brought them. They were all in Ellie's huge farmhouse kitchen, complete with Aga, drinking tea and eating vast slices of chocolate cake that Virginia had made with her mother's help. Clare had popped home, to hang up her new clothes and change into her jeans and a rugby shirt but had found no joy in the morning's post. The girls were entertaining the two adults by showing them their collection of model ponies all of whom had their own saddle and bridle plus an array of accessories that a top class model would have been envious of. Different coloured head collars, winter and summer rugs, leg and tail bandages, each had to be demonstrated in turn. Clare was supplied with sticks of red and green plasticine and commissioned to make carrots which would then be fed to the ponies in buckets made out of egg box sections. While she was busy concentrating on this, Lydia had Virginia in fits of laughter as she made droppings from some brown plasticine and solemnly placed piles of them behind each pony. Ellie rolled her eyes and grinned at Clare, while she topped up their cups.

'So, how's work?'

Clare laughed out loud.

'You've only been off two days, Ellie. Much the same as when you asked last night!'

Clare did relent and proceeded to tell her about her morning, describing Sam's video, her surgery and of course Ed's new girlfriend. She waxed lyrical about the blouse that she'd bought and how she was longing for an excuse to wear it.

'That's easy,' cried Ellie. 'Come for supper on Saturday. Bring David and I'll invite John and Faye, Ed and this new girlfriend of his, so we can all have a look at her and Sam. Has he got a girlfriend? He can always bring her along if he'd like to.'

'That sounds wonderful. Unfortunately, David won't be able to make it; he's away at the moment.'

'Away?' echoed Ellie. 'On another conference?'

'No,' explained Clare and went on to tell Ellie what had happened. Ellie was aghast and full of sympathy.

'Clare, you poor thing. I feel so responsible. Look, I'll talk to David when he gets back. Even better, Ian will be back then too, so we'll all get together as a foursome and have dinner or something.'

Clare was quite keen to change the subject.

'In answer to your question, Sam doesn't have a girlfriend at the moment, as far as I can gather.'

'Now that I find amazing. He's so bloody good looking; I'd have thought he'd be fighting them off. But, as far as Saturday is concerned, that's fine, you can pick Sam up on your way.'

It could be good fun,' agreed Clare. 'How about if I bring some food? I could make some salads, or a pudding.'

'Brilliant,' Ellie agreed. 'Leave it with me and I'll contact everyone this evening, or failing that tomorrow morning at work. What is it now?'

Lydia and Virginia were desperately trying to attract their mother's attention.

'Can we take Clare out to see Smudge? She's not seen him for ages. Lydia can ride. She can ride without the leading rein now.' This last comment was proudly directed at Clare, who looked suitably impressed and admired how supportive Virginia was of her sister, rather that jealous.

'That's excellent progress. Shall we go out now and get Smudge ready, Lydia? Your mum and sister can join us in a few moments.'

Lydia needed no persuading, grabbed Clare by the hand, scattering tiny carrots in all directions and pulled her out of the kitchen. They ran together down the path from the back door, across the yard to the fence. Smudge, alerted by the noise, lifted up his head from grazing, pricked up his ears and started to amble over towards them. Clare was touched by his tolerance as Lydia fumbled with the head collar which she first had upside down, then inside out and then twisted. All the while, the little pony kept his head still and waited. Finally, with more than a little help from Clare, Lydia triumphantly led him out of the paddock, tied him up and started to groom him. Ellie appeared, helping her other daughter out very cautiously and Smudge diplomatically whinnied when he saw them. Lydia did indeed walk round the paddock completely unaided and was preparing to trot when Ellie lost her nerve and asked Clare if she would run alongside at a discrete distance.

'I can't wait until I can ride again,' moaned Virginia, as they were all making a fuss of Smudge as Lydia removed his tack.

'Don't worry,' Clare assured her, 'you'll catch up in no time.'

'Maybe when I'm better, as I'll need to do lots of practice to be as good as Lyd, Daddy will buy us another pony, so we've one each,' she dreamed.

'Don't push your luck,' muttered Ellie, smiling at Clare.

They really were lovely children, thought Clare as she drove home, full of chocolate cake, covered with Smudge's dribbles but not caring in the least. She could still hear their laughter as she went into the house which in contrast seemed deathly quiet. Still no messages from David.

Unable to contemplate the thought of more food, Clare picked up some medical journals and read through them. She wrote up some notes on Sam's progress, including the details of Alexa Thetford. She tried to keep an almost daily diary of events, highs and low, so that she had plenty of evidence to back up the report she would be obliged to submit at the end of his training.

After a couple of hours useful work, she threw some washing in the machine and then rewarded herself with a glass of wine As she carried it into the lounge the phone rang and Clare's heart lurched in her chest. The caller display told her it was a local call and she instantly recognised the voice as Ellie's.

'Clare, it's me. I've spoken to John and Faye and they can come on Saturday. Ed's promised to come and thinks that Hannah should be able to come too, though he says it's a bit much her having to meet everyone at once. I can't ring Sam as I don't have a number for him, so would you ask him and let me know as soon as you can please?'

'Of course I will. I'll see him in the morning. I'm going to bring salads and bread, is that ok?'

'Perfect. Faye's doing her famous meringues and I'm just going to make a big pot of chilli con carne with rice or baked potatoes. All nice and easy with no last minute preparations. I can easily do another dessert- the girls will help, they like cooking.'

'Mmmm, it all sounds delicious. I'll be in touch.'

'Looking forward to it. Oh, Clare, any news from David?'

'No, nothing,' replied Clare, slowly.

'Clare –'

'Don't worry, I'm not. Speak to you soon.'

Clare sat down in her favourite chair and curled her legs up under her, wondering what time of day it would be in New England and what David might be doing. Half a glass of wine later, drunk rather too quickly, she told herself to count her blessings. Work was going quite well, she'd bought some new clothes that she was exceptionally excited about, she'd had an enjoyable afternoon at Ellie's and there was the prospect of Saturday evening to look forward to.

Emboldened by the alcohol, she decided to ring Sam then and there, figuring that Ellie would need to know numbers so that she could make catering plans. She fetched her diary, thumbed through the address section, picked up the telephone and dialled his number. She let it ring for a considerable length of time and was on the verge of giving up when a voice at the other end said hello.

Clare was rather taken aback at the voice was a woman's and she wondered if she had the wrong number. Temporarily thrown, she was lost for words and the woman repeated her hello.

'Oh, hello,' Clare stuttered. 'Could I speak to Sam please?'

'Hang on, I'll just get him,' was the reply and she heard the phone being put down on a table or something similar.

Moments later Sam's cheery tones greeted her.

'Hello, Sam, it's Clare. I hope I'm not ringing too late, or disturbing you.'

'Hi, Clare. This is an unexpected surprise. No, you're not disturbing anything. I'm just having supper with er my er aunt. She's on her way up to Scotland on holiday.'

''Well, I'll not keep you,' promised Clare. 'It's an invitation really. All the partners are going to Ellie's on Saturday evening for a bite to eat and we wondered if you could join us. I told Ellie that I would let her know as soon as possible.'

'Saturday? Let me have a quick think. I've no plans at all for this weekend, so that would be really nice, thank you very much for including me.'

'Wonderful,' said Clare. 'If you wanted to bring anyone with you, they'd be most welcome as well.'

'Thanks again, but it'll just be me.'

'Okay, I'll let you get back to your meal and I'll see you in the morning. Goodnight Sam.'

'Sleep well, Clare.'

As Sam turned to go back into the kitchen, where he and Becca had indeed been having supper, he found her leaning against the doorway, obviously listening to the call.

'Who was that?' she demanded, barring his way.

'Clare, my trainer.' Sam pushed past her to go back to eat. 'Come on, your dinner's getting cold.'

'What did she want?'

'There's a practice get together this weekend and they've invited me.' He helped himself to more shepherd's pie.

'Are you going to go?'

'Yes. Becs, your food. Eat.' He indicated with his fork for her to sit down, rather harshly.

She did as he asked and picked up a knife which she used to move her food around the plate, while she considered the situation.

'Darling, why don't you tell them about me? I heard you on the phone just now. Why did you say I was your aunt, of all people?'

Impatiently, Sam put down his cutlery and pushed his now empty plate away from him.

'Just give me time, Becs. Don't pressurise me. I've not said anything about you as the right moment hasn't arisen. I was hardly going to announce your existence over the phone just then, was I?'

'I don't see why not. It sounded as if you were asked if you wanted to bring someone with you. And,' she paused for effect,' I am supposed to be your fiancée.'

'Leave it Becs. I'll tell them when I'm ready. Maybe when all this business with you is sorted out, we could go out with them or something. Maybe invite them here? Now, I'm going to have a beer. Want one?'

'Sam, I'm pregnant. You know I shouldn't have any alcohol.'

'So what? You won't be pregnant for much longer will you? You can have what ever you want. Raw eggs, soft cheese, liver....'

'Sam, that's so unkind,' Becca told him, trying hard not to give in to the rush of tears she felt flooding her eyes.

He was unrepentant however and took the top off two bottles and handed her one.

'Remind me, when's your appointment at the clinic?'

Dreading this moment, Becca took a deep breath in.

'I've cancelled it.'

Sam almost dropped his beer.

'You've what?' he raged.

'I've cancelled it,' she repeated before adding hastily,' I've made alternative plans.'

He looked worried.

'And what might they be?'

'I'm going to stay with Alice for a while. I've cleared it with Imogen and she's given me all next week off. I'll go on Sunday and she's arranged an appointment for me at a clinic near her. It means I'll have someone with me the whole time. Before and after, this makes me feel a little better about things. You'll be busy working, so I thought it was a good idea.'

'When did all this happen? More to the point when were you planning to tell me?'

'Only this afternoon,' Becca was able to say quite honestly. 'I just felt I needed some female support.'

Mollified, Sam thought the idea through.

'That's quite a good plan Becs. It'll be much better for you to be with Alice as you say. Take as much time as you need. I can always square it with work for you if needs be.'

Becca was surprised that Sam had taken this so well. He and Alice had a mutual loathing of each other, which Becca could not understand at all, so she had expected Sam to argue and make the usual spiteful comments about her friend which he usually did. She was even more surprised when, for the rest of the evening, he proved to be the model boyfriend as he cuddled up to her, massaged her feet and generally lavished attention on her.

Chapter Fourteen

Saturday passed in a flash as Clare shopped in the morning and then spent most of the afternoon in the kitchen, making a green salad, a tomato and sweet corn salad and some coleslaw, followed by a choice of dressings. She listened to an excellent play on the radio and then, as an afterthought, rushed back out to the off licence this time to buy wine and beers. Ellie had told everyone to arrive at about six, because the twins had begged to be included in the revelries and their wish had been granted on the condition that they promised to go to bed at nine.

There had still been no word from David in any shape or form and Clare, if she were honest, felt angry with him. It was not like him to bear a grudge and although that part of her fretted from time to time that something might have happened to him, increasingly that fear was being replaced by annoyance. She ignored the fact that she had behaved no better, having made no attempt to contact him, which some might have said was inexcusable when she not only, of course had his mobile number, but also a copy of his entire itinerary which included contact details for all the hotels. Clare had calculated that he would be in Boston that weekend but disallowed further speculation by turning the volume on the radio up louder as if to block out her thoughts.

Looking forward immensely to the evening, she wallowed in the bath and concluded that as it was highly likely that David would be having a fantastic time, there was absolutely no reason why she should not do the same. Stepping out of from her ablutions, she pondered on what to wear as Ellie had stipulated casual dress only but the temptation was far too great and she reached for her new blouse and trousers. She had, after all, promised to show Ellie. She slipped on the blouse and marvelled over the soft and sensuous feel of the fabric. Parading in front of the mirror, she worried, with her head tilted to one side, that the neckline was a little too low. Trying on a camisole with a lacy border underneath ruined the effect completely, so, throwing caution to the wind, she consigned it back to the drawer and mad a mental note not to lean forward too much. The trousers fitted like a dream and she chose open toed sandals, yellow and white gold geometric earrings and a delicate gold necklace to accessorize.

Ready with five minutes to spare, she had just time to gather together her contributions to the feast before the front door bell rang. She had decided to book a taxi, not wanting to risk drinking and driving, well aware that alcohol tended to flow freely at Ellie's parties. Climbing into the car, she told the driver Sam's address, having arranged to pick him up as his house was on the way. It was a cloudy evening with more than a hint of autumn in the air and trees and plants bore the signs that change was on the way.

Sam was waiting outside his front gate. He waved when he saw the taxi approaching and leapt in beside Clare, kissing her each cheek, before it had even had a chance to stop entirely.

'You're nice and prompt!' Clare was flattered by his greeting. 'I hope you haven't been waiting long.'

'Hardly a minute,' he reassured her, trying to peep into one of the containers she was balancing on her knees.

'I love the look of your house, or should I say your brother's house.'

'Pardon?' Sam was perplexed but quickly recovered. 'Oh yes, it's beautiful, isn't it?'

'How long has he lived there?'

Sam thought about his answer.

'You lose track of time, don't you? It must be several years now.'

He changed the subject adroitly and they chatted politely for the rest of the journey. Clare was thinking how odd it was that it seemed hard to chat socially to someone you never stopped talking to in a work situation. She asked whether his aunt was still staying and heard that by now she should be in the Highlands.

Lydia was waiting at the door for them. Sam assisted with carrying things in from the taxi while Clare paid and arranged a time for the return trip. As she went into the kitchen to find Ellie, she was just in time to see Sam disappearing out of the back door with an over-excited Lydia, evidently en route to see Smudge. Virginia had arranged herself in the lounge, where she was under strict instructions to stay quietly and was being entertained by John and Faye.

Pour yourself a drink,' Ellie called from the walk in pantry before emerging with a pile of plates and a bowl of rice that she had cooked that morning.

'Wow!' was her reaction when she saw Clare, who had just taken her coat off. 'That's beautiful. Just look at me in my jeans and sleeveless shirt. You make me feel very dowdy.'

Clare appreciated this statement, knowing full well that Ellie not only looked stunning as she was dressed tonight but had that enviable ability to look chic and desirable in anything from a bin liner to an expensive evening gown. She twirled round, proudly.

'Just remind me not to lean too far forwards!' she warned. 'What can I do to help?'

'Everything' s under control. Take your drink through and join the others. I'll be in in a minute. Where's Lydia? Oh she is impossible at times. She was all clean and tidy and I bet she's hugging that pony again.'

'I think she's taken Sam with her,' Clare remarked, 'I'll go and retrieve them shall I?'

'Would you? I've just a couple of last minute things to do and there's the bell. It must be Ed and Hannah.'

Clare walked out to the paddock and predictably found Sam and Lydia engrossed in Smudge.

'Come on you two, dinner's ready,' she called.

Reluctantly, Lydia allowed herself to be dragged away from her pony. Half way to the house she ran on ahead, having thought of something else she would like to show Sam. He and Clare arrived at the back door simultaneously. Solicitously, he opened the door for Clare and as she went in, she felt his hand run down her back, touching her as light as thistledown.

'I love your top,' he whispered as Ellie handed him a beer and ushered them through to the lounge.

They were greeted by the sound of much laughter which suggests that someone has just said something really funny and Clare immediately went to kiss Virginia before she went over to Ed and Hannah. Ed performed the introductions and then excused himself, saying that he wanted to fetch drinks. Hannah asked for orange juice. She was very petite but muscular in a wiry sort of way. Clare could imagine her with no difficulty in Lycra, abseiling down a rock face. She had very short cropped hair, in a practical, no nonsense style but it suited her small, freckly face. Devoid of any traces of makeup she had a natural healthy glow, the sort often seen in those who liked to spend a lot of time outdoors. Clare tried hard to put her at ease but made little headway. Despite asking about her job, where she came from and how she met Ed, her questions were all answered with responses that were brief and succinct and which did not encourage further conversation. Hannah looked uncomfortable in a tailored, dark blue dress which Clare suspected she usually wore for work. She kept shifting in her high heels so Clare suggested they sat down to make her feel more comfortable but she declined. When Ed reappeared with the drinks, he put his arm around Hannah protectively and Clare was pleased to see how spontaneously she leant against him in an affectionate manner.

Ellie summoned everyone through to the kitchen to help themselves to food. Faye asked Virginia what she would like and came back with her plate before fetching her own. Lydia insisted that Sam sat with her and her sister, so Clare found a spare seat next to Hannah who had finally agreed to sit down, albeit on the very edge of the chair. The room was virtually silent apart from the appreciative murmurs of people eating good food. True to form, wine and beer was provided in unlimited amounts and by the time they got round to feeling like dessert, everyone, apart from Hannah, who had religiously stuck to non- alcoholic drinks, was distinctly a little merry.

Faye's meringues proved to be as good as ever. Crunchy to bite into, they melted into nothing after a moment on the tongue. Sandwiched together with thick, whipped cream and then drizzled wickedly with melted chocolate they were awarded many oohs and aahs of satisfaction. As an alternative, though most people found room for both, Ellie had made a fresh fruit salad, which contained all manner of different fruits apart from apple as all of these had been smuggled out to a certain pony half way through the afternoon.

John groaned for everyone when Ellie brought in chocolates and fudge to nibble on while they drank their coffee. Clare declined all but the hot drink as by now her trousers were feeling uncomfortably tight. She went, at Faye's request, with her into the kitchen where they started to clear and wash up. It had been Faye's intention to try to find out more about the problems Clare and David were experiencing but, giving nothing away, Clare denied any difficulty at all and claimed emphatically that she was totally fine and that by this time next week David would be home and normality restored. Faye, unconvinced by her bravado, took the matter no further. Like her husband she had a huge soft spot for Clare. She felt that she and John had taken Clare and David under their wing when they first arrived in Lambdale and had nurtured them and watched them settle in. John had worried her when he had told her how Clare had been recently, the ridiculous hours she was putting in and how tired she had been looking. Tonight, though, Clare looked sensational and did, she had to admit, seem to be quite happy.

Clare was determined not to let anything spoil her evening. She had eaten well, perhaps too well and laughed more than she had done for as long as she could recall. Whilst she dried the dishes that would not go into the dishwasher she thanked Faye for her concern and tried repeatedly to change the topic of their conversation. For reasons that she could not explain, she kept thinking of the feeling she'd experienced then Sam had stroked her back. She berated herself and forced herself to drink more coffee hoping it would sober her up and extinguish the alcohol-fuelled thoughts she was having.

Their taxi arrived just after eleven and ignited the end of the party. John and Faye collected their coats and said their goodbyes, Faye kissing Clare and reminding her that she was only a phone call away if she ever needed a friend. Ellie hugged everyone and thanked them for coming.

'It's been a wonderful evening, Ellie,' enthused Clare. 'Thank you so much. Ed, can we drop you and Hannah somewhere?'

'No thanks, Hannah's car in down the road. See you Monday.'

'Goodbye then. Lovely to meet you Hannah. I hope we see you again soon. Sam, are you ready?'

Clare and Sam fell into the taxi, Sam clambering in first. They spent the journey giggling about the evening.

'What did you make of Hannah?' asked Sam,' she seemed a bit stand offish to me.'

' I think she was just completely out of her depth meeting all of us at once like that. It's really difficult being the only person at a party who doesn't know anybody else. It's easy for someone like you because you're charming, confident and an extrovert but we're not all like that.'

'You're always so understanding, aren't you Clare? I really admire the way you've so much time for everyone. You're a lovely person.'

He squeezed her hand but let it go.

The taxi drew up at Sam's house.

'We're here already,' exclaimed Clare. 'Look, there's a light on in your house.'

But as she spoke, it disappeared, leaving the house in darkness.

'Oh, it's gone out!'

'You've had too much to drink,' joked Sam.

'Not so much that I'm seeing things,' retorted Clare indignantly, before bursting into another fit of giggles.

'You're right. It's one of those automatic timers. Lights come on and go off to dissuade would be burglars. My sister's very safety conscious.'

'Your sister?' queried Clare.

'I mean my brother,' Sam hurriedly corrected himself and then tried to open the taxi door.

'Sorry mate, it gets stuck. Meant to get it fixed earlier but didn't have the time. Can you get out of the other door?' The driver sounded apologetic.

'Shove up Clare,' Sam coaxed and she opened her door and got out. He shuffled across the seat and climbed out.

'See you Monday, Clare,' he said softly and kissed her on the cheek, just once but lingering rather longer than she expected and pressing his body against hers ever so slightly for a fraction of a second.

Reeling a bit, Clare watched him go up the short path to his front door, turn and wave. Smiling to herself, she got back in the taxi and closed her eyes as it sped away and headed for home.

She fell into bed, too tired to take off her makeup and jewellery or hang up her clothes which she discarded in an undignified heap half way across the room. Her head spun as she rested it on the pillow but she was barely aware as she fell asleep almost instantly. She woke an hour later, parched, with a thumping headache and a sore ear where her earring had dug in.

'Did you have a good time?' asked Becca, who had put the bedroom light back on when she heard Sam come in.

'Marvellous, thanks. Delicious food, chilli, guacamole, meringues, loads to drink, you name it. I must ask Ellie for some recipes.'

Did you tell them about me?'

'What is this, an inquisition? Look, I'm tired, I need to sleep. What time is your train tomorrow?'

'Two.' Becca pulled a face.

'Okay, I'll run you to the station.'

With that he put out the light, leant over and gave her a perfunctory kiss and then by his posture, made it quite clear that he wished no further interruption.

Chapter Fifteen

Clare could hardly believe that it was Thursday already. The week had passed in a flash and the weekend's party seemed like months rather than days ago. She'd felt terrible for most of Sunday, creeping round the house, holding her head before repeatedly admitting defeat and crawling back into bed with pints of water and paracetamol. By the end of the day, the bedroom looked as if a typhoon had blown through it. The bed linen was tangled and looked in need of a wash, sections of the Sunday papers were strewn everywhere and a trail of half empty mugs decorated the carpet by the bedside table, where there was a piece of cold toast with a solitary bite out of it. Other than ring Ellie to thank her and compare hangovers, Clare had done nothing at all but was rewarded on the Monday morning when at least she could genuinely state that she felt infinitely improved.

The week so far had jogged along quite pleasantly. Clare had enjoyed her surgeries, full of the usual unpredictability. Her tutorials had gone well and other than to mention how much he had enjoyed Saturday evening, Sam had made no reference to it. His work continued to be exemplary and Clare, after some discussion with John, decided that she could relax a little and stop checking each and every one of his patient contacts.

In the evenings, she had cleaned the house with a vengeance from top to bottom and shopped to stock up the fridge and freezer. David was due back in two days time and she viewed this prospect with some considerable trepidation, made worse by the fact that he had not been in contact at all with her. There had been one momentary rush of optimism when Clare had spotted a postcard lying on the hall floor with a pile of letters but it turned out to be from some friends they had not seen for months.

The only fly in the ointment had been Prudence Kerfoot, who had rung repeatedly for the last three days, resulting in a visit each time. Her asthmatic wheeze over the phone had convinced whoever had taken the call that she was in great distress and Clare had had to drop everything and rush round. Needless to say, by the time she arrived, even though it was only minutes from the call professing crushing chest pain and breathlessness, Prudence had been asymptomatic but delighted never the less to see Clare, who she had then held captive for some twenty to thirty minutes. She had allowed Clare to examine her and check her blood sugar, all the while gossiping on about the cats, some noisy neighbours and as usual, the parlous state of her carers.

By the third visit, Clare had felt herself beginning to run out of patience and had started to speak quite sternly to Prudence about wasting her time, causing the latter to assume her hurt look which had made Clare feel wretched. She hoped that a compromise had been reached as she had negotiated with Prudence and agreed to visit her regularly once a week. The patient had seemed delighted with this prospect and Clare had left with an arrangement made for after the weekend.

As Clare got ready for work that Thursday morning, an insipid sun shone into her bedroom. It promised to be a busy day. Elliot was taking Sam on a course about practice management and John was due his half day, which left Clare and Ed holding the fort for the afternoon. Only two days to go, thought Clare, as she reached for a cardigan, then after the weekend, Ellie would be back at work and then there should be the prospect of life calming down. After a quick coffee and bowl of cereal, she left the house, not forgetting to divert all telephone calls, just in case.

With no tutorial that morning, Clare saw extra patients and steadily worked her way through a list of familiar faces who presented with new or well established problems. At coffee time, she was delighted, if stunned, to see that Prudence had not requested a house call that day and Clare allowed herself a few moments to bask in the fact that maybe she had solved the problem. She would visit weekly for a few weeks, build up Prudence's confidence and then back off, gradually increasing the time between each encounter. John and Ed commented on her absence from the house call list and Clare simply smiled smugly at them. Much to her amazement she had finished her house calls in time to drive to the hospital to an educational meeting on latest developments in gastro-enterology. This meant that she had to sacrifice lunch but it was a chance to hear some expert speakers talk on their specialist subject. Rushing back to the surgery afterwards, she arrived just in time to grab a quick drink and a digestive biscuit before starting on her afternoon appointments, all of which, as usual were fully booked with a couple of extras added on the end.

Three hours of intense work later, Clare, surgery finished, paperwork done and nothing outstanding on her 'to do' list, put on her coat, packed up her bag and made her way through the empty waiting area. Feeling her stomach rumbling, she wondered what to have for tea. Gary, answering the phone as it rang, waved to her as she headed for the door.

'Dr Jennings! It's for you,' he called her back. 'It's Dr Curtis. He's asking if you're still here.'

'Thanks Gary.'

Clare leant over the reception counter to take the phone from him.

'Hello Sam,' she greeted him, 'you just caught me.'

'Clare, I've got some great news. I couldn't think of anyone better to share it with than you. Do you remember me telling you that I'd done a project on falls in the elderly? I've just heard today, it's going to be published in the BMJ!'

Clare was suitably impressed.

'That's wonderful. I'm so pleased for you Sam. You must be thrilled. I'd love to read it. Can you bring it in tomorrow?'

'Yes, I will. I'd be interested to hear your opinion. No, wait, I've a better idea. Why don't you pop round on your way home and see it. We could perhaps have a quick drink to celebrate. If you've time, that is.'

Sam sound exuberant, with good reason.

'I'd love to,' Clare accepted readily. 'I'm just leaving now. I'll see you in ten minutes.'

'Perfect.'

Clare had barely time to knock on the front door before it was opened and he was ushering her in. He took her coat which she removed while she looked round appreciatively at the hallway.

'This house is as lovely inside as it is outside.'

'Come into the kitchen. Or would you like to see the rest of the house?'

Clare blushed.

'Sorry, I didn't mean to be nosey.'

She followed him into the kitchen and sat down at the table on the chair he offered her. He went over to the fridge and produced a bottle of champagne triumphantly.

'I've been saving this for a suitable occasion and what could be better that this?'

Sam expertly removed the cork and then reached up into a cupboard for two flutes which he then filled in stages, waiting for the bubbles to settle.

'Here you are,' he presented Clare with one glass.

Clare took it and then raised it to Sam.

'Congratulations, Sam. You've done really well.'

They tested their drinks.

'Oh, that's lovely,' breathed Clare, taking another sip.

'My favourite,' Sam told her.

He reached across the table for a folder and, opening it, extracted a sheaf of papers which he handed to Clare.

'This is it,' he announced, proudly.

Clare started to read, punctuating her progress with sips of champagne. It was a very good paper, she told him. Well researched and written, impressive statistics and some thought provoking conclusions that would doubtless inspire considerable debate.

'I'm so glad you're impressed,' Sam said. 'Your opinion is very important to me. Let me refill your glass.'

'Thank you, I must remember that I'm driving though. So how was today, was your course good?'

'Interesting, I think I would say,' deliberated Sam. 'There was a lot that just went way over my head but Elliot has promised to do some more work with me in the next couple of weeks and then hopefully it will make more sense. How was work today for you?'

Clare amiably chatted about her day as she started to feel the early warning signs that she was drinking on an empty stomach, slight giddiness, ravenous hunger and a surge in her self-confidence. Sam watched her as she visibly relaxed. She didn't object when he offered her more champagne.

He made her laugh a lot. They giggled as they had done in the taxi coming back from Ellie's, finding tiny things outrageously funny as they continued to drink.

'I don't know about you, but I could eat a horse,' Sam told her.

'Not Smudge!' cried Clare and the two of them dissolved into more laughter, before she agreed that she was starving.

'Could I make you something? Or do you have to get home?' asked Sam.

'No, I don't have to get home,' repeated Clare. 'Do you cook?'

'A few basics. Come on, let's see what I've got. You sit there and enjoy the champagne. Luckily I went shopping this afternoon on my way home.'

In a matter of minutes, he had put French bread, cheeses, pate and grapes on the table. He broke off a hunk of bread and passed it to her.

'Tuck in,' he commanded her.

She needed no persuading. She generously buttered her bread and then bit into it scattering crumbs all over which made them laugh again. Sam picked up the bottle only to find that it was empty.

'Oh no!' giggled Clare.

'Never fear,' replied Sam, leaning back in his chair, so that he could open the fridge door without getting up. 'Ta ra!'

He opened another bottle of champagne, slightly less expertly this time.

'Oh my goodness,' said Clare, with her mouth full, 'I'll never be able to drive home now.'

'Who cares! Get a taxi!' Sam waved his glass about wildly. 'Or stay here.'

They continued to eat and drink. Ice cream was produced, which Clare tried to refuse but Sam insisted that she should try some and fed her a little on his spoon, all the while looking deeply into her eyes.

Clare stared laughing again and gave in to temptation, so he dolloped some of the ice cream into a bowl for her, splashing it on the table as he did so. Clare wiped it up with her finger and was about to lick it off when she changed her mind and she offered it to Sam who gently took it from her.

Somewhere not far away something was ringing and it took Clare a couple of moments to realise that it was her mobile phone in her bag. Jolted back to reality she frantically searched through her things to find it.

'Hello!' she gasped.

'Is that you, Dr Jennings!'

Clare was horrified. It was Prudence. It took her a moment to comprehend how she had managed to contact her but then realised that all the calls to her house were diverted to her mobile phone. She slapped her hand over the lower half of the phone and mouthed to Sam who it was. He roared with laughter which made her laugh too.

'Dr Jennings, are you there?'

Clare hiccoughed.

'Yes, Prudence. It's not really a very good time to talk, I'm afraid. I'm very busy.'

Clare looked at Sam and pulled a face.

'I'm so sorry. It's just that I feel so unwell. I've a terrible pain in my tummy and back. It won't go away.'

Sam, who had moved nearer to Clare to hear the conversation, rolled his eyes and passed Clare her glass, from which she took another drink.

'Prudence, you're always saying that there's something wrong. I'm sure you're just anxious and that everything's fine. Just try to relax. Make yourself a cup of tea and take some deep breaths. Your other pains go away quickly, I'm sure this one will do too.'

'Oh I don't think it will. It's ever so bad. I've never had pain like this before. I feel quite faint.'

'I expect it's nothing,' repeated Clare, 'try those things as I suggested.'

'Would you come and see me?' Prudence pleaded.

Sam shook his head emphatically and Clare had to cover her mouth so that Prudence would not hear her trying not to laugh.

'Not this evening Prudence. You know the arrangement we made last time I saw you, well let's just stick to that. I'm going to have to ring off now. Good-bye.'

Sam took the phone from her and switched it off.

'What was all that about?' he asked, incredulous. 'Why on earth does she have your number?'

Clare looked sheepish and tried to explain but the more she did so the more ridiculous it sounded.

'You're beyond belief,' Sam told her. 'Here you deserve more champagne. Want some more ice-cream? You have to admit, it is very good indeed.'

Clare, who was slightly concerned by her forthrightness to Prudence acquiesced and agreed to both, putting her worries firmly to the back of her mind and trying to recreate the conviviality they had been enjoying. But the mood had been lost to some extent and they finished their meal in near silence.

'Can I ask you something?' Sam said, as he scraped the last of his pudding from the bottom of his bowl.

Clare nodded, draining her glass, which was then filled again for her.

'How come you're not in a rush to get home? Is your husband away? He didn't come to Ellie's either.'

Clare pondered on how to reply.

'He went on the holiday we were both supposed to go on. He was really angry with me because I said that I'd cover for Ellie, without discussing it with him.'

Angrily, she took a huge gulp of champagne.

'I wondered. You've had a hard time. Would you like some coffee?'

'I think I'd better! I've drunk an awful lot.'

Sam stood up and filled the kettle.

'When's he back?'

'This weekend.'

'You must be looking forward to it.'

'I'm half dreading it, if I'm honest. He hasn't rung or written once. He's obviously still furious with me.'

Sam turned to look at Clare and saw huge tears rolling down each of her cheeks. He went round the table to where she was and crouched down beside her as she desperately tried to wipe her tears away with her hands. She looked at him. He stood up, taking her hand as he did, so that they were standing facing each other.

'You need a hug,' he told her, putting his arms around her. She allowed herself to lean against his chest, her hands still over her face while she wrestled with a mixture of feeling drunk, unhappy but something else which she failed to identify.

Sam squeezed her gently and held her for almost a minute. She listened to his heart beating. He unwrapped his arms and put a hand on each of her shoulders. Clare, with a final wipe of her nose with the back of her hand, tentatively looked up at him. He gazed down at her and half smiled before leaning towards her and gently, ever so gently, kissing her on the lips.

He drew back to see her reaction and when she made no attempt to move, he kissed her again, this time parting her lips with his tongue and feeling her start to respond. He kissed her cheeks, her chin and her eyes before returning to her mouth. As Clare felt her insides melt into nothing she offered no resistance when he quietly started to undo the buttons on her blouse and peel it back from her shoulders which he then licked and caressed. To his delight, he found that Clare was undoing his shirt, exploring his body with her nervous hands. He lifted her up and sat her on the table and continued slowly to slip off her clothes, kissing her, stroking her as he did so, encouraged by her murmurs of pleasure. He laid her back on the table, leaning over to kiss her breasts and stomach, helping her wriggle out of her trousers and underwear. Quickly he undid his belt and slipped his own trousers and underpants down to his ankles. Refusing to hurry, he softly kissed a receptive Clare all over, sending tingling paroxysms of desire which she had never known before shooting through her body like flashes of lightning. Eventually, it was Clare who, unable to wait any longer, pulled him down roughly on top of her, begging him to enter her. As he did so and started to move inside her, they heard the champagne glasses shatter as the hit the floor. Neither of them cared, too overwhelmed by the exquisiteness of the moments as they neared orgasm. Clare, beginning to cry out with ecstasy, made Sam plunge deeper and deeper, intent on their reciprocal pleasure.

Someone screamed, but it was not Clare.

Seconds away from the most incredible climax she had ever experienced Clare's world was catapulted into chaos when Sam suddenly stopped and looked round.

Becca was standing at the door, mouth open, shrieking.

Sam leapt back and stood, looking completely stupid with his trousers round his ankles and a half erect penis. Clare, suddenly very sober, could not believe what was happening. She sat up and frenetically tried to cover herself up with her blouse.

'Hello Becca,' Sam said. 'You've rather caught us in the act.'

'What's going on?' yelled Becca. 'Who's that? Oh my God, it's the doctor!'

152

Sam hastily pulled on his clothes and threw the rest of Clare's to her. She scrabbled into them, fully believing that she was going to die with embarrassment. Becca watched them speechless.

'We weren't expecting you, Becs. You could have phoned or something,' complained Sam.

'Why? So you could have done this earlier and then hoped I'd never find out? I can't believe that I'm seeing this.'

Clare, now fully dressed felt she should say something.

'I'm so so sorry Rebecca. This must look terrible. I had no idea that you knew Sam.'

'Know him? He's my fiancé, or so I thought.'

Clare's face lost all its colour as she instantly put two and two together. She sat down heavily and put her head in her hands. Her head ached partly from the champagne but mostly from the enormity of the situation. Her tongue felt rancid, dry and too big for her mouth. Her heart raced and her stomach churned. How had this happened? She dared to look at Sam, who was watching Becca, with a slightly mocking look on his face.

'I should go,' grabbing her bag, Clare made for the door.

Becca moved to one side to let her pass.

'I'm so sorry,' she repeated, knowing how inadequate that sounded.

She ran down the little path and fumbled with her car keys, her hands shaking so much that she could not insert the key in the lock. Finally, she opened the door, got in and drove off, veering dangerously near to a parked car in her attempt to get away as quickly as possible. The fact that she got home in one piece was nothing short of a miracle as she failed to stop at junctions, signal or look in her mirror. The only thing on her mind was to drive as fast as possible and get back to her own house where she could hide away, preferably for ever.

Clare ran indoors and upstairs, where she took off her clothes and stood for fifteen minutes in the shower, sobbing hysterically while she did so. She put on her dressing gown and wrapped her hair up in a towel before sitting on the edge of the bed going over and over again what had happened and as she did so, each time it seemed worse and worse. Even though she was warm from the shower, she could not stop shivering. Hot tea did not help as she could barely swallow. She ran downstairs to her doctor's bag and looked inside. Picking out a small bottle of tranquilisers, she took two straightaway and put a further two in her pocket in case she need them later. She paced about waiting for them to work. How could she face Sam in the morning? How could she have let Rebecca down like that? Not that she had known she was involved with Sam. But then that meant that Sam was the father of Rebecca's baby. The one she was going to have terminated because Sam did not want it. And what about David?

Clare could not begin to make sense of anything. There was no way out of this impossible nightmare. She had ruined her life, David's and Rebecca's.

Almost imperceptibly, she noticed that the shaking was settling a little. Her mobile phone rang and she picked it up to answer.

'Clare?' said a voice which sounded a long way away.

'David!' gasped Clare. 'Is that you?'

'I'm in Boston. Waiting for my flight. I thought I'd just give you a call and say I've been a fool. I love you Clare and I can't wait to see you tomorrow. What's wrong Clare, are you crying or is it just a bad line?'

Sobbing again, Clare cried, 'Oh David, I'm so sorry, please forgive me.'

She heard his voice, laughing softly, the voice she'd missed so much.

'Don't be daft Clare. We're as bad as each other. You sound exhausted. I bet you've been overworking. Get some sleep. I'll be back with you in less than twenty four hours.'

He rang off and she was left, clutching the phone, her shoulders heaving with weary sobs as the effect of the alcohol and the diazepam combined to make her increasingly sleepy. She managed to drag herself back up to bed where she climbed under the duvet, having first searched out one of David's favourite jumpers to have with her and cuddle up to, so that she could imagine that he was near her. As she closed her eyes, visions of the evening ricocheted round her brain with a fierce intensity that gradually started to fade as she fell into a deep but troubled sleep.

Chapter Sixteen

Clare was woken from sleep by the autumn sun streaming in through the window, as she had never thought to close the curtains. Screwing up her eyes to see the clock, her heart sank when she saw that it time to get up. Slowly, as the drug-induced sleep cleared, her mind focussed on the day ahead but then zoomed in with ferocious intensity to the previous evening. Tempted to hid under the duvet, Clare forced herself to get up and went to make a cup of tea which she preceded with a large glass of water, as although her body fought every swallow, she knew she was dehydrated and needed it. Clasping her cup, she wandered out into the garden, but despite the brightness, there was a chill in the air and she quickly returned to the warmth of the house. Unable to sit down, she wandered hopelessly from room to room, touching the possessions she and David had worked so hard to own and picking up photographs of the two of them that symbolised their life together. She sipped at her tea and tried to imagine what it would be like having David back that evening. She doubted that she would be able to look him in the eye, for fear of him seeing guilt written all over her face.

Reluctantly, Clare went to dress, choosing loose fitting black trousers and a baggy black polo neck jumper to hide in. She stood and stared into the mirror, despising what she saw. It was impossible, she decided, for her to get through the day. She had no idea what would happen when she saw Sam, what she could say to him, let alone how she would cope for the rest of his attachment. Her eyes were red, their lids puffy and nothing less than a complete mask of make up would even begin to hide them. Looking at her hands, trembling, she seriously considered ringing in sick, which would at least give her a long weekend to think. But conscience dictated to her that she had to go to work. She knew too well the consequences of one of the doctors calling in sick at the last minute and felt she could not do that to her colleagues.

Somehow, she managed to navigate safely to the surgery, where seeing that Sam's car was not yet in the car park, she rushed indoors and told the receptionists only to disturb her if it was an emergency. At least that way, she should be safe for a couple of hours and busy seeing patients.

Gary and Elizabeth gave each other a look as Clare hurried in.

'Shall I make her a coffee?' Gary suggested and Elizabeth nodded.

Several of the patients commented to Clare that she did not look well. She told them she thought she might be coming down with a virus and thanked them for their concern, cringing at the prospect of what their reaction might be if they knew the truth. Half way through the surgery, she took half a diazepam tablet, as her nerves were about to explode and the adrenalin rush she got each time she saw there was an email waiting for her. In doing so her feeling of self-loathing increased.

Finishing off, her mobile phone bleeped and she quickly checked to find a text message from David saying that the plane had landed safely and was waiting for his luggage. Clare gulped and fresh tears trickled down her face. She wiped them hurriedly with one of the tissues usually reserved for her distressed patients, sniffed loudly and tossed her hair back. She knew that she had to go upstairs to check on the day's paperwork which would mean seeing all the others, including Sam. Her partners would immediately suspect a problem it she avoided them. So, trying to look nonchalant, which was a million miles from how she felt, she went up to join them, persuading herself that she could act as though it was a completely normal day. Reaching the door to the coffee room, she heard chattering within and the sound of the kettle boiling. Clare put her hand on the door handle, gritted her teeth and went in. A quick glance around the room showed her that John and Ed were in there with Ellie, but there was no sign of Sam. Feeling a huge sense of relief, Clare greeted her female colleague enthusiastically and heard that Ian was back from Milan and was at home with Virginia so that Ellie could come in and catch up for a while. Inevitably, Ellie asked Clare if she had heard from David and at least this time she was able to reply in the affirmative.

'He's probably driving up the motorway as we speak,' she added.

'I bet you can't wait to see him,' Ellie replied.

'Um, no,' agreed Clare, keeping a wary eye on the door lest it should open to admit Sam.

'Sam's gone on some house calls,' John informed her, as if reading her mind. He seemed very keen to be up and off, so I didn't like to dampen his youthful enthusiasm! He told me to tell you that this morning's surgery had been fine and that he'd catch up with you later.'

Oh, good, thanks,' breathed Clare, feeling more relief.

'Promise me one thing Clare,' began John, 'that you and David will sit down this weekend and plan some time off, together preferably. If that's not possible, then you definitely need a break. You look terrible again today. '

Clare nodded and made a big fuss of getting on with her paperwork. Whilst she was secretly delighted that Sam had gone out, she knew that he had to be faced and the longer she left it, the harder it would become. For now, however, she was glad to have a temporary reprieve.

House calls completed, Clare headed for the shops to buy in some of David's favourites for supper – tender steaks from the local butcher plus some of his special pork and ale sausages and a selection of cheeses from the delicatessen. In the latter she reached into the freezer for ice cream but suddenly stopped short, experiencing a horrifying flashback to the previous evening. Rapidly discarding that idea she opted for two slices of gateau instead. Armed with her purchases she had time to drive home and put them away, plus warm up a bowl of soup and make a slice of toast for lunch. She managed half the soup before feeling far too full to eat any more but the toast ended up cut into symmetrical cubes and on the bird table in the garden.

Clare took her time, checking that everything in the house was tidy and just as David would want to find it and then still had time to sit and watch the clock before leaving with just enough time to get to work and hurry in to start her afternoon surgery.

She was particularly attentive to all her patients, even more so than usual, her aim being to prolong matters as much as possible and finish so late that there was no way anyone would be left in the building apart from the receptionists. Ironically, the patients repeatedly refused to collude with her desires and, while grateful for all the health promotion she attempted to offer them, they obviously had other items on their agendas for the day than simply visiting the doctor. The consequence of this, plus one patient who failed to attend was that Clare finished somewhat uniquely on time and bizarrely found herself with no referral letters to write either. Why this should happen today of all days and never when she desperately wanted to be away on time would forever remain one of life's unsolved mysteries.

She froze when a tap on the door was followed by Sam entering.

'Can I come in?' he asked.

'Of course,' Clare replied trying her best to sound normal. Her heart was in her mouth and she suspected that her pulse was too rapid to be counted. Keeping strictly to her role as trainer she forced a smile. 'Have you had a problem? I'm so sorry that we missed each other this morning but it was good of you to go out on those visits.'

'Clare,' Sam spoke softly, almost affectionately, 'we have to talk about last night.'

Clare avoided his eyes, afraid that he might be able to exert some hypnotic influence over her.

'I'm trying very hard to put last night firmly out of my mind. I think you should do the same.'

Sam reached out to put his hand on hers but she jerked away as though stung.

'I feel dreadful about last night Clare. I had no idea that Becca was going to come back home. She wasn't due until the weekend. I'm so sorry.'

Clare pulled a face.

'That really doesn't make me feel any better at all, Sam. The way I see it is that I got horribly drunk, so did you and we ended up having... well you know what happened and in the midst of all this your pregnant fiancée walked in on us. Nothing can make that any better.'

'Don't worry about Becca, she'll come round,' Sam tried to console Clare, who stared at him incredulously. 'She has done before.'

'What do you mean? Has this happened to you before? Look Sam, I am married, happily married.'

Sam raised his eyebrows as if to challenge her.

'Are you sure about that?'

158

'Yes, I'm quite sure about that. David comes home today and I can't wait to see him. He must never, ever find out about this as it would break his heart and I could never do that to him. You must promise me that you won't say anything, please.'

'Okay,' Sam agreed simply.

'But what I can't understand is that you told me, more that once that you didn't have a girlfriend. But it turns out that you do and what's more it's someone who confided in me, trusted me and respected my opinion. Between us, we must have destroyed her life. How can you live with that?'

Clare was becoming really angry now but Sam continued, unrepentant.

'Becca and I have a very open relaxed relationship. It's never been serious from my part. I'll talk to her over the weekend, I promise and she'll be fine about it all, believe me.'

'Sam, I can assure you that I will have the greatest difficulty believing anything you ever tell me from this moment on.'

Sam got up, walked towards the door then came back and crouched at Clare's feet, one hand on each of the arms of her chair, so that she was imprisoned.

'Then you won't believe me when I tell you that yesterday evening, you and I, for me, was just wonderful and I wish with all my heart that we could be together again. I had no idea when I came here as your registrar that this would happen but it has and I can't ignore it. I've never met anyone like you, Clare.'

Clare felt afraid by his proximity but he stood up again and went back to his chair. She watched him as he went, wishing he would go.

'I think you should go home now Sam. When we next see each other on Monday, we are going to act as if none of this has taken place. You'll be my registrar; I will try to be as good a trainer as I can to you. I hope sincerely that Rebecca can emerge from this chaos and that you will help her do so.'

Clare leaned over sideways to pick up her bag, hoping to emphasise the fact that she wanted this conversation to be over. Sam moved towards her so that when she returned to her original position he was able to kiss her lightly on the lips before she realised what was happening. He left the room, leaving her shaking all over.

Clare waited over ten minutes before daring to leave her surgery in case Sam was waiting for her in the car park. She found herself driving home by a long and circuitous route, willing herself to calm down and relax. Half a mile from home, she stopped in a lay-by and combed her hair and refreshed her lipstick. As she turned in her road, she saw David's car in the driveway, looking as if it had never been away. As she parked her own car, David appeared at the front door, arms outstretched, ready to envelop her in a hug. Clare had tears streaming down her face before she had even got out of the car and when she felt the familiar warmth of his arms around her and smelt his aftershave mingled with unrecognisable hints of sunshine and sun screen she could do nothing other than bury her head in his chest and sob hysterically. He held her close.

'Hey, what a welcome,' he laughed, lifting her head and kissing her.

'Oh David, I'm so sorry, so sorry. I've been so stupid. It's been awful without you. If only I'd come with you, everything would be alright.'

David hugged her more tightly.

'Everything is alright now Clare. I've missed you so much but I'm home now and you're here so we're back together and that is all that matters. Come on in now or all the neighbours will be talking about us!'

Clare allowed him to lead her into the house and they went into the kitchen where he had started on some preparations for supper having spotted the steaks in the fridge. He poured her a glass of champagne.

'This calls for a celebration,' he announced. 'I bought this at the airport. To us!'

Clare had a small sip and tried hard not to think of the last time she had had champagne.

'Let's go in the lounge and have this, then we can make supper together when we're ready. I've loads to tell you, lots of photos to bore you with but first, how are you?'

Clare took a larger gulp.

'I'm fine, or at least I will be now that you're back.'

David beamed with happiness.

'You look so tired Clare. I know you, you'll have been working all hours while I've been off. We've got to make a determined effort to have more time together in the future. I've had lots of ideas while I've been away. I suppose it's the first time I've had when I've been able to stop and look critically at our lives.'

'That sounds wonderful,' Clare whispered. 'Your being away has made me realise quite a lot of things as well. It's so good to have you back.'

They sat together and talked, or perhaps more accurately David talked and Clare listened as she snuggled up against him, leaning on his shoulder with her eyes closed. He told her in detail about his trip, people he had met, the ones Clare would have loved, the ones she wouldn't. He described the views, the colours, the towns, bringing it all to life with his photographs so that Clare could actually feel that she was there. He had brought her all kinds of presents from a key ring shaped like the Liberty bell to a necklace of polished semi-precious stones, the same colours as the leaves on the trees in the Fall. There were little boxes of chocolates and fudge, a book of traditional recipes and chunky cardigan in various shades of blue. Clare was overwhelmed.

'I wanted to buy you something from everywhere we stopped, so that at least you'd have the souvenirs, if you couldn't have the trip. But you will have the trip too, one day, as I promise you we will go there together, in the not too distant future.'

Later, Clare watched while David made their supper, feeling guilty as she had planned to do everything for him as he must be starting to feel the effect of jet lag. He had insisted though, saying that as long as he kept going he'd be fine, but once he allowed himself to relax, he'd probably fall asleep for hours. Supper was delicious. David ate heartily, enjoying English cuisine once more and Clare picked at hers, making the excuse that she was so excited to see David that she couldn't eat. It was ten o'clock by the time they had finished and cleared away by which time it was clear that David was beginning to droop. They took cups of coffee up to their bedroom but David never even started his as he was fast asleep as his head felt the softness of his pillow. Clare curled up next to him, listening to his rhythmical respirations, her arm resting gently over his body protectively until she finally fell asleep as well.

She woke repeatedly during the night, lying awake for a while each time before she was able to fall asleep again, finding solace in moving close to David so that she had actual bodily contact with him, which made her feel safe. She watched him sleeping, blissfully unaware as her guilt consumed her more intensely. He slept soundly, over tired but happy to be home and back in bed with his wife.

When Clare finally opened her eyes at seven o'clock, she slunk out of bed, taking great care not to disturb David and tiptoed out of the room and downstairs to make tea. It was a grey start to the day and held little promise of sunshine. She pulled her dressing gown more tightly around her as she waited for the kettle. Sitting alone in the kitchen, she sipped her tea slowly. It was too early to wake David, who needed to rest so she passed the time reading the newspaper from start to finish and started the crosswords, one of which in Saturday's edition was on general knowledge. This gave her something to focus on rather then giving in to the meanderings of her mind which, however hard she tried to control them, would inexorably veer back to her infidelity with Sam and the disastrous involvement of Rebecca.

David finally stirred just after ten. Clare heard him on his way to the bathroom and interpreted this as a signal to make fresh tea, squeeze oranges and make toast. Decorating the tray with a late rose which she'd found in the garden and balanced precariously in a tiny crystal glass, she carefully carried his breakfast upstairs. She found him looking sleepy and disorientated, sitting on the edge of the bed, holding his socks. He needed no persuasion to roll back under the duvet, be propped up on all their pillows and served his breakfast.

Clare kissed him on the cheek.

'Good morning. How did you sleep? I could do you some eggs if you'd like.'

'No need,' David told her, downing the orange juice in one swallow. 'This is just ideal. Come and sit with me and share it. Fetch another cup.'

Clare declined saying she had had her breakfast. David patted the bed beside him and Clare climbed across and lay back with him. He told her what he'd been having for breakfast in New England, where the choice had been enormous and he'd indulged in huge amounts to set himself up for the day's adventures, planning not to eat until the evening meal but then of course, not been able to resist the cakes and pastries that appeared midway through the afternoon.

'I'm sure I must have put on pounds,' he reflected, patting his stomach, which looked no different to Clare. 'I did try to exercise each day, even if it was just a good walk or a swim.'

He finished his toast and put the tray on the floor. Clare moved so that he could put his arms around her and nuzzle her neck.

'What would you like to do today, my darling?' he asked her.

'I don't mind. Whatever you'd like to do. You must still be quite tired. I'd be quite happy just to stay at home and relax.'

'That's not very exciting. I thought we could go for a drive out and have lunch. Nothing too hectic as, yes, I do feel pretty shattered, but I'd like to go out with you.'

'I'd love to do that David. You choose where we go.'

They lay cuddled up together, while David thought.

'It's good to be home,' she heard David say, slurring his words as he fell asleep again.

They had a delightful day out. Clare drove, so that David was spared the driving and they ended up about sixty miles from home at the seaside. Parking the car, they clung to each other as they battled against the wind walking down the beach, watching surfers in wetsuits brave the waves and ecstatic dogs bounding in and out of the water. The sun was gracious enough to shine, albeit in a rather half-hearted way that had little warmth but it made the sea look blue and sparkling. Clare picked up razor shells and pointed out sea anemones in rock pools as she teetered on the slippery seaweed-clad boulders. David laughed as he tried in vain to make pebbles bounce across the water and pretended to push Clare in. He was pleased to see some colour in her cheeks at last, to see the lines of worry and angst disappear and the hunted look in her eyes dissolve as she truly forgot about everything except the moment they were living in.

Appetites augmented by the sea air, they sought out the best café they knew of for fish so fresh that once you'd tried it, nothing else would ever come close and golden chips with crisp exteriors but soft and fluffy centres. Even Clare ate well, David was pleased to see. They spun out their cups of tea for as long as they could before deciding that they should head for home. Clare could tell that David was wilting somewhat and was torn between wanting the best for him and not wanting to break the magic of the day. As they drove home, her anxiety increased with every mile that brought them closer to Lambdale.

David switched on the television to watch the football results and started to wade his way through the pile of letters waiting for him. Clare, who had never been much of a sports fan, curled up on the settee next to him, needing to be near him. They spent a leisurely evening together, watching a play, David basking in being reunited, Clare tussling with her guilty conscience.

David slept deeply again that night but it was not until the daylight was just beginning to peep through the small gap in the curtains that Clare fell asleep, to be woken some time later by David bringing her a cup of tea. He sat beside her, stroking her hair, studying her in detail.

'What is it Clare?' he finally asked her. 'There's something wrong, I can tell.'

Clare tried to brush off his concern.

'Nothing really, it's just work and I'm really tired. I've not slept well while you've been away.'

'You stay there as long as you want today. I'm just going to do some paperwork and then perhaps spend some time in the garden. I'll cook later on, so you can just rest all day.'

'Why are you always so nice to me?' Clare wondered out loud. 'I really don't deserve this.'

'Of course you do. The holiday and all that went before is behind us now and we're not going backwards any more, we're just going to plan for the future.'

'I can't think of anything I'd like more,' Clare affirmed, genuinely meaning what she said.

In the end, she stayed in bed until nearly lunchtime, half relishing the luxury of having been given permission to snooze and read, half worrying that she should be doing David's washing and ironing rather than leaving him to do it. They ate sandwiches and fruit before spending the afternoon in the garden, weeding and pruning and generally preparing it for the winter. Clare was aware that as it got later in the day, a feeling of dread was taking an increasing hold on her, nausea rising in her throat. Pretending to read the papers while David was roasting a chicken and peeling potatoes to accompany it, she kept watching the clock, willing time to stand still so that it could just be the two of them and everyone else would go away. She wondered what Sam and Rebecca were doing, what they had said to each other, if they were still together as a couple. Clare fervently hoped that they weren't. Rebecca deserved someone better than Sam, someone who was honest, kind and supportive.

When David called her to the table, she had failed to be seduced by the delicious aromas of traditional roast chicken with crispy potatoes that Clare could never manage to do quite as well as him, peas and carrots, courgettes, stuffing and gravy. David poured her a glass of chilled white wine and set down her starter of sliced melon. As she looked at it what appetite she had evaporated. Each mouthful, which should have tasted exquisite as the soft fleshy fruit collapsed to release its intensely sweet juice sat like lead on her tongue before landing with a jolt in her stomach making her want to retch.

David shook his head sadly as he removed her half finished plate. Tenderly, he replaced it with a larger plate on which he had elegantly arranged her main course. Clare drank her wine, fighting with her self control and complimented the chef as cheerfully as she could David chattered on about anything and everything he could think of, more anecdotes from his holiday, some ideas he'd had for the house and even some snippets he had read from the newspapers. Clare forced herself to listen, repeatedly saying to herself that there was still over twelve hours to go before she had to go to work and that she must try to be as natural as possible for David's sake. Observing him eating and drinking, her heart ached with love for him; he looked so well after his break, tanned and stress-free. If only she had gone with him then she would have looked the same. She wondered what his reaction would be if she were to tell him about Thursday evening. He was so kind and caring that he would probably try to forgive her which would make the hurt that she would see in his eyes even more impossible to bear.

By finishing the lion's share of her chicken, Clare was able to excuse herself from dessert on the grounds that she was too full. David accepted this and ate apple pie with custard on his own. They washed up together, Clare encouraging David to tell her more details about his trip rather than risk steering towards more familiar and infinitely more treacherous territory.

At half past ten, David suggested bed and Clare reluctantly followed him. They lay in bed, cuddled together, Clare wrapped in David's arms. When he began to kiss and stroke her with more intent, she wanted to break away and be on her own. Afraid though that a rebuttal like that would generate suspicion and accusations, she allowed him to make love to her but lay, eyes tightly closed to blot out visions of the other night and her humiliation.

Chapter Seventeen

Monday morning surgery was chaotic. Clare, who had never felt quite so unlike doing her work, had to call on her wits to be able to deal with it. She'd clung to David as he'd stood at the front door, ready to leave for the hospital, trying to find reasons for him to say for a few more minutes. He'd looked so smart in his dark grey suit, crisp white shirt and wine red tie. Trying hard not to cry, she'd listened to his heart beating as he held her close to him, kissing her newly washed but not dried hair and repeatedly reassuring her. He'd made her promise that she would speak to John that day and arrange some time off, stressing that it was vital that she did that right away, hoping that she would not realise how concerned he was for her health. She looked thin, wracked with some personal secret that was consuming her from within, just as a cancer would.

Mrs Mandeville brought Clare into the real world with a crash. Presenting with symptoms of redness and pain in her left eye, with some loss of vision, Clare spent nearly quarter of an hour, liaising with the ophthalmologists at the hospital and arranging an emergency out-patient appointment for her. Mr Passmore was an overweight fifty five year old antique dealer with a plethoric complexion and a trouser waistband that seemed to cut into his corpulence, both of these the legacy of far too much rich living, admitted to thirst and tiredness. Checking his blood sugar confirmed the diagnosis of diabetes, which he was extremely reticent to accept and it tested all of Clare's communication skills to the limit and cost her a great deal of time in the process.

At this point, Clare, not normally superstitious, gave passing thought to the idea that things always come in threes and as if on cue, in came thirty one year old Diana Taylor who took a further thirty minutes as she droned on about how very tired she was all the time. Between the three of them, these patients plus the other seventeen who together constituted the whole surgery and wanted a variety of different things such as antibiotics for viral illnesses, anti-obesity drugs and smoking cessation advice caused Clare to finish very late indeed and exhausted.

There were several house calls for her exclusively and Clare made a mental note to postpone her visit to Prudence until the following day, when hopefully things would be quieter.

Clare was still preoccupied with her patients as she made her way upstairs for a much needed drink. Entering the coffee room, she was taken aback to see Sam sitting there alone, reading a book.

'Oh,' gulped Clare.

'Good morning,' Sam greeted her, looking infuriatingly normal as far as Clare could tell. 'You've had a hard surgery. I'll get you a drink.'

'Thanks,' Clare accepted and sat down, thinking to herself that she would drink her coffee as quickly as she could as then make her excuses to rush off on her calls.

'Here you are. Biscuit?'

Clare chose a custard cream and set about biting off one biscuit so that she could lick the creamy bit in the middle. She tried to drink but it was too hot.

'Where's everyone else?' she asked.

'Gone out on visits,' Sam replied. 'I'm the duty doctor today, waiting for urgent calls.'

'Of course,' Clare agreed. 'Any problems with your surgery?'

'No, quite straightforward, thanks. I did have a slight problem with a rash but it was one of Ed's regulars, so I asked him to come and have a look at it.'

'What was it?'

'Lichen planus. In the mouth as well. I've never seen that before.' Sam paused. So, how was your weekend?' he continued, catching Clare off guard as she hoped they were concentrating on clinical matters.

'Fine, thank you. David got home safely on Friday, so we've had a wonderful time together,' Clare informed him, putting emphasis on the last three words.

'Good, I'm pleased for you.'

'How about you? How's Rebecca? Did you talk to her?'

'Yes, at length. Most of the weekend was spent talking actually.'

'What did she say?' Clare asked, afraid to find out.

'I think we're finished. We both got very upset. She'd had the abortion on the Wednesday, so that didn't help matters. I suggested she move out for a bit, to give us both some breathing space so I think she'll be going this week sometime.'

'That's so terrible, I feel so guilty. Do you think I should go and see her?'

'I wouldn't if I were you. I don't think that she'd be too thrilled with that idea.'

'Oh dear,' Clare sighed.

Sam, much to Clare's surprise, returned to his book, so she took the opportunity to scrabble her things together and get ready to go out, much as she might have wanted to stay and find out more. Maybe, she wondered, he was going to do as she'd implored him and put it behind them. Not that this would ever restore their working relationship to what it once had been but it might make his last four months a possibility.

It was raining heavily as she trudged round on her visits. The traffic was very busy and temporary traffic lights seemed to have sprouted up all over the place overnight. The windscreen wipers on her car seemed to have developed a most irritating squeak and by mistake she went to a wrong address and got half soaked as she stood at the door waiting in vain for someone to answer her frantic knocking.

Knowing that it was foolish, but feeling that she was under some strange sort of compulsion, she drove past Sam's house with the weird thought that she might see Rebecca and then have an excuse to talk to her. The house looked all shut up, not even a window was open. She then drove to the dress shop and crawled past, trying desperately to see past the clothes on display but this was equally unrewarding. Feeling impotent, Clare wended her way back to work, to dry out, write up notes and generally gather her composure before the rigours of the afternoon took a hold.

She remembered her promise to David and spent a few moments with Elliot Douglas, asking if he would look at some dates that she might be able to take as days off without causing any disruption. Elliot, previously briefed by John that Clare should be allowed whatever time she requested, promised to get back to her that afternoon before closing.

Surgery was full of Clare's regulars, returning for follow up and chronic disease management. There were some cervical smears to be taken and one unfortunate lady with an infected sebaceous cyst, bright red and almost glowing with heat, which Clare agreed to incise immediately for her. In doing so, the foul smelling pus shot out and splattered her top leaving her with a dreadful smell pervading her nostrils but a very grateful patient, now relieved of pain.

As she was leaving, Clare paused to say good bye to the receptionists, all of whom looked worn out after yet another busy day. Elizabeth was on the telephone and Clare heard her telling someone to come straight down to the surgery and the doctor would wait to see her.

'What's that all about?' inquired Clare.

'It's all in hand, Dr Jennings,' answered Elizabeth. 'You get off home. It's just a patient who says she can't wait until tomorrow but Dr Bonnington knows all about it and is going to see her.'

'Are you sure?'

'Go home, Dr Jennings! Dr Bonnington has finished surgery and is just waiting for this last patient. There is honestly nothing for you to do.'

Clare laughed.

'I think I get the message, Elizabeth. I'll be off then. See you tomorrow. Oh, by the way, could you put Prudence Kerfoot down for a visit tomorrow? I promised her I'd pop in early this week.'

'I'll do that, Dr Jennings. We've not heard from her for a few days have we? Let's hope that's a good sign. Poor lonely old soul. Good night!'

David was home by the time Clare reached the house. He still looked tanned and fit but not quite as relaxed as he had done twenty four hours previously. She quizzed him about his day, sympathising with him about the amount of work that had been waiting for him.

'I'm sorry Clare but I've agreed to be on call tonight. I know it's not really my night but, Jim, my senior house officer has gone home with flu or something and none of the other juniors were available to cover for him. Let's hope I don't get called in, then we can have the evening to ourselves.'

He studied her carefully and was pleased to see that she looked a little calmer. He encouraged her to talk about her surgeries and Clare found herself glad to have the chance to tell

170

him about her busy day and the various clinical challenges she had been faced with. They made the supper together, Clare chopping vegetables for a stir fry while David took the meat off the chicken carcase and cut it into strips. Eating off plates balanced on their laps they watched the evening news after which Clare volunteered to do the clearing up so that David could go into the office and deal with some outstanding work that he had brought home with him. As she was putting the last of the cutlery in the drawer, she heard the telephone rang but it was answered before she could get to it. Assuming that it must be for David, as he did not call her, Clare wiped down the worktops and went back into the lounge to read unless she could find some diversion on the television.

David appeared at the door.

'No prize for guessing that was the hospital. Do you know, it already feels that my holiday was weeks ago. It's hard to believe that this time last week I was on the other side of the Atlantic. I've to go in and see someone. I'll try not to be long.'

Clare was too used to this comment to take it too much for granted.

'Anything interesting?' she asked supportively.

'Very bad depression, suicidal,' he replied. 'See you later.'

He kissed her on the top of her head and she reached up to stroke his face.

'Take care,' she called as he left the room.

David took Clare's car to the hospital as she had, as usual, parked it at such an angle that he did not feel he could reverse his own out safely. He put on the CD player and smiled when he heard what she had been listening to. Several tracks later, including his favourite one, which he had jumped forward to, he arrived at the hospital and gave thanks that visiting time was over as he was able to park close to the front door and not go round to the back of the building and the staff car park. The porter on the front desk welcomed him gravely and commented on the weather. David walked into the Accident and Emergency department, passing by a disparate selection of people waiting patiently to be seen. Some had make shift bandages round their hands; one was holding a packet of frozen peas on his knee. Children of all ages were running about, throwing magazines and comics on the floor and pestering their long-suffering parents for drinks and crisps from a machine in the corner. Several heads looked hopefully at David as he crossed the room and went toward the reception desk.

He waited behind an angry man who was raving at the poor girl behind the desk as he had been waiting for over two hours and when was the doctor going to see him. Finally giving up and turning to go back to his chair, he gave David the chance to introduce himself to the girl who pointed wearily to some doors and told him to go through them.

Three nurses were busily writing notes and two doctors were musing over the appearance of an ankle x-ray. The Sister in charge greeted David warmly.

'I'm so sorry that you've had to come in, Dr Jennings but we're really worried about this patient. Dr Clarke has seen her briefly and doesn't want to send her home without a psychiatric assessment tonight. We'd no idea your SHO was off sick.'

That's fine, Sister. It's not a problem. I'm glad to help. Mind you the bed state in the psychiatric wing is pretty deplorable, so let's hope we don't have to admit her.'

The Sister smiled broadly. David was well known and popular. His calm manner and seemingly inexhaustible patience made him a welcome sight on this busy Monday evening.

'She's through here. I've put her in the little room we keep for consultations like this, so it's perfectly private and I'll make sure you're not disturbed.'

Her shoes made tap dancing noises as she marched briskly down the polished corridor floor. Opening a door into a small, windowless room, David saw a young student nurse sitting next to his patient. She stood up nervously at the sight of the senior nurse and the consultant.

'Thanks, Ruth. You can go back now to the department and set up some minor injury trolleys.'

Ruth looked as if she would rather stay where she was.

'Run along now! Right, now then dear,' Sister leaned over to the patient and patted her on the knee,' here's the psychiatrist I was telling you about. He's very kind and understanding and he's here to help you. So try to tell him all about yourself.'

She stood back so that David could enter and sit in the chair that Ruth had been using.

'This is Rebecca Howarth. If you need anything, ring 2101. I'll get Ruth to bring the two of you a cup of tea.'

She left the room in one bound and closed the door with a bang just as David said, 'Hello, my name's David Jennings, I'm the psychiatrist on call tonight.'

David looked at his patient and his heart melted. He could see that she was a vividly attractive woman but tonight her hair was matted and dirty, her face puffy and a pale grey colour. Her fingernails were all bitten and she was now systematically chewing off the skin around each nail. Dressed in a filthy shirt which was buttoned up asymmetrically and stained track suit bottoms, he noticed she had flip flops on her feet which looked purple with cold. Her hands, as she raised them to her mouth were trembling. Her shoulders were hunched and her gaze fixed rigidly on the skirting board of the opposite wall. Repeatedly she would bring her knees up to her chest and hug them, rocking a little back and forth. She refused to look at him.

Some time passed in complete silence as he waited for her start to talk. He tried one or two questions to try to encourage her but she remained non-committal.

David was writing one or two notes about her appearance when she spoke.

'I want to die. I have no reason to live.'

'Tell me about it. I can help you. Why don't you want to live anymore?'

Rebecca studied her knees intently.

'I have nobody, nothing at all. What I did have has been taken from me.'

'Go on,' David tried to coax her gently, but she hung her head and disappeared in the curtain of hair that had escaped from its slide. She started to weep noisily.

'How long have you lived in Lambdale?' he tried prompting her, looking at her address on the empty folder which constituted her hospital notes.

'We moved here at the end of July.'

'Where did you live before that?'

'Brighton.'

'How long did you live there?'

'Most of my life.'

'So why did you move up here? Were things going wrong in Brighton?' David suggested.

Rebecca took a quick look at him and wiped her face on her sleeve.

'It was supposed to be a fresh start.'

'Why was that necessary?'

'I don't know if I can talk about it. I'm a disaster, I'm so hopeless.'

Rebecca shook her head slowly from side to side in despair and started gnawing at her fingers again.

David passed her tissues which he found under the table.

'Tell me why you think that,' he said to her softly.

'I've been so stupid. You wouldn't believe how stupid I've been.'

'Try me. I'm a good listener. Remember this is confidential. Just between you and me. You'll feel better if you tell me and I'll know how best to help you. Take your time.'

'I don't know where to start,' wailed Rebecca.

'Start anywhere you like. We can always go back further if we need to. Why don't you talk about Brighton, were you happy there?'

For the first time, Rebecca nodded.

'Yes, I was. I went to school there and then went on to college to do a course in child care. I love children. I was living at home with my parents. That was ok I suppose but they've always been quite strict.'

'Do you have brothers or sisters?'

'No. My parents are great but quite old now. They were in their late forties when I was born.'

'So what happened about your course? Did you finish it?'

'No, I should have finished this summer.'

'What happened?'

'I met my boyfriend, or rather my fiancé, or at least he was my fiancé until this weekend.'

'How did you meet?'

'At a party given by one of my friends, Alice. She lives in the Midlands now.'

'Tell me about your boyfriend,' asked David.

'The first time I saw him, I thought, how fantastic looking he was. He was gorgeous, very confident, outgoing. All the things I wish I was. I fell in love with him as soon as I spotted him but I never thought he would look twice at someone like me. So I tried to pretend that I was like him, an extrovert.' Rebecca laughed cynically. 'I can look quite attractive when I try.'

'I'm sure you can,' David agreed. Rebecca smiled ruefully.

'I couldn't believe it when he came over and started talking to me. He said I was the most beautiful girl in the room. He took me home that night and we started seeing each other every day. Those first few weeks were like nothing I've ever known before. He was kind, attentive, generous...' she tailed off.

'Did you parents like him?' David wondered.

'At first. He charmed them just as he did me.'

'What went wrong?'

'I got pregnant,' Rebecca told him flatly. 'He told me to have an abortion. That he would arrange it and pay for it. I didn't know what to do so I told my parents. They were horrified. Then Sam – that's his name- told me he was moving up here. He asked me to come with him and move in with him but it was on the condition that I had the abortion. I was so in love with him I would have done anything to keep him, so I ignored my parents and had the abortion. They haven't spoken to me since. I've tried ringing a couple of times but they just put the phone down and though I've written, I haven't had any replies.'

Rebecca's shoulders heaved and shuddered. She started to pick tiny pieces of tissue off and roll them between her fingers to make little balls which she then arranged in a line on the table. David said nothing, waiting for her to continue. When the tissue was completely destroyed, she put her legs down and plucked at the material of her trousers.

'Just before we came up here, I found out that he'd been having an affair with the wife of one of the people he was working with. I'd wondered why he'd had this change of heart about where to work, as when I first met him, he told me he was staying in Brighton for the best part of a year. He promised me that this was a one-off, that it would never happen again, that it was this woman who made all the running. You know the sort of thing and I, like a stupid, stupid idiot believed him. How could I? I must have lost my senses.'

There was a quiet knock on the door and the student nurse appeared with tea for the two of them. David poured Rebecca a cup and pushed it towards her, followed by the sugar bowl.

'We came up here and found the most beautiful house to rent that I loved immediately and to start with Sam did seem to have reverted back to the man I first met. He was working hard, liked the people at work and he was very loving to me. I got a job in a dress shop in the town and loved it. I really thought this was it and that we would have a future together.'

David let his tea go cold, not wanting to move in case Rebecca stopped talking.

'Then, the worst possible thing happened.'

'What was that?'

'In the flurry of the house move, I forgot to take some of my pills. I found out I was pregnant again. I thought it would be different now because we had the house, Sam had this good job and seemed very happy but when I told him he was furious. He told me I had to have another abortion as he wasn't ready for children or settling down. Then he proposed to me and said that we could plan to get married after the abortion and that we'd have a family in the future. I so wanted to believe him that I agreed. I thought I loved him and that maybe in a strange way he loved me. I told myself that there was no way he would have proposed to me if he didn't love me. I went to stay with my friend Alice. She'd arranged an appointment for me at a local private clinic. She tried to talk me out of it. She's never liked Sam. Perhaps I can see why now. We had a bit of a row and when I came out of the clinic, after the abortion, things were really difficult between us, so I decided to come home last Thursday. I didn't tell Sam I was coming, as I wanted to surprise him. Ha!'

'Go, on Rebecca, you're doing really well.'

'This all sounds so terrible. I got the train home and a taxi to the house. When I went in I heard noises in the kitchen, so I opened the door. That's when I found them.'

'Who did you find?' David asked after a pause.

Rebecca looked at him, her tear-stained face the epitome of despair.

'Sam and Clare.'

'Who's Clare?'

'He works with her. She's his boss, I suppose.'

David's mind was beginning to race. The names were frighteningly familiar. Before he could ask anything, Rebecca shouted out.

'They were making love in the kitchen, on the table. Right there, in front of me!'

David felt his mouth go dry. He couldn't bring himself to speak.

'I screamed at them to stop. Sam just laughed. Clare looked horrified. I could feel sorry for her but I don't. I hate her. I trusted her. She was going to help me. I feel so betrayed by everyone. Sam and I have rowed all weekend. He's told me to leave and I have nowhere to go. I've spent all day planning to kill myself as there is nothing left now and I don't deserve to live. I went to the doctors this afternoon and saw Dr Bonnington who was very kind. She arranged this appointment for me.'

David had heard enough. He took control of the consultation and steered it in the direction he wanted it to go, asking about Rebecca's childhood and adolescence. There was no doubt that she was so distressed that he felt she might do something to harm herself that evening and as she had nowhere to go to, he felt obliged to admit her onto one of his wards for the night. They had spent more than two hours talking. Rebecca looked absolutely worn out. He walked with her up to the ward and introduced her to the psychiatric nurse in charge. Rebecca was just being led away to her bed when David called after her.

'Just one other thing, Rebecca, what did you say that Sam did for a living?'

David knew what the answer was going to be before he was told. He prayed fiercely for seconds, willing her not to say what she did.

'He's a doctor. He wants to be a GP.'

Chapter Eighteen

David walked down the ward, oblivious to the patients who were coming up to him, wondering who he was, or those who were scrutinising his every move from their beds in the small four bedded units on either side of the corridor. Struggling to keep his composure, he dialled the entry number of the security lock on the door to the doctors' office, went in and leant back against it as it closed. Taking several deep breaths, he went over to the desk and after some further controlled respirations, opened up Rebecca's file and began to write the lengthy psychiatric notes that were necessary following his interview with her. Keeping his professional approach, he carefully documented her past medical history, details of her childhood, premorbid personality and social history. It was only when he came to the details of her presenting problems that he found his pen unwilling to write, his normally small, precise, italic handwriting stuttering, making facile spelling mistakes. As he approached the final events leading to Rebecca's irreversible plunge into the depths of despair, he was totally unable to put pen to paper. After repeated attempts to do so, he threw his expensive fountain pen against the opposite wall and collapsed, sobbing onto the desk. He doubted he had ever cried like this before. Having given way to his pent up feelings, he was unable to rein them back in and it was with some sense of relief that he wept noisily. Thinking of Clare, sitting at home waiting for him, made him feel physically sick. Worn out by the exertion of expressing his grief he sat back in his chair, chin on his chest, eyes closed. Unaware of the door opening, David did not notice Kevin, one of the nurses from the ward coming into the room. Kevin had heard him crying but had been unsure whether or not he should intrude on this patently very personal moment. Now that David was quiet, Kevin felt it prudent to enter, offer help and consolation if needed.

David professed to have a bad migraine, not realising that the volume of his sobs had been audible to others.

'Can I get you anything, David? A drink? A painkiller?'

'Nothing – but thanks Kevin.'

'I'm just down the ward if you need me,' Kevin promised him, hesitating before taking his leave.

'Oh, there is one thing,' David called after him.

'Yes?'

David quickly scribbled on a piece of paper which he held out for Kevin.

'This is my home number. Could you ring my wife and tell her that I've decided to stay at the hospital tonight.'

'Sure, I will. Shall I tell her about the migraine?'

'No, just say that it's very busy.'

'Okay.'

Kevin paused in case David was about to add some further message but when nothing was forthcoming he left David to his thoughts.

Some half an hour later, David appeared at the nurses' station, left Rebecca's now completed file and having said good night to Kevin and his team, walked off the ward. His footsteps echoed around the whole length of the corridor as he made his solitary way to the doctors' mess. Only a harassed-looking very junior doctor bustled past him, stethoscope around her neck, her nose in a book, frantically reading up what she was expected to do at her next destination, totally unaware of David as he stepped to one side to get out of her way. In the mess, he booked into one of the on call rooms, made himself a cup of black coffee and then sat with some of the other doctors watching the late news. At midnight, the majority having left, either for their beds or back to their duties, David wearily trudged to his room, splashed cold water on his face and then lay on top of the bed, fully clothed. He put out the light and stared into the dark.

Clare was relatively surprised to receive the telephone call from Kevin. She was well used to David coming back late, even waking the next morning to find that she was still alone in their bed. It was rare that he rang and even more unusual for him to get someone to pass on a message for him. She felt exceedingly sorry for her husband, his first day back at work and then having to cover the on call overnight. He'd be exhausted the following evening when he came home. She also felt quite sorry for herself as she'd hoped that they would have spent the evening together, using it to perpetuate and build on the wonderful feeling of togetherness that they had rediscovered over the weekend. That, together with the tiny glimmer of optimism that Sam was not going to want to refer back repeatedly to the previous week made Clare feel minimally more confident about keeping her infidelity secret from David and was just beginning to start to relax more in his presence. But, resigning herself to the fact that she was to be on her own, she had a bath and an early night, actually enjoying reading the novel that she had started over a month ago but which had been discarded since she and David had rowed and he had gone away on his own. Just before she put out the light, Clare contemplated trying to ring David. After all, he had made the effort to send her a message so it seemed appropriate that she should be similarly considerate. Dialling his mobile number she waited while it rang and rang unaware that David was listening to it as the shrill tone shattered the silence of his black environment.

While Clare slept peacefully, David, insomniacal in his despair welcomed a summons to an admission at three in the morning after which he abandoned the thought of even trying to rest and paced around the seemingly interminable corridors of the hospital trying to decide what to do.

Clare woke refreshed, in time to have breakfast and get dressed at a leisurely pace. Arriving at work she found that Sam had arrived before her, in anticipation of his tutorial. He'd spotted her driving into the car park and had made her a cup of coffee. Clare eyed him guardedly but he seemed to be behaving quite naturally as they took their drinks down into Clare's surgery and settled down to start their teaching session. The topic for the day was to discuss the health issues surrounding middle aged men; a subject which had arisen after Sam had had a challenging consultation with a man with impotence who was only in his early forties. Relishing her role as tutor, Clare realised with some satisfaction and a great deal of relief that Sam had prepared well and was raising clearly thought out ideas and suggestions. She found that they were laughing together at times in a perfectly normal way and her confidence grew the longer he stayed strictly within the boundaries of being a registrar.

Winding up, Clare summarised what they had covered and identified some learning points for Sam to take away with him and read up on. She was writing a list of these for him when he said,

'Becca's left Clare. I thought you should know.'

Clare stopped mid word.

'When?'

'Yesterday,' replied Sam. 'When I got home in the evening she'd gone. She's still got to pick her things up but she won't be coming back to stay. She'd left her keys.'

'Oh,' faltered Clare. 'Where's she gone?'

'I don't know. Back to her friend Alice in Stratford probably. Maybe even her parents in Brighton.'

'Oh,' repeated Clare feeling bewildered, not knowing what to think or say.

Tactfully Sam gathered up his things and Clare hurriedly finished her list and gave it to him.

'Let me know if you want to talk,' he whispered and left the room.

Clare stared at her desk, at the paperweight which contained a tiny ammonite. She couldn't decide whether Rebecca leaving was a good or a bad thing. True, it was hopefully one less person in this disastrous equation which must be good, but she still felt appalled by how she had let Rebecca down. Whilst leaving Sam was undoubtedly the best move, Clare could not ignore the fact that she was the catalyst that had caused their break-up and guiltily she visualised the scene in the kitchen when Rebecca had walked in.

With extreme difficulty she forced herself to turn her attention to her patients, trying her best to satisfy their needs and demands. Her penultimate patient brought her a home-made lemon drizzle cake which Clare took with her to share with the others.

Elizabeth stopped her as she passed the reception desk and handed over a clutch of messages. Skimming through them Clare smiled as she read that Mrs Murphy had rung to thank her for helping her get a disabled parking badge, frowned when she read that Mr Pocock had a huge bruise on his arm where the nurse had taken blood from him and what was the doctor going to do about it and finally groaned out loud when she read that social services had rung to inform the practice that they had been unable to visit Prudence Kerfoot since before the weekend as she had refused to answer the door on any of their attempts. Clare knew that she was going to have to be strict with Prudence when she visited later. However intrusive she, Prudence, found regular visits from carers or people delivering meals, she needed all of them and their continuation was non-negotiable as far as Clare was concerned if Prudence intended to continue to live on her own.

She passed Ellie on the stairs, on her way to start surgery, looking wonderful in a pencil skirt and a figure-hugging polo-necked top.

'Clare – I'm just off to start. Can we have lunch today? It'd be great just to have a chat and catch up.'

'I'd love that Ellie,' Clare answered, warmly.

'Great, I'll meet you upstairs at one. Must rush, I've got a coil to fit.'

So saying, she flew, as best as she could in her tight skirt, down the remaining stairs.

Visits were light that day, so Clare took her time over coffee and paperwork. Once Sam had opted for the nursing home run and John and Ed had picked up the requests from their own patients, Clare found herself left with a bereavement visit to an elderly lady whose husband had died after a protracted hospital stay and Prudence. She chose to do the visits in that order and spent nearly an hour listening to Mrs Sparrow, a tiny lady bent over by her osteoporosis, her fingers deformed by her arthritis, telling her how it was a blessing that George, her husband was no longer suffering. Blighted by a lifetime of heavy smoking and diabetes, he'd had both legs amputated and could barely lift a cup to his mouth without struggling for breath and complaining of angina. Clare could do nothing but agree. His was no life towards the end, merely an existence, trapped in a hospital bed or the chair beside it, kept alive by intravenous solutions, insulin and nebulisers, with nothing to do but watch the clock waiting for visiting time and the arrival of his devoted wife. Nonetheless in spite of Mrs Sparrow's remarkable objectivity, Clare was needed to offer consolation as the widow wept. Unable to get away, Clare was shown wedding photographs from fifty two years ago when George had been a tall, rakish chap with a mischievous grin and a twinkle in his eye, his bride, a shy but pretty brunette, standing up straight in a polka dot covered dress with huge shoulder pads.

Saddened, Clare offered help and support whenever Mrs Sparrow wanted and encouraged her to contact the surgery if there was anything she thought Clare could assist with.

'There is one thing, doctor,' started Mrs Sparrow.

'What's that?' asked Clare.

'It's all these tablets and medicines. There's bags of them. Could I give them to you please? Perhaps they'd be of use to someone else. It seems a terrible waste just to throw them out.'

So saying, she limped into the back room and reappeared with two large carrier bags stuffed full of bottles and boxes.

'Of course I'll take them for you. Is this it? Goodness, there are all sorts in here,' Clare opened one of the bags and peered in.

'Thank you doctor and thank you for coming. You've been very kind.'

Mrs Sparrow stood at the front door to see her off, watching Clare as she put the carrier bags in the boot and only going back inside when Clare had started the engine of her car.

Driving back to the surgery, Clare tried to imagine what it must be like to have been married for over five decades. Thinking fondly of David, willing him not to have had too bad a night, she fervently hoped that one day she would find out.

Clare hurried down the street to Prudence's cottage. There was a cold feel to the breeze that day and it was definitely not one for standing about. She knocked loudly on the door and turned the handle to go in as usual but found to her surprise that it was locked. Presuming that this was to defy admission to social services Clare knocked again, more loudly. She tried to peer through the letter box but there was a piece of thick green woolly material covering over the inside of it, presumably acting as a draught excluder.

'Prudence,' she called. 'It's Dr Jennings. Can you let me in?'

There was no answer but Clare thought she could hear one of the cats miaowing. She banged on the door with her fist.

Beginning to feel annoyed, she walked to the end of the terrace and round to the tiny path which led up to all the back yards. She had no problem identifying which one was Prudence's house as it was overgrown and a mess. A used cat litter tray festered by the back door. Weeds grew out of the cracks in the concrete, aetiolated and eccentric. Several old bin bags, stuffed to beyond their limits had burst, belching out old cans, slices of mouldy bread and plastic trays that still bore traces of the meals they had once kept warm. An enormous pair of dully grey pants hung menacingly on the washing line next to some elastic stockings that were intertwined as if in an erotic dance and a tea towel full of holes.

Clare ducked under the washing and fought her way to the back door. Peeping through the filthy window she could just make out the silhouette of Prudence's head as she sat in her chair, the television flickering away in front of her. Clare tried knocking on the window, with no more success than she'd had at the front. Rattling the knob, she found that the back door was open but that there was something heavy leaning against it, preventing it from opening. Clare pushing, tentatively at first and then more aggressively until, finally surrendering, the door gave way. Clare had to steady herself on the grimy draining board to prevent herself from falling headfirst into a box of toilet rolls and incontinence pads.

She choked as her nostrils were deluged by a putrefying stink. The piteous mewing of Millie and Minnie could be heard over the blare of the television which was extolling the virtues of a particular make of stair lift. Realising that something was very wrong, Clare instinctively clasped her hand over her mouth and nose and slowly made her way into the back room. As she opened the door, the two cats shot out and flew into the back yard. Clare, who had rarely seen them do more than saunter, was taken aback by their speed. She called out to Prudence who was in her chair, legs apart, up on her foot stool. One look was all that Clare needed to know that Prudence was in no state to answer back. Her face, bloated and suffused with blood was dark purple in colour. A congealed rivulet of brown liquid ran from one corner of her mouth down her chin and neck. Her open eyes bulged, unseeing, devoid of life. One hand tightly clutched her angina spray, the other hung over the chair arm. Her mottled skin was cold despite the fact that the gas fire was on full, exacerbating the stench of death and decay. Rotting cat food that was rancid and pungent, lurked behind her chair, inedible even for the starving cats.

Clare made a quick exit and retreated to the back yard and had to stand for a few moments gulping in fresh air before scrabbling in her bag for her phone. She rang the police and promised to wait for them, preferring to do so at the front of the house, where there would be reassuring signs of everyday life.

True to their word, the police arrived promptly and Clare explained what had happened. Answering their questions, she told them that she'd last seen Prudence alive the previous week and gave them a synopsis of her medical problems. Thanking her, they allowed her to go and with one last glance at what remained of Prudence, Clare hurried back to the surgery.

Chapter Nineteen

Ellie was reading while she waited for Clare. Sam, glued to the computer doing some sort of search was also in the coffee room. They sat in companionable silence, each intent on their work, which was abruptly interrupted by the door being flung open.

'Oh my goodness,' announced Clare, bursting into the room and collapsing onto a chair.

The other two looked up simultaneously from what they were doing and focussed their attention on her.

'Prudence Kerfoot is dead. I've just found her, decomposing in front of her fire.'

'I'm sorry,' commiserated Ellie, 'but it was bound to happen sooner or later. She's been living on borrowed time for years. It won't seem the same without her ringing every day. Still, it'll free up a lot of time for you, Clare.'

'I know,' agreed Clare,' but it was a shock to find her like that. The smell was dreadful.' She sniffed her sleeves, 'I can still smell it now.'

'How long had she been dead?' asked Sam.

Clare shrugged her shoulders.

'I don't know. The fire was full on and I'm hopeless at forensic medicine. A couple of days perhaps? I'd meant to visit yesterday but it was so busy I put it off for a day. I wish I'd gone now, even though I know she'd still have been dead.'

'What about those two cats of hers?' asked Ellie.

'They're all right. Hungry but alive. The police are going to contact the local branch of the cats' protection league.'

'Did she have any relatives at all?' inquired Sam.

'I know she divorced many years ago but she's never mentioned anyone else in all the time I've known her,' Clare replied, sadly.

'Yes, it's tragic really,' Ellie agreed. 'Anyway, let's go and have lunch. I thought we could go to that new delicatessen. It's got a tiny restaurant at the back of the shop. I noticed it the other day when I was shopping in there.'

For a moment Clare wished that she could distance herself from the emotional aspect of her job like Ellie could instead of feeling almost on the verge of tears for Prudence who had died alone with no one to look after her.

Keen to escape from work for a while, Clare, carrying only her purse, held the door for Ellie and the two women made their way out and across the market square to Delicious, the slightly pretentious name of their lunch venue. Clare noticed that the first four letters on the sign were in bright orange and the others in green. Quite clever, she thought.

Seated at a trendy hexagonal table, they took their time studying the large menus before deciding on a baguette with coronation chicken and a hot ciabatta roll with chicken and avocado. As soon as their order had been taken, huge cups of cappuchino appeared before them to sustain them while they waited.

'Mmmmm,' murmured Ellie, 'just look at those pastries.'

'How's Virginia?' asked Clare.

'She's doing brilliantly now, thanks,' was the enthusiastic reply. 'She's so much more cheery now that Ian's back, though I expect it has helped that he has, inevitably, promised to buy them another pony as soon as she's fit to ride.'

Clare laughed. She loved to hear about Ellie's domestic life. She scooped up some of the foaming coffee with a spoon and licked it appreciatively.

'How is Ian? Is he back for quite a while this time?'

'Yes, for a couple of months at least. So by the time he's off on his travels again, Virginia should be fine and normality restored to the Bonnington household – if there is such a thing! What about David, how was his holiday? How were things between you when he got back?'

'David's great. He had a wonderful trip by the sound of it and some of his photographs are breathtaking. I can't tell you how it felt to see him again. We've had a fantastic weekend, just the two of us, talked for hours, walked on the beach. Everything's really good again.' Clare was emphatic.

'Excellent,' pronounced Ellie. 'You do look a bit better than you did. Have you sorted out some holiday time for yourself?'

Clare pretended to groan.

'Has John put you up to this? There seems to be some conspiracy to get me away from work. No, seriously, I've had a word with Elliott and he's going to work something out for me. I'll probably just be at home as I doubt David will be able to manage much more than a long weekend off, but that's fine. The poor soul had to be on call last night on his first day back. His SHO went off sick and no one else could cover at short notice. He's not been back all night, so he must have been run off his feet. He's so thoughtful though, he got one of the nurses to ring me to say he'd not be back.'

'Really? I wonder if he saw the patient I sent down to the hospital,' mused Ellie.

Two large plates of food arrived and were deposited in front of them. Not only were their orders enormous but accompanied by chips and salad.

'Who was that?' Clare's mouth was full. Her ciabatta roll certainly lived up to the name of the shop.

'I was just about to go home when a girl rang, begging to see someone. She was extremely depressed and talking quite seriously of suicide.'

'That's terrible,' empathised Clare. 'Depressed about anything in particular?'

'The usual suspects. Catastrophic relationship, roller coaster emotions, a termination she didn't want to have deep down.'

Clare felt her blood starting to chill in her veins and froze, her sandwich half way en route to her mouth.

'Anything else?'

'Not much that I could get out of her. All that she did tell me was just the sketchiest outline. Most of the time she just sat mute, crying and staring at the floor. I really felt that she was seriously at risk so I sent her up to A&E for a psychiatric assessment.'

'David was called in to see someone mid-evening who was very depressed,' Clare admitted.

'Then it was probably her,' Ellie concluded matter-of-factly. 'Hang on, you've seen her a couple of times I think. Before all this happened. You might remember her. What was her name? Rachel? No. Rebecca? Yes that's it. Rebecca Howarth. For some ridiculous reason her name made me think of a school trip I went on years ago when we were reading Jane Eyre. This sandwich is to die for. I'm going to have to let my belt out. What's up? Aren't you eating yours?'

'It's lovely,' Clare managed to mutter, inadequately while her mind careered off in all directions. She took a small bite and chewed but her throat had closed off and the doughy mouthful seemed to swell in volume the more she moved it around her mouth, making her want to gag.

Vaguely, Clare was aware in the distance of Ellie chattering on. Clare hoped that she was nodding and smiling sufficiently and appropriately to convince Ellie that she was listening attentively. Frantically she was trying to work out the sequence of events that Ellie had just recounted and come up with a viable alternative outcome.

Perhaps, she told herself, Rebecca had not attended the hospital and has just left Lambdale. Perhaps she had gone to a different hospital. Perhaps the doctor in A&E had been less impressed by her mental state and had discharged her. Perhaps there had been another psychiatrist apart from David on call. Perhaps David's SHO had made a miraculous recovery but David had chosen to stay at the hospital in case, not wanting to disturb her by coming home late. And just perhaps, if David had seen Rebecca, maybe she might not have mentioned any names.

None of her ideas made much sense, if she thought logically other than the forlorn hope of the first one.

'Clare, are you all right?' Ellie's insistent tones jolted Clare back to reality. 'I take back what I said earlier about you looking better. You look as if someone's just walked over your grave. You've not heard a word I've said.'

'I'm so sorry Ellie, I was miles away. I just remembered something I've forgotten to do,' Clare heard herself lie.

'It must be something very important. You worry too much. You've got to leave work behind sometimes you know.' Then more kindly, 'is it something I can help with?'

'No, no, you know me,' Clare tried to laugh it off, but there was no conviction in her laughter. 'I always want things to be perfect.'

Ellie called for the bill.

'I'd wondered about sharing a pudding with you but you've barely touched your sandwich. Come on, let's go back to the surgery.'

Ellie continued to talk as they wandered back, trying desperately to coax her friend out of her introspection. As they went into the building Clare thanked her and excused herself, almost running to her surgery. Trembling she rang the hospital and asked to be put through to David's office. His secretary answered promptly.

'Hello Lillian, it's Clare. Is David there?'

'Hello Clare? Did you enjoy your trip to the States? It sounds wonderful. Yes, he's in his office, I'll just put you through.'

Clare waited nervously.

'I'm sorry; he must have slipped out when I wasn't looking. Do you want to leave a message?'

Clare's heart sank. She knew that David had to walk past Lillian's desk to get in and out of his office. Perhaps she was mistaken and he hadn't been there at all but then again perhaps he did not want to talk to her. It was clear that Lillian knew nothing of David going on holiday on his own.

'No, thanks, I'll try later perhaps. It's not urgent.'

Clare slowly and deliberately replaced the receiver. A voice in her head told her that there was now little doubt that David had found out about her and Sam. That was why he had not come home the previous night and why he was now avoiding talking to her. A second voice spoke over the first and suggested that David had just left his office and Lillian hadn't noticed. It was, after all, the approximate time for clinics to start or he could easily have been called to an emergency on the ward. Clare put her hands over her ears trying to block out the argument going on inside her but it raged on and on, spiralling out of control.

Her door opened, producing a welcome disturbance and one of the health visitors scurried in, wanting Clare's room to do her clinic. It was Clare's half day and the afternoon stretched out emptily in front of her. Any plans she might have had were annihilated by the trepidation of going home and facing David. She was faced with the dilemma of whether to pretend all was normal in the hopes that David had not met Rebecca at all (still a remote possibility), do likewise but dismiss Rebecca's claims as the rantings of someone with a serious mental health problem or pre-empt any possible confrontation by admitting her guilt and trying to explain what had happened. The first two prospects seemed equally futile and dishonest. The third was at least the truth. None of them, however, could ameliorate the pain that David would be experiencing.

As she left the surgery, Ellie waved to her from behind reception and Clare toyed with the idea of going to speak to her in confidence and asking her advice. She even started to walk towards her but Ellie's attention was diverted to Joan, who obviously had something pressing to discuss.

Clare drove homewards but stopped in the little parking area by the start of the riverside walk that she and David had been on many times. Fishing her thicker coat out from the back seat of the car, she slipped it on and buttoned it up to her chin, more aware of the cold than she had been earlier. Plunging her hands deep in the large pockets, she proceeded to amble along the dusty path towards the water's edge. Turning right onto the track that ran parallel to the river, she continued, lost in her own world, unaware of the beauty of the water, tumbling over the rocks, twinkling in the occasional sunshine. She sat on a bench, donated as a memorial to a much loved spouse and gazed into the distance. Gradually she realised what she had to do, the only solution that would lay comfortably in her conscience. She had to tell David everything. It was the only way she would feel any better and the very least he deserved. The prospect was daunting to say the least.

Mind made up, Clare walked briskly back to the car and drove straight home. It was unlikely that David would be home before six or seven which gave her at least three hours to tidy up, make a meal and plan how she was going to tell him.

Letting herself in, the house seemed cool and hostile. She noticed that the post had been picked up from the mat which could only mean one thing, that David had been home. Ignoring the fact that his car was not outside, Clare checked in the kitchen and his study in case he was there and then ran upstairs to the bedroom. The wardrobe doors were partly open and most of his clothes had gone. Hysterically, Clare checked drawers and found them empty and rushed into the bathroom where again, all signs of his existence had gone. She flew back downstairs and back into the kitchen, this time noticing an envelope on the worktop, just next to the day's post.

Clare picked it up, instantly recognising his handwriting. She took it through to the lounge and sat on the settee. With fingers like soft rubber she struggled to open it and extract the notepaper within.

'Dear Clare,

'When I saw you for the very first time, I fell in love with you and knew that there would never be anyone else for me in my life. Over the years, that love has grown as we've both worked hard, achieving a lot but only because we've known that the other was there, loving, supporting, always non-judgemental.

'We overcame all the obstacles that caught out our friends and now we have the jobs we always wanted and a house that we both adore. We've put hours of time into making it just the way we want it.

'We've always been so close, able to read one another's thoughts and emotions. I have always believed that if I had you by my side then anything would be possible.'

Clare paused to wipe away the tears that were streaming down her cheeks.

'What went wrong Clare? Was it the difficulty with the IVF? Why did we grow so far apart without realising what was happening?

'My holiday without you was the longest two weeks of my life. All I could think about was you and coming back to you. I couldn't believe that I'd left on such unpleasant terms, something you and I have never done before.

'It would appear that you did not reciprocate these feeling while we were apart. Did you plan for us to be separated? How long have you been sleeping with your registrar?

'I cannot comprehend the change in you. This is not your normal behaviour. You have always maintained that you deplore infidelity yet you are now guilty of that same sin. For me to find out the way I did must surely be the cruellest twist of fate. Had you hoped to keep this from me and carry on as usual? Truth always comes out, you should know that.

'I cannot come back home. I don't know what the future holds for you, me or us. I shall be working as normal but please have the decency to grant me the respect I ask for when I say do not contact me. I need time and space from you. Wait for me to contact you. I will, I promise, when I am ready but I have no idea when that will be or what I will have to say to you when I do.

'Love David.'

'Oh David,' whispered Clare, 'what have I done?'

Numb, Clare re-read his letter until she knew every word by heart and each time the pain grew exponentially. Pulling her knees up to her chest, she lay, curled in a ball, like a large foetus, images flashing through her mind. She too could vividly remember the day they met, feeling very much the naïve sixth form schoolgirl overwhelmed by the prospect of medical school. David had been so kind to her, putting her at ease, emphasising all the positives, making her more determined to do well at her A level exams so that she could earn her place with the next intake. Then when she first started, how he had sought her out in the coffee room and asked her out for a drink.

She thought of their wedding day, how handsome David had looked, how proud her father had been to lead her up the aisle and how nervous she had felt in her stunning ivory silk dress and the ridiculous tiara that her mother had persuaded her to balance on her head. She could hear David whispering to her as they met at the altar, assuring her of her beauty and his undying love. Closing her eyes she was transported back to the moment they emerged from the church, laughing as they clung to each other while relatives and friends tossed rose petals over them, blood red to match the flowers in her bouquet. Dizzy, wonderful memories of their first dance at the reception, totally oblivious of the hundred or more guests as the moved, rather than danced, as one, her head on his shoulder, his arms tight around her. The honeymoon with long white beaches and brilliant blue seas, stretching forever to merge with the horizon and cosy evenings laced with glasses of Guinness. Heady days, both of them inebriated, not by alcohol but by their love for each other and then back to work. But even that had been a joy, snatching time together when they could, mutually supportive of their long hours and examinations. Clare recalled their delight at David's successful application for the consultant's post, which was equalled when she was offered the partnership at Teviotdale. They'd drunk the champagne that she'd bought and life had seemed perfect, the two of them invincible.

How wrong could she have been? This is what it must be like when you're drowning, Clare thought, it's like watching a replay of my life with David. Clouds encroached on her sunny memories as she remembered the repeated monthly agonies oscillating from the optimism that she might be pregnant this time to the inevitable let down that she wasn't. Despite the diagnosis of unexplained infertility, Clare had always felt that the blame lay with her and as time progressed and no conception was forthcoming, she knew that she was becoming withdrawn and starting to isolate herself from David. She could see the fleeting look of dismay when she told him that she was still not pregnant before he rapidly and loyally replaced it with one of comfort and solace.

Clare's thought were now on an irretrievable downward spiral, ever accelerating and dragging her with them as she tried to fight against it. She desperately willed herself to block them out but, insistently, they eroded deeper into her mind and images presented before her of Sam's first day, how good looking she had thought he was but so self-assured. Her reticence about the IVF had culminated in David going away on his own and then there was her stubbornness, Ellie's party and of course the Thursday evening she went to Sam's house. As if to inflict more punishment, she forced herself to go through events as they had happened. Innocent chatter and laughter –at least it had been on her part- mistakenly drinking on an empty stomach and feeling her inhibitions melt away as she became horribly drunk. She could taste the ice cream that they'd shared before sharing far more that she cared to recall.

But something else was tapping on the edge of this vision, niggling away at her, needing to be considered and Clare racked her brain to identify it.

Slowly she realised that her phone had rung and that she'd hoped it might be David. But it hadn't, it had been Prudence. The content of the conversation suddenly became clarified. This had been no ordinary call, but Prudence in pain, needing help and advice, only to be dismissed and turned into a comic figure by giggling, drunken Clare and Sam. The one time she had ignored Prudence had turned out to be the time she really needed someone. Now she was dead, the mode of her demise unclear but possibly painful and frightening and worst of all preventable.

Clare wept, her whole body heaving with sorrow for David, for Prudence and for herself. Why had she not gone to Prudence that evening or at the very least followed up the call the next day. If only she had done, Prudence might still be alive. Never before had she let her personal life take precedence over her work and cause the latter to suffer. She had let Prudence down and she felt despicable.

Spent form thinking and crying, Clare eventually uncurled and pushed herself up into a sitting position. She still had David's letter in her hand and was amazed to see that it was almost dark outside. She shivered and tried hugging herself and rubbing her arms to generate some heat, without success. Leaving the letter on the table, she stumbled into the kitchen, vision blurred from her sore, red eyes and swollen lids and switched on the light and the kettle. She spotted a jumper of David's in the ironing basket by the back door and pulled it on snuggling into it, trying to smell his scent but being met only by the aroma of fabric conditioner.

Having made a cup of tea, she took it back to the lounge, sat and sipped repeatedly from it, too hot to take a proper mouthful. She was startled by the sound of the telephone and almost burned herself spilling her tea in her wild efforts to find out who was calling. It was Ellie's voice that greeted her.

'Hello Clare, it's me. You sound terrible, what's wrong?'

Not ready to share her problems, Clare resorted to lies, assuaging her conscience with the fact that there was some truth in them.

'I feel terrible,' she agreed. 'I think I must be coming down with something.'

'You poor thing. No wonder you were so quiet at lunch and hardly ate. Look, I'll not keep you, I was only ringing to ask you and David over but that can wait. You take a couple of days off. I'll sort it at work, ok?'

Gratefully, Clare acquiesced.

'It's probably just a virus or something,' she mumbled.

'Well, we both know how debilitating they can be. We spend enough time telling people how to look after themselves, so how come we're so notoriously bad at taking care of ourselves? Keep warm, drink lots of fluids and I'll ring you at the weekend. Don't think of coming back to work this week. Take care, give my love to David.'

So saying, she rang off and Clare fell heavily back on to the settee with relief at having been given the opportunity to remove work from the insoluble dilemma she was faced with. Glad that she did not even have to contemplate how she might cope with seeing people at work, she drank the remains of her tea and put on the television which she neither watched nor heard as she sat trapped in her own mesmerising world of confusion.

Chapter Twenty

For two days, Clare was barely aware whether it was night or day. She lived in the lounge only venturing out to bring down a duvet and to make occasional cups of tea or coffee. Eating was out of the question. Slopping around in an old pair of pyjamas and David's lambs wool dressing gown she felt no inclination to shower, wash or even brush her hair. Previously rather dismissive of daytime viewing, she mindlessly sat through all manner of programmes. She learned how to purchase a property in Spain, how to decorate her own house so neutrally that it would instantly be bought by someone and how to transform her garden. Re-runs of popular series from two and three decades ago were interspersed with quizzes, cartoons and tear-jerking American made-for-TV dramas which had her weeping uncontrollably, as did advertisements which featured tiny puppies or kittens.

Much as she willed the telephone to ring or her mobile to signal the arrival of a text message, she was continuously disappointed. At a particularly low ebb she had sent a barrage of messages to David, begging him to get in touch. The post lay on the hall floor, unopened, having been scoured for any hint of David's handwriting and then discarded. Dust accumulated on flat surfaces and mugs multiplied in the sink waiting to be washed.

Thus she existed, like a hermit, avoiding contact with reality, cocooned in her makeshift bedsit.

On the Friday morning, she woke from a deep sleep, weak from tiring dreams. She had been able to see David in the distance, standing with his back to her and as fast as she tried to catch up with him, the further away he seemed to become. When finally she had reached him and put out a hand to touch him, he had turned but it had been Sam's face who had looked down on her, laughing, mocking.

Eager to escape from the vestiges of her dream, she went over to the window and half opened the curtains, recoiling like a vampire as the autumn sunlight was able to stream in. She sought safety back under the duvet and put the sound back on the television, which she'd left on all night, the flickering screen acting as her companion.

Dozing some hours later, she was blearily aware of someone knocking and ringing simultaneously at the front door. Afraid to face anyone, she pulled the duvet up even further to her chin, silenced the television and sat, as still as a rabbit caught in the headlights of a car, waiting for her visitor to assume that there was no one at home and depart. All went quiet and Clare heaved a sigh of relief and returned to her cookery programme. But a banging on the window made her jump and turn to look over the back of the settee. There was Ellie's face, nose pressed up against the pane as she strived to look inside the darkened room, hand waving frantically.

'Clare, it's me. Can I come in?' Ellie's words were muffled by the double glazing.

Clare considered hiding and staying silent but knew that Ellie would probably have seen her, so reluctantly she made her way and unlocked the back door.

Ellie made her usual vibrant entrance, preceded by a breeze of the gentle, flowery perfume that she wore to work. She took one look at Clare and then slowly reviewed her surroundings.

'Whatever is going on?' she exclaimed.

Clare stood, ashamed, trying to avoid Ellie's eyes as they took in the sad sight before them. Unwashed, dishevelled, greasy hair, her face swollen and blotchy from hours of crying and poor quality sleep. It required little of Ellie's intuition to diagnose that this was more than a viral illness. She slipped off her jacket, rolled up her sleeves, went over to Clare and gave her a huge hug; this one small act of kindness was enough to make Clare start weeping again. Ellie held her until the worst had subsided and then gently let her go.

'Go and have a shower and wash your hair. I'll tidy up here and make us a coffee. Go on, off you go.'

She herded Clare out of the kitchen and watched while she plodded upstairs before turning back and starting to tackle the washing up. Peering into the lounge, she rescued another three half drunk mugs of cold tea and consigned these to hot soapy water as well. There was nothing in the fridge apart from some milk and a tub of magarine but Ellie found some bread in the freezer, so set about making toast which she then adorned with baked beans just as Clare returned, looking somewhat refreshed but clean in a T shirt and jeans, her wet hair combed back from her face.

'Here, sit down and eat this,' ordered Ellie. 'Tea or coffee?'

Clare did as she was told and started to toy with some of the beans, surprising herself with how good they tasted and how hungry she suddenly was. Ellie let her finish in silence, pleased to see her having something. Throwing open cupboard doors in a theatrical manner, Ellie found chocolate biscuits which she decanted onto a plate and placed on the table with the two mugs of coffee. She sat opposite Clare and watched her as she solemnly dipped her biscuit into the hot drink and then sucked off the chocolate.

'Thanks, Ellie,' Clare spoke softly.

'How are you feeling? That was some virus you've had.'

'Yes,' agreed Clare, trying to preserve the illusion, 'I'd not wish it on anyone.'

Clare looked up and caught Ellie's eye, instantly understanding that they both knew that she was not ill in that sense.

'I think maybe we should talk about things, don't you?' Ellie suggested and slowly Clare nodded in agreement.

'You've not been ill have you?' Ellie went on.

Clare shook her head and ran her fingers through her wet hair.

'Is it you and David?'

Large tears started to fall down Clare's cheeks at the mention of his name.

'Come on Clare, you can tell me. You know I'll help if I possibly can.'

With this invitation, Ellie lapsed into silence and waited for Clare to begin. It took her some minutes to decide how and where to start but once she began to speak, it was as if some cathartic process had been unleashed and she found herself telling Ellie all about David, Sam and Becca. If Ellie was shocked or surprised, she was too professional a counsellor to let it show. She simply uttered murmurs of encouragement to enable Clare to let all her pent up emotion out. When Clare had finished, she hung her head, hopelessly.

'What sort of person am I?' she asked.

'You're still a good, wonderful person,' Ellie assured her.

'I don't think so. Look what I've done. I've ruined two relationships and in doing so I've lost the most important thing in my life, David. I doubt that he'll ever forgive me for what I've done.'

'Do you know where he is now?'

'Not really. He said in his letter that he would be carrying on working so he might be living in at the hospital I suppose. I tried to contact him but he won't reply.'

'Clare, if there's one thing I'm sure of, it's that David will be back. He loves you far too much to give up on you for this one indiscretion. This wasn't your fault; it was that bastard Sam taking advantage of you when you were lonely and vulnerable. You must realise that and start believing it.'

Clare looked unconvinced. Ellie reached out and clasped her hands in hers, squeezing them tight, as if to transfuse her positivism into Clare.

'Give him some time, Clare. He'll be in touch for sure. He'd be horrified to see you looking the way you are doing at the moment. Let's concentrate on sorting you out first and then, if you've still not heard from him, then we can decide on the best way of communicating with him. Don't worry, Clare. I know you're devastated by all that's happened, anyone would be, but you can get through this, emerge from this gloom and then you and David will be stronger than ever.'

'I so want to believe you,' pleaded Clare, 'but right now, I cannot see any hope at all.'

'Right, let's start as we mean to go on. You and I will tidy up the mess in the lounge. Then we'll go out to the shops. I need to go anyway and you certainly do. When did you last eat for goodness sake? After that, you'll come back for a meal at mine. Don't worry, Ian won't ask any awkward questions and the twins will be simply overjoyed to see you.'

Clare almost smiled. Ellie was at her most formidable when organising people and not easy to disobey. Clare stood up and started towards the sink.

'You go and blow dry your hair, it's sticking up at the back and you know you can't bear it when it does that!'

Clare hugged Ellie in gratitude. Ellie, returning the gesture was again horrified to feel how thin and frail Clare felt without the padding of the dressing gown.

Tidying up, Clare, whose hair was now under control and helping her look almost human, showed Ellie David's letter. Ellie raised one eyebrow questioningly to confirm that she was allowed to read it and then skimmed through the words.

'He wrote this when he was hurt and upset,' she announced. 'Once he's had a chance to calm down, you'll get the opportunity to explain things. But for now I would do as he asks and just leave him to his own devices. I'm sure it'll only amount to a few days at the most.'

Bustling in her most efficient housewife mode, Ellie had Clare dusting and vacuuming and restoring the room to normality. She kept up a cheery light-hearted conversation, which needed little input from Clare but was enough to keep her interested. Partly about work, Clare learned that the post-mortem on Prudence showed that she had died from a massive heart attack and that death would have been more or less spontaneous.

'Did they say how long she'd been dead?' asked Clare, feeling guilt starting to creep back into her veins as she thought about her last phone call with Prudence.

'Difficult, perhaps three or four days. Don't worry about it Clare, there was nothing you could have done. Even if you'd gone to see her when she rang you that evening, you know what she was like, she'd have refused, as always, to go to hospital. I know how hard you're taking this but you're only finding it worse because it's all ravelled up with the rest of your troubles. Try to see things in perspective if you can.'

Clare looked tortured and unconvinced. Ellie laughed.

'OK, so that's impossible at the moment. Well in that case, just trust me on this one! Are we done here? That certainly looks more like the room I've spent so many happy evenings in. I'd finished in the kitchen, so let's hit the shops.'

Clare allowed herself to be led to Ellie's car. She felt rather like a pit pony emerging from the mine or like a patient recovering from a major operation as she made heavy weather of getting into the passenger seat.

'It's a good job I had to swap my half day this week,' Ellie declared, fastening her seat belt and then driving off at what Clare felt was an alarming rate. As the houses flashed past them, Clare reflected on the past week, which felt like so much longer and had literally turned her life upside down.

She really did not have much enthusiasm for shopping and idled down the aisles in the supermarket pushing her trolley while Ellie picked multifarious items off shelves and out of freezer compartments, insisting that they were all necessary, while at the same time doing her own shopping with a dexterity that was positively awesome. At the check-out, all that was required of Clare was to pay, which she did by handing over a credit card, unaware of how much she was spending and not really caring. She was then marched into the coffee shop and sat at a table to wait until Ellie returned with a pot of tea for two and a large Danish pastry which she ordered Clare to eat and refused to share even the tiniest morsel of.

They drove back to Clare's house at the same speed and Ellie waited while the shopping was all put away. Instructing Clare to arrive at her house no later than half past six, Ellie sped off into the distance leaving Clare reeling from her whirlwind of an afternoon.

Overwhelmed but inspired by Ellie and with the evening ahead to aim for, Clare tried to relax and work her way through the mountain of mail that had been piling up. Tenderly, she put letters and journals for David in one pile and rather than fretting about what to do with them, she decided that she would simply wait and ask Ellie's advice. She felt so much calmer now that she had unburdened herself and had consequently acquired an ally. She wrote some cheques for outstanding bills and picked through some general practice journals of her own. With one eye on the clock, Clare showered again and dressed in some smart but casual trousers, which she noticed felt much looser that they ever had done before and a cerise coloured V-necked cardigan which was deliciously soft and made her feel cosy.

Feeling ridiculously nervous, she drove carefully to Ellie's where she was met with hugs from them all. Whether Ian had been told the exact nature of her problems, Clare never knew but he gave nothing away and was the epitome of the good host, pouring her a drink and regaling her with stories from his trip to Milan, illustrating them with photographs which made Clare yearn to go there, preferably with David. The twins were ecstatic to see her and fought with their father for her attention so that they could update her with all their news.

They ate around the kitchen table, Ellie determined to keep things as ordinary as possible. She produced a home-made fish pie, creamy potato concealing a melange of cod, prawns and hard-boiled egg in a rich cheese sauce. Keeping a wary eye on Clare, Ellie was relieved to see her starting to unwind in the family atmosphere, even joining in the laughter as Ian had the girls giggling uncontrollably with some of his silliest jokes. For dessert, there was lemon mousse, which melted on the tongue with almond shortbread biscuits. Clare did her best but could barely manage any pudding and apologised to Ellie who winked at her and mouthed 'well done.'

On finishing, Ellie refused Clare's offer to wash up and sent her with the twins to watch one of their favourite DVDs. By nine o'clock, Clare could feel her eyelids drooping and sleep fast approaching, the combined effects of a good meal and the warm room. Yawning, she made some comment about having to get home before she fell asleep to which Ellie suggested that she stay the night. Virginia and Lydia, who had managed somehow to avoid their own bedtime, yelled their support for this motion and begged her to stay. Clare pondered on the big empty house waiting for her and the prospect of another night which she would surely spend on the settee and accepted with alacrity. Ellie scuttled off to find a nightdress and before she knew it, Clare was in the spare bedroom, cosily curled up under the bedcovers, luxuriating in the treat of a hot water bottle. Feeling about six years old, Clare watched as Ellie smoothed the covers over her and then sat on the bed beside her and stroked her hair.

'Thanks for a lovely evening, Ellie,' she said softly.

'It's been great to hear you laugh. Try and get some rest now- don't interrupt, I know it's early, but you need to. Have a lie in, I'll tell the girls to keep the noise down as much as possible but I expect they'll be bursting to visit you in bed. They do love you Clare, we all do. It breaks my heart to see you like this. Sleep well, good night.'

Ellie kissed gently on the cheek and then stood up and walked to the door, giving Clare the chance to wipe away the solitary tear that dribbled down her nose, surreptitiously. Left alone in the dark, Clare listened to the strange, unfamiliar sounds of the twins going to bed, protesting to the last before admitting defeat and settling down. Then later, Ian locking up before coming upstairs with Ellie, the two of them laughing and talking softly, making Clare feel envious, before closing their bedroom door after which the only sound which broke the silence was the hypnotic ticking of the grandfather clock on the landing. Clare found this reassuring, as though it was the heart beat of someone protecting her and she lay listening to it, counting the beats and waiting for the hourly chimes. It was the early hours of the morning before she dropped off.

Waking, it took Clare a while to realise where she was. Glancing at her watch, she saw that it was not yet six o'clock but further attempts to sleep were unsuccessful. She climbed out of bed and rooted through the bookcase, crammed with paperbacks of all shapes and sizes, for something to read.

Trying to concentrate was enough to have her dozing again and Clare was awakened by the sound of subdued giggling outside her bedroom door, followed by a very polite tapping. Asking her visitor to come in, she watched while the door opened to admit Lydia, walking extremely carefully and slowly, intent upon the tray that she was carrying. Expressing delight, Clare attempted to get out of bed to help but was ordered to stay where she was. With obvious relief to both of them, the tray arrived safely on the bed and Clare held it steady so that Lydia could climb up and sit beside her. Clare admired her breakfast – a glass of orange juice, only partly spilled, toast, butter and marmalade and a little cafetiere of coffee, all arranged beautifully neatly and shown off to the best advantage by a tiny posy of flowers in an egg cup.

'I made the toast,' Lydia informed her, proudly. 'And I went in the garden and picked the flowers for you.'

'This is wonderful,' Clare thanked her. 'Thank you so much. Would you like to share my toast?'

Lydia, obviously hoping for this, nodded enthusiastically.

'Where's Virginia this morning?' Clare asked as she generously buttered a slice of toast, checked that Lydia wanted marmalade and then divided it into four equal fingers so that they could share.

'Dad's taken her to the doctor for a check up on her leg,' replied Lydia, munching away, paying no attention to the crumbs that were flying in all directions. 'They'll be back soon. Would you like to see Smudge after breakfast? Are you staying all day? I hope you are. Can I have some more toast?'

'Of course, help yourself. And yes, we'll go and see Smudge. How is she?'

'She's ace. Dad's going to get us another pony as soon as Ginnie's able to ride again. Won't that be brilliant?'

'Wow, you are lucky! Will I be able to come and see the new pony?'

'Yup. You can come and help with the mucking out,' Lydia decided confidently.

Clare laughed.

'Gosh, thanks for that.'

Amicably, they finished their toast, Clare listening while Lydia kept up a running commentary about school, friends and ponies.

Pushing the tray to one side, Clare threw back the bedclothes.

'Right, this is it. Give me ten minutes and I'll join you downstairs.'

Lydia scrambled off the bed and ran across the room.

'I'll be out with Smudge, come and find us!' Like a small typhoon she tore through the door and Clare heard her galloping down to the kitchen.

Having no other clothes, Clare was forced to dress in her trousers and cardigan from the night before and took the tray with her as she set off in pursuit of her small companion. Ellie was loading the dishwasher and looked up, smiling as she spotted Clare.

'Sleep ok?' she asked.

'Not too bad,' Clare lied.

'Good. Did you have enough breakfast? Can I get you anything else?'

'Plenty, thanks. Enough for two in fact!'

'I told her not to pester you, but I knew she would. The instructions were to creep in, leave the tray and come back down here straightaway.'

"Not to worry. Anyway, I have an assignation with Smudge now. Then I'd better be getting back home, I suppose.'

Ellie stood up and faced her.

"Look Clare, I think you should stay a bit longer. You seem better just for having had some company and distraction for a few hours. It can't be doing you any good to be on your own. Why don't you nip back home, take Lydia with you, she'll keep you company, collect a few things and then come back and spend the rest of the day and tonight with us. I tell you what, I'll do a big roast dinner tomorrow in the afternoon and then you could head off back in the evening.'

Clare hesitated; she very much wanted to stay.

'I'm not sure, Ellie, I don't like to impose...'

'Great, then that's settled. Go and see Smudge and then the two of you-that's you and Lydia not you and Smudge, go and get your stuff.'

'If you're sure..'

'We'd all love it.'

Ellie gave Clare a quick hug and then chuckled.

'Looks like you're wanted.'

'Come on Clare,' cried an impatient Lydia, half in and half out of the back door. 'Borrow Mum's boots. I've tied Smudge up. She's quite dirty, she's been rolling but she's longing to see you.'

Ellie watched as the two of them made their way to the stable, Lydia jumping around, keeping up a continuous flow of chatter and Clare, rather more sedate, holding her hand, smiling and nodding. She felt so desperately sorry for Clare and wished frantically that her problems would soon be resolved. She contemplated ringing David herself, but a warning voice admonished her and she decided to wait a little longer and see what transpired naturally.

Lydia was delighted to act as chaperone for Clare. She made Clare drive past her school and then past the equitation centre, even though it was several miles off their route. At her house, Clare supplied Lydia with lemonade and more chocolate biscuits than her mother would probably approve of while she ran upstairs and rapidly, with little thought, rammed some things into an overnight bag and changed into jeans and a jumper.

'Ready,' she announced breathlessly arriving in the kitchen.

Lydia eyed her up and down, critically.

'That was quick. I like your jumper. It's a pretty colour. Did you get it in Lambdale?'

'Thank you. I bought it in Harrogate actually.'

Lydia nodded, knowingly.

'I thought as much. Mum likes to go shopping there.'

'Have you had enough to eat?' Clare was agitating to leave the house.

'Yes, I think so. I might just take a couple more of these biscuits. One for me to eat in the car and one for Virginia.'

'That's a good idea. Help yourself.'

As Clare started the car, she could tell that Lydia was building up to asking her something.

'Clare?' she began.

'Yes?'

'Do you think we could possibly go back past the farm shop that sells all the brushes and bridles and horse stuff?'

'I don't see why not. Was there something you needed?'

'I think Smudge might need a new head collar and some crunchy carrot treats,' was the serious reply.

'Then let's go and see what they've got. I'd like to stop somewhere as well and get some flowers for your mum, so let's get going!'

Clare allowed Lydia to direct her to the saddlers and then stood over her while she agonised over the head collars, unable to decide which one would suit Smudge the best. Finally deciding on the green one, Clare tried to lead the way to the counter which was not easy as Lydia insisted on examining everything on the way such as brushes, rugs and riding boots. Then, while Lydia was prevaricating over crunchy apple or crunchy carrot treats, Clare picked up a bag of each and indicated to the assistant that she was ready to pay. As Lydia was digging deep into her pockets trying to find her pocket money, Clare suggested that she pay as a thank you to Smudge for letting her stay and Lydia agreed whole-heartedly that this was a splendid idea. They eventually reached their destination having stopped twice more, once for flowers and once for chocolates. Lydia, spotting her father's car in the drive which implied that he and Virginia were back, went running into the house, shouting greetings. Following at a more sedate pace, Clare searched out Ellie, who was reading the paper, spread out on the kitchen table and drinking a cup of coffee.

'Everything ok?' Ellie inquired.

'Yes I think so. It was a good idea of yours to take Lydia with me. Here, some flowers for you. Just to say thanks.'

'Those are gorgeous. There was no need but I know you know that. There's a vase in that top cupboard, if you can reach it.'

The day passed in a flash. There was little left of the morning but just enough time to play a board game with the twins. In the afternoon, Ellie and Clare stayed with Virginia while Ian took Lydia out for a ride. They all had a lazy sort of supper, eating pasta off plates balanced on their knees while they watched television, passing round garlic bread and a bowl of salad. The twins were cajoled into going to bed at a reasonable hour by the promise that Clare would come up and read to them. Kissing them good night and arranging various stuffed teddies, dogs and other toys in a very specific order on either side of them, Clare was filled with longing for children of her own. She hated herself for turning down the offer of assisted conception, purely on selfish grounds. Maybe if she could contact David and say that she had changed her mind, it might make a difference and he would come home, though she suspected that she had caused so many ructions in their relationship that, if it was remediable, then it would take far more than that alone to restore the status quo.

She sat half way up the stairs, thinking of David and what on earth she was going to do. He'd been gone for almost a week but it seemed like forever. Monday and work loomed horribly close. Even at Ellie's, safe among friends, Clare felt like a spare part. Ellie and Ian were their friends, not just Clare's and it seemed incongruous to be staying there, but not having David there, not even mentioning his name but thinking about him constantly.

Ellie, wondering what was keeping Clare so long and hoping that it was not her daughters being naughty, appeared at the foot of the stairs and instantaneously saw the downswing in her friend's mental state.

'Are they asleep?' she asked brightly. 'Come and have a drink with us. Ian's just opened a bottle of wine.'

Clare burst into tears.

'I don't know if I can do this any more, Ellie. It's been so lovely being here with you all. You've all been so good to me. Your children are marvellous and you and Ian make me feel so welcome. I'm dreading going home, I'm dreading going back to work and I cannot even contemplate the thought of seeing Sam again without feeling physically sick. I just want to wake up next to David and find out that this has all been some awful nightmare. I miss him so, so much and I'm so scared that I've lost him forever.'

Ellie went up and sat on the stair below Clare, putting her hand on her knee and patting it.

'Let's just take this one day at a time. Try to relax a bit while you're here. You never know with work, it might help. It'll give your day some structure; it sounds so much easier to be at home hiding but in fact it's so counterproductive. You'll have to concentrate on your patients and you love doing that. As for Sam, we'll all rally round and help.'

'But Ed and John must never find out what's happened. I'd not be able to look them in the face again if they did,' uttered Clare, aghast at the prospect.

'They won't,' Ellie reassured her. 'There's no reason why they should. You and I will come up with such a good plan they won't suspect a thing. Trust me. I promise. Now, let's go and join Ian. He's found a film on TV for us to watch.'

Ellie stood up and help out her hand to Clare.

'Just give me a minute, Ellie. I need a moment to myself.'

Ellie nodded, understanding and left her. Clare sat and listened to Ellie and Ian chatting and the sound of a cork popping then wine glugging from the bottle into glasses. She blew her nose fiercely.

'Clare,' called Ellie, 'the film's starting.'

Dutifully, Clare made her way reluctantly into the lounge, where Ian leapt to his feet to hand her a glass of wine and then tactfully suggested that they dim the lights, ostensibly to add to the cinematic atmosphere but really to save Clare and her blotchy tear stained face from embarrassment. They were aware that, for most of the film, Clare continued to cry almost silently but at least she stayed with them, secure in their proximity.

Chapter Twenty One

Ellie, thought Clare, is one of the most remarkable people I know. She's a great doctor, always looks fantastic, never puts on weight, never lets worries get the better of her and manages effortlessly to juggle full time work with a busy, fulfilling home life. So far that Sunday morning, Ellie had provided them all with breakfast, changed all the bed linen, done two loads of washing, conquered a teetering pile of clothes waiting to be ironed and helped the twins with their homework. Somehow, while doing all of these things, she had managed to mastermind the cooking of a proper lunch and had now called them all to the table and was serving up roast beef, Yorkshire puddings (home made of course), the crispiest roast potatoes imaginable and two sorts of vegetable. Managing to look entirely calm and tranquil, she passed the gravy round and urged them all to start while their meals were hot. Clare could hear her own plate groaning under the weight of the food on it. Her appetite had deserted her. After another early awakening, she had been aware of increasing anxiety as the morning advanced, aware that the clock was ticking and work was looming ever closer. Hidden behind the Sunday papers, as Ellie had assured her there was nothing she could do to help in any way, Clare had barely read a word, her eyes burning into the print but not seeing it, her mind hyperactive, accusatory, self-deprecating.

Watching the others, doing justice to their food with their healthy appetites and wishing that she was on her own, Clare pushed her food around gently with her fork. Suddenly she wanted to be back at home and have her own belongings around her and be quiet.

'Just eat what you want, Clare,' Ellie, ever observant, said. 'Don't be put off by the gannets that constitute my family. You'd think they all had tapeworms!'

'Ugh,' cried the twins in unison, instantly told off for speaking with their mouths full.

'It's really delicious, Ellie,' began Clare. 'It's just that......'

'I know, it's fine. Lydia, Virginia, Ian, has everyone got plenty? There's loads of potatoes left.'

'Aren't you hungry Clare?' asked Lydia, innocently.

'Not really. I'm not used to big meals like this,' Clare explained.

'Don't you and David have roast dinners?' Lydia continued.

'Sometimes. It's a lot to cook for just two of you. We like roast chicken though.'

'Eat your dinner, dear,' Ellie instructed her daughter and smiled at Clare sympathetically.

The meal was excruciating for Clare. Willing them all to eat quickly, they did exactly the opposite and after the initial onslaught to assuage the edges of their hunger, they proceeded to decelerate, take their time to stop, talk and laugh, just as a family meal should be. When their plates were at last empty, two of them, Ian and Virginia replied in the affirmative to Ellie's offer of second helpings and to Clare, when they appeared, these looked every bit as large as the first ones.

Eventually, Ellie cleared away the plates and the family sat, replete and content. She said nothing as Clare handed her a plate of untouched food. Hoping that the meal was over, Clare was on the verge of suggesting that she should be leaving when Ellie announced that there was apple crumble for pudding and who wanted custard.

The thought of firstly refusing any and then having to watch everyone else enjoying theirs was the final straw.

'I think I'll go home now. I really think I should,' Clare apologised. 'Sorry to interrupt your meal, but I need to go.' There was urgency in her tone which slightly scared Ellie.

Rushing out of the room, ignoring the upset on the twins' faces, Clare missed the anxious glances that passed between Ellie and Ian. By the time she returned down with her possessions hurriedly squashed into her bag, Ellie was waiting for her in the hall.

'I've delegated the custard making to Ian,' she explained. 'Are you sure you have to go?'

Clare nodded.

'Take care then. Drive safely and I'll ring you this evening to see how you are.'

Ellie gave her a quick hug.

Clare tried to smile but grimaced and unable to speak resorted to a wave as she ran out to her car, jumped in and started the engine.

She drove nervously and had difficulty getting her key in the lock because her hand was shaking so much. But the house was just as she and Lydia had left it, feeling cold and rather forlorn. Clare quickly checked for messages but was not overly surprised to find none and so went upstairs to unpack her bag. Her bed looked so inviting that she was unable to resist the temptation to lie down on it and then envelop herself in David's half of the duvet. Weary beyond belief, she closed her eyes and dozed comfortingly for what remained of the afternoon.

It was dark outside when Clare blearily roused herself and she felt hot and sticky. A long hot shower helped her to feel better and thinking that there was no point in putting proper clothes back on, she slipped into her nightdress and David's dressing gown. Sitting on the stool in front of the mirror, Clare combed out her wet hair and slicked it back from her face, which stared back at her, thin and pale, dark rings beneath her eyes, cheekbones too prominent to be attractive. Exploring the top drawer, she opened up a number of little jewellery boxes and sentimentally gazed at gifts she had received from David over the years to mark anniversaries, birthdays and surprises when he just wanted to tell her that he loved her. There on the top were the diamond earrings, glittering, breathtaking but barely worn as Clare knew she did not deserve them.

I need to be busy, she thought. All this wallowing in the past can't help. I'll have a cup of tea.

She closed the drawer and made herself go downstairs. In the kitchen, while filling the kettle, her hand slipped on the handle and water splashed out of the tap, off the side of the kettle, spraying Clare and leaving her nightdress soaked and clinging to her skin. Cursing and on the point of going to change, she was startled by the doorbell ringing.

'David!' she cried out loud, not realising that he had a key and would have let himself in.

She rushed to the door and flung it open.

'Hello,' said Sam.

Clare recoiled as if struck by lightning.

'What are you doing here?'

214

'I was worried about you. You were off sick last week and no one seemed to know when you'd be back. Joan gave me your address. So, how are you?'

'I'm okay now. I should be back at work tomorrow, all being well. I've just had some awful sort of virus. I expect I picked it up from one of the patients. There's been a lot of this about; I expect you've seen plenty in your surgeries.' Clare gabbled on, trying to keep calm.

'You still look a bit rough,' Sam commented, walking past Clare into the hall. 'This is very nice.' He looked round appreciatively.

'I'm just a bit tired, that's all,' Clare replied. 'Do you want a cup of tea? The kettle's just boiled.'

'That'd be great.'

Pleased to have something to do, Clare made heavy weather of making a solitary mug of tea which she put on a plate with a few biscuits and placed on the table in front of Sam.

'Help yourself,' she offered.

Clare sat on the edge of her chair, twirling the end of her dressing gown belt around her index finger, first clockwise then anticlockwise. Sam crunched on biscuits noisily and slurped his tea, clearly thirsty.

'Becca's gone back to her parents, Clare. She's picked up all her possessions.'

Clare stayed silent.

'There never was any future in our relationship. She knew it wasn't serious.'

'That's not what she told me,' Clare contradicted him. 'I thought you were supposed to be engaged.'

'Ah,' murmured Sam. 'I think she rather got the wrong end of the stick there. I'm sorry about that. Anyway, she's left, so that should make life a bit easier for you.'

'Hardly,' Clare responded, looking at the carpet.

'Why's that?' asked Sam.

'Surely you know what happened?'

Sam shrugged his shoulders, innocently.

'She saw Ellie at the surgery who referred her for an urgent psychiatric opinion.'

'Perhaps that was a good thing; it would help her to move on.' Sam suggested.

'Don't you understand? It was David who saw her and she told him what happened.'

'Oh, shit.' Sam seemed genuinely horrified.

'That could qualify as the understatement of the year,' Clare told him, her voice edged with bitterness.

'Hang on Clare – I never meant for him to find out. How was I to know that was going to happen?'

'He has taken all his things and left me. I haven't heard from him for a week. I don't even know where he is. You are responsible for this. I think you should go now.'

'Let me stay Clare,' Sam urged her, 'I can help you. I still find you very attractive, you know I do. Maybe now that you're on your own, we could get together a bit.'

'How dare you!' cried Clare, jumping to her feet. 'I want you to leave please.'

'She walked into the hall to emphasise her point. Sam got up and followed. In the hall, he reached out to touch her shoulder. She whipped round and her dressing gown fell open. Simultaneously, the door opened to reveal David, standing on the doorstep.

Time froze.

He surveyed the scene before him. Clare's nightdress was clinging to her body, revealing her contours, her erect nipples and Sam, close to her with his hand on her shoulder.

'David!' screeched Clare, shattering the silence. It's not what it looks like. Tell him Sam.'

David glanced briefly at each of them in turn, then closed the door on them, went to his car and drove off into the darkness.

Clare chased after him, standing on the drive, screaming at the top of her voice.

'David, please come back!'

The tail lights of his car disappeared around the corner.

Clare turned, distraught, to Sam.

'This is all your fault,' she hissed. 'How could you? He was coming back to me, I know he was. But you've ruined everything – again. Get out now! I never want to see you again!'

She virtually pushed Sam across the threshold and slammed the door in his startled face before sinking to the floor and sobbing hysterically, hugging her knees to her body, wailing and rocking back and forth.

With a sudden spurt of energy, she rushed to the telephone and maniacally dialled David's mobile number but an impassionate voice informed her that his phone was switched off and cordially invited her to try again later. Clare did try again, but immediately, time after time, getting an identical response on each occasion, becoming increasingly frustrated and desperate, missing the correct numbers and swearing out loud.

Finally, worn out, she allowed herself to rest from her efforts and was rewarded by the almost ringing of the phone.

Clare snatched up the receiver and held it tremulously to her ear.

'David, thank you, oh thank you for ringing me back. It's all a terrible mistake; it wasn't what it looked like.....'

'Clare, is that you? It's me, Ellie. Whatever's been going on?'

Feeling overwhelmingly disappointed, Clare let out a huge sigh and sob.

'Clare?' repeated Ellie, concern mounting in her voice.

'Yes?' was the monosyllabic reply.

'Tell me what's happened. Has David been in touch?'

Clare took the phone to a nearby chair and having made herself as comfortable as she could, recounted events to an astounded Ellie.

'Oh Clare, how awful for you. It's all such a terrible mix up. No wonder you're so distressed. Would you like me to come round?'

'No. Thank you. I want to be on my own. You've done enough for me already. Just when I thought everything was going to be sorted out. Now, instead, it's all worse, far worse and I didn't think that was possible.'

'Try to calm down. This will work out and David will understand. Was that you trying to ring him? 'I've been trying to get through for ages but the line's been engaged all the time.'

'Yes, but his phone isn't switched on, so I can't even leave a message.'

'He probably needs time Clare. Leave it for now. Try again tomorrow. Why don't you ring him from work when I'm around in case you need any moral support?'

'I don't know what I'd do without you, Ellie. You've been such a good friend to me.'

'And you'd do the same for me. Have you had any supper?'

'No, I can't face food.'

'Well, I think you should try to have something. You didn't eat any lunch, although you pretended to, so go now and have at least some soup or toast, something light. Have some hot chocolate and then curl up with a good book in bed, I'll see you in the morning.'

'I can't go to work,' Clare announced, flatly, emphatically.

'You must try. We talked about why it would help, earlier. You'll be among friends the whole time and that will help too.'

'I can't face Sam, though. I've just screamed at him that I never want to see him again as long as I live.'

'Are you due to do a tutorial tomorrow?' Ellie asked.

'No,' admitted Clare.

'Fine. Go straight to your surgery and leave Sam to me.'

'What are you going to do?' Clare was frightened by the purposeful tone in Ellie's voice.

'Just rearrange his teaching schedule a bit. I think he'd benefit form having more of an input from the other partners. Ed has always said he'd like to be a trainer some day. Well this is his chance to do some tutorials and see how he gets on.'

'That could be wonderful Ellie, if it could be arranged.'

'Consider it done. We'll set up something for the next couple of week, just until you get your feet back on the ground and pointing in the right direction and then we can review it.'

'Ellie?'

'Don't even try to start saying thank you again! Go and have some supper and a warm drink. Think about Lydia and Virginia having theirs – I'm just about to go and put the milk on for them. Try and get some sleep. Lots of love from us all.'

'Goodnight Ellie,' Clare put the receiver down and felt very alone. But, determined not to let her friend down, she did as she had been instructed and made some toast, liberally spread her favourite raspberry jam on top and boiled milk for cocoa. Taking these up to bed, she sat up, eating, drinking and trying to concentrate on a detective novel. Much to her surprise, she soon felt drowsy and feeling slightly guilty at not having brushed her teeth, Clare slid down under the duvet and was asleep within seconds

She woke early, just before five, instantly wide awake and already full of trepidation for the day ahead. As predicted, her mouth felt dry and tasted horrid. Searching for distractions, she headed downstairs, made tea and plonked herself in front of the television for the next two hours.

Trying to estimate what time Sam would be in and so avoid him, she showered and then dressed in loose black trousers and a black twinset. Normally she would have enlivened this ensemble with a colourful necklace but that morning, it looked so incongruous to Clare that she settled for a more discrete choker made of tiny gold links.

As she arrived at the surgery, Clare was convinced that her heart night rupture spontaneously, so frantically was it beating within her thorax. Suspecting that to everyone, her inner turmoil was clearly transparent, Clare gingerly entered the building and was relieved to be greeted by Gary, Elizabeth and Joan in exactly the same way as they did every day. They were preoccupied preparing for the morning surgeries of the day, opening post and putting out prescriptions to be signed. To them the sight of Clare was not only welcome, as they had been concerned about her being off sick and how her absence had made appointment availability really tight, but also a normal landmark of the morning.

Clare made it to her surgery and closed the door thankfully, feeling that she had triumphantly succeeded in some life threatening task rather than simply come to work. Logging on to the computer, she started to make her way through a long list of waiting emails and was cheered to find that after an initial rather rocky start, feeling afraid before she opened up each message, her normal professional behaviour seemed instinctively to return and the run up to her surgery starting became more tolerable.

She steeled herself for the first patient, a Mrs Thompson who wanted to discuss the pros and cons of immunisations for her baby. After a hesitant start, Clare felt that she made a reasonable attempt to listen and advise. Certainly her patient seemed happy to accept her doctor's opinions.

The next few patients all had simple, acute problems such as tonsillitis, a flare up of psoriasis and an infected ingrowing toenail. As she dealt with these, Clare's confidence started to grow; she felt back in the swing of things and silently acknowledged that Ellie was right with her sage advice.

Clare even smiled welcomingly as she asked Mr Barron to come in. Sadly this charming gesture, designed to put him at his ease, did nothing to appease the rather grumpy mood he had woken up in and which had not been helped but his wife's revelation of how she had scratched the side of his car the previous evening reversing in the car park by the cinema.

'I'll come straight to the point, Dr Jennings,' he barked. 'My wife's made me come; she booked the appointment. I hardly ever come to the doctor so I'll make the most of this and tell you about a few things.'

'Of course,' answered Clare, accommodatingly, still trying to achieve the feeling of some rapport.

'Well the first thing is this lump in my armpit.'

He then underwent a series of bodily contortions which involved pulling up his shirt and twisting to reveal the affected part of his anatomy without actually removing any clothes. Clare was happy to reassure him that he had a simple skin tag that needed no further treatment.

'Then there's my nail. My wife says it's a fungus but what does she know? I've told her she's talking rubbish.'

Clare examined his feet and discussed the likely accurate diagnosis of Mrs Barron.

'Humph. Then there's another thing.'

He looked acutely embarrassed.

Clare made encouraging noises.

'Things don't seem to be working properly. You know what I mean? In the bedroom department. Are you with me?'

Astutely, Clare interpreted this to be a problem with erectile dysfunction and took a careful history, offered to examine him (which he declined) and discussed how best to investigate with a view to discussing the most appropriate treatments.

Armed with a form to take to the nurses for blood tests, Mr Barron started to put his jacket back on.

'I sometimes get this ache, just here,' he pointed to the left side of his chest. 'It's only been over the last few weeks, if I get out of breath or rush. I don't suppose it is anything. I wasn't going to mention it but as I'm here...'

Clare's heart sank. Tempted to defer this problem to another day, she realised that this could be a potential heart problem and visions of Prudence flashed before her. Certainly, as she took a history from Mr Barron, it seemed likely that this was the case. His ache was related to exercise; he was a smoker and had a strong family history of heart disease. Instigating all the necessary tests for him took some time but she was rewarded by him shaking her by the hand and thanking her for her help, though still not smiling at her.

Now running over thirty minutes late, Clare's temporarily slightly restored better humour had expired. She longed for a cup of coffee and some respite form the demands and intricacies of her patients. Her head had begun to throb and she felt slightly nauseous.

'You're running very late, doctor,' complained Felicity Lester, a sour-faced woman in her thirties, dressed in an uncomfortably tight black suit with sheer black stockings and perilously high heels with viciously pointed toes. 'I really don't think this is acceptable. Some of us have important jobs to go to I'm going to be late for an extremely vital business meeting now.'

On cue, her mobile phone rang and she fished it out of her bag to answer it.

'Please don't use that in here,' advised Clare, her hackles on the rise, fighting the temptation to answer back. 'I'm sorry I've kept you waiting but some of my patients this morning have needed a lot of my time. How may I help you?'

'I'll be very quick. I need some antibiotics.'

'For what, exactly?' inquired Clare, patiently.

'I have a sore throat. I've a presentation to do tomorrow to fifty people so I must be well for that.'

'When did you sore throat start?'

'This morning.' Felicity was showing signs of increasing irritation. 'If you just look at my records, you'll see that I always get antibiotics when I want them.'

'Do you feel unwell with it?' Clare continued, unabashed.

'No. Usually I get erythromycin, I think it's called. I'm allergic to penicillin.'

'Do you have any other symptoms?'

'No. I only have to take about four of the tablets and then I'm better.'

'May I examine you?' suggested Clare.

Felicity demurred to this request and Clare found, unsurprisingly, nothing abnormal.

Knowing that there was an uphill struggle pending, Clare leant forward slightly to capture her patient's full attention.

'You have a mild viral infection. I would suggest that you gargle with some soluble aspirin, rest and drink plenty of fluids.'

'But I need antibiotics.'

'It would not be appropriate to prescribe them today. You should save them for when you really need them.'

'I need them now,' Felicity demanded and banged her fist on Clare's desk to drive her point home.

'I can assure you that you do not. If you would just try my suggestions for two or three days, I think you will find that you get better.'

'Give me some erythromycin. I insist that you do.' Felicity's narrow, pursed lips did nothing to improve her appearance.

Clare cogitated. The easy way out was to capitulate. The consultation would be over, the patient would be happy and this rude woman would be out of her room in seconds.

'No, I'm sorry. You're not getting antibiotics from me.'

Felicity Lester reached down and snatched up her handbag, furiously.

'I have never been spoken to like that in my entire life. Call yourself a doctor? You're not fit to look after a rat. Let me assure you, your bedside manner is sadly lacking. You'll be hearing about this, mark my words.'

'I really couldn't care less, you stupid woman,' murmured Clare, under her breath, she thought.

'I heard that.'

The pictures on the wall shuddered in the wake of the door being slammed shut.

'Why on earth did I say that?' Clare asked herself.

If Clare's next patient was baffled by his doctor's thorough interrogation and touching concern, plus offers of all sorts of advice that had never been on his agenda, he was too polite to say anything. He was, however, astonished to be quizzed about his smoking and drinking habits, have his blood pressure, weight and height checked, be offered a chest examination and an ecg, when all he had made an appointment for was to ask for a repeat prescription for his elderly mother's sleeping pills. When Clare then moved on to talk about his prostate gland and more intimate matters concerning men's health, he blanched visibly and interrupted her, firmly thanking her for her contribution and bolting for the door.

Thus Clare stumbled through what was left of her surgery and bade the final patient farewell with considerable relief. There was a knock on the door and Ellie came in, bearing two mugs of coffee, a most welcome sight.

'Are you done?'

Clare nodded.

'How did it go? You're very late finishing. I've been keeping an eye out for your last patient leaving.'

'Mixed, really,' Clare pondered on her answer. 'Some dreadful ones, some not quite so bad.'

'It was bound to be hard going because you've been off. We all know how patients wait for us and store their problems up. It'll get easier as the day goes on.'

Clare looked unconvinced.

'Have you seen Sam?' she asked.

'Yes, he's gone out on visits. There are rather a lot of them today, so he was keen to make a start. I've told him that Ed is keen to do some teaching with him for the next fortnight and that it will be good for him to have a male perspective on the practice. He took it very well, in his usual cool and charming fashion.'

'Huh,' grunted Clare.

'Did you sleep last night?' Ellie was keen to change the subject.

'To start with. Your suggestion of cocoa seemed to work. I woke up early though, so I still feel shattered and sick.'

'You look it.' Ellie was candid. 'It's scary how tiring emotional problems can be. What about David, do you want to try ringing him now?'

Clare checked her watch.

'It's probably not a good time. He does ward rounds all Monday morning and they go on for hours. I don't think he'd relish being disturbed by me. I'll maybe try later.'

She took a drink of her coffee. 'You say there are a lot of visits?'

'I'm afraid so. I could help you with yours if you like.'

'No, I'd better do them. I've a long list of phone calls to make too.'

'Right, I'll leave you to it. I've got to go and start surgery, I'm already a little late. See you this afternoon.'

'Thanks Ellie.'

It was with a heavy heart that Clare dutifully ploughed her way through what seemed like an interminable list of telephone calls. Never at her most confident when trying to assess symptoms without seeing a patient, today was so bad that she was catapulted to new heights of indecision. Simple headaches just might be brain tumours; indigestion a heart attack, rashes could be the start of meningococcal septicaemia. The only way that she could resolve her diagnostic dilemmas was to suggest that these patients came into the surgery that day for more conventional face to face consultations which she knew would lengthen not only her but everyone's afternoon surgeries and make her deeply unpopular with her partners. Clare also ended up with two extra visits which, added to the six that were already booked for her, meant that what was left of the morning (not a lot) and all the early part of the afternoon was spoken for as she drove around Lambdale and part of the surrounding countryside tending to the housebound.

Chapter Twenty Two

A week later, Clare felt even more tired and nauseous. Her sleep pattern was atrocious. While every cell in her body screamed with exhaustion and desire for rest, her mind would not sanction it. With the chronic fatigue came the inevitable dulling of all her emotions and negativity injected itself subliminally into her psyche. Anorexic, she tried to survive on endless cups of black or very dark brown coffee in the hopes that the caffeine might provide some stimulation and large glasses of wine in the evening to act as a sedative. The former worked a treat but brought with it the unpleasant side-effects of edginess and palpitations; the latter just precipitated more sorrow and dejection.

Somehow, she had managed to cope at work. Her surgeries all over ran and she was acutely aware that the standard of medicine that she was practising was a far cry from her normal. Her inability to make decisions had now crept into all facets of her daily life and she over-investigated, asked for far too many follow up appointments and rang patients at home after seeing them to check how they were.

She wrote ridiculously long notes after every encounter and her referral rate to consultants shot through the roof.

Her partners watched her anxiously. They saw weight drop off her on an almost daily basis and despite Ellie's best interventions, Clare continued to turn up for work in the same clothes each day and showed no signs of washing her normally gleaming hair.

Clare had tried to ring David many times. She had used his mobile number, afraid to have any contact with his secretary, for fear of what she might have been told. Though he never answered, at least his phone was switched to voice mail, so that she could leave messages, which she did, dozens of them. Sobbing, crying messages, screaming, incoherent messages and flat, impassive messages, all imploring him to come home or at least make contact.

True to her word, Ellie seemed to have dealt, albeit temporarily, with Sam. Clare rarely saw him as she spent most of the time in her surgery rather than going upstairs to join in the general chat, another feature of concern to her colleagues.

When she did come up against him, briefly, she was never on her own, being either in the safety of the receptionists or in the waiting area, which was rarely empty. He gave nothing away, greeting her courteously, his face relaxed and smiling, pleased to see her, telling her how much he was learning from Ed. If anything, this made Clare feel more unnerved. She felt she could have coped better if he had ignored her or even shown signs of hostility. From her own point of view, the anger she felt towards him had not subsided one iota; the merest mention of his name made bile rise in her throat. The sight of him made her cringe with horror and disgust at what had happened between them.

At home, things were no better. As soon as the front door was opened, any visitor could tell that all was not well. There were three houseplants, wilting with thirst and an irregular pile of post, swept to one side and left. Clare had regressed into her one room habitat. The duvet had been dragged downstairs and lay untidily on the settee, her bed, her chair, her world. The table in front of this piece of furniture was littered with mugs, half empty with cold coffee festering in them. Dust gathered again on the surfaces, the curtains had not been opened beyond the slightest chink; the carpet was littered with papers, magazines and dried up tissues.

Ellie had visited one evening, with the twins, confident that they, if anyone, would be able to bring a smile to Clare's face. She had warned her friend about their visit, expecting her, as usual, to have pushed the boat out and bought far too many gooey cakes and chocolate biscuits with which to ply her children. On their arrival, there had been nothing, the kitchen had looked like a room in a show house, with no signs of use and the fridge, into which Ellie had peeped when Clare was not looking, was empty apart from some cheese that was aromatically displaying a hideously dusky green sheen. Clare had spent most of the visit sitting, shrouded in her duvet, the television in front of her switched on, blaring out some inane chat show that she seemed to find fascinating. Lydia and Virginia had hardly been recognised and Ellie quickly had taken them away, upset by their puzzled faces, having no idea why one of their favourite people was behaving so peculiarly.

Ellie had rung on her return home. She had invited Clare for the weekend again, promising all sorts of family entertainment, a trip bowling followed by a pizza, the sight of Lydia and Smudge tackling their first jump and if Clare fancied it, a trip to the shops looking for clothes. Clare had come up with a selection of excuses, none of which Ellie believed for a moment but had decided not to force the issue and simply had told Clare that if she changed her mind, she only had to ring. Unhappy at the thought of severing all contact, Ellie had continued to phone, diligently, each evening, slightly dreading the response she would get and keeping a very close eye on her friend at work.

Following Ellie's call the previous evening, Clare had felt inspired to try to change. She was determined to have an early night, get some proper sleep, even if it was assisted by a sleeping pill from her bag and get up in good time to shower, do her hair and make up and put on some bright, cheerful clothes. As it was, after three glasses of wine and one temazepam tablet, things had started to go horribly wrong. Rather than go to sleep and wake early, Clare had been unable to get off to sleep at all and had tossed and turned for many hours before finally surrendering to a deep sleep and waking from disturbing dreams just as her surgery should have been starting. Soporifically, she reached to the adjacent chair for her clothes from the night before, which were creased and in need of a wash. There was no time to shower and the fact that she was going to be rushing and late seeing her first patient was just about the worst start her day could have had. Scraping her fingers through her greasy hair so that there was the hint of a style; at least there was if you had a vivid imagination, she rubbed her cheeks and eyes, looked round for her bag, which she had abandoned on the other side of the lounge and then had to think where her car keys might be.

As she was leaving the house, the telephone was ringing. Correctly anticipating that this surgery, frantic to know where she was, she let it ring and miserably drove to work, blaming road works for her tardiness and asking Gary to bring her a cup of strong coffee.

Her surgery went rather better than she expected. Patients were sympathetic that she was late and did not overstay their welcome. One or two asked if she was alright, knowing her well enough to tell that there was something seriously amiss. The loss of eye contact, empathy, interest all spoke volumes. But to Clare, it was a relief when each consultation ended, ticking each one off from a list as it was completed.

She was drearily looking through the house call list when the phone on her desk rang. Answering it, she was surprised to hear John's voice.

'Clare, have you got a moment?'

'Yes of course,' she replied, trying to sound normal.

'Perhaps you could pop along to my surgery.'

'Of course,' she repeated. 'I'll just be a couple of minutes.'

She rushed to the toilet, feeling sick again, blaming the combination of the wine, the sleeping tablet and Gary's inability to make good coffee.

John's surgery was totally different to Clare's. The walls were magnolia and covered with dozens of family photographs - Faye, their children at all ages and now their grandchildren. The family dog featured prominently and even the cat had been captured in one admittedly rather blurred snapshot. His desk was cluttered with ornaments, some from grateful patients, others from his grandchildren; papier mache dinosaurs, clay ashtrays and souvenirs from as far apart as Blackpool and Australia. Regardless of this apparent disarray, he knew exactly where everything was and could lay his hands on a particular paper or letter in a trice. John sat in a large, old armchair. He had jettisoned his modern stylised chair as soon as they had moved into the health centre, insisting that he could not consult in anything other than the chair he had been using for years. He was sitting back in this, his hands in front of him, fingertips touching, when Clare entered. His heart gave a lurch when he saw the state that she was in. Ellie had hinted to him that all was not well at home for Clare but had refused to go into details.

'Ah, Clare, come in and sit down. Shall I get one of the girls to bring us a coffee?'

'No, I'm fine, thanks,' Clare hoped she sounded convincing.

John leaned forward, putting his elbows on the desk.

'Thank you for coming in. I know you're busy but we need to have a chat.'

'Is it about Sam?' Clare blurted. 'I know I haven't been doing much teaching recently, but Ed had said he wanted to see what it was like being a trainer, so I thought.....'

'No, it's not about Sam. He's a very capable registrar, who seems to be doing very well here after that initial worry with Alexa Thetford. If Ed wants to teach him for a bit, so long as you are overseeing it, then that's fine. You know as well as I do what training involves and your responsibilities.'

Clare felt a weight slip from her shoulders. She had been sure that this was what John had wanted to talk to her about.

'It's you I'm worried about, Clare.'

'Me?'

'Yes, you.'

Clare gazed at him, her pale face lined with worry.

'I have quite a lot to say, Clare. All of it causes me considerable distress as I know that this is completely out of character for you.'

If it were possible, Clare became even paler.

'I have been very concerned about you for some weeks now. Since you covered for Ellie when her daughter was sick. How very characteristic of you that was. Always there for everyone else, work colleague or patient, never afraid to work, loving your work, putting it –rightly or wrongly- first, above everything else in your life, including David. He's a fine man, Clare, not that you need me to tell you that.'

Clare bit her bottom lip, determined not to start crying.

'Over the last few weeks I have watched you become sadder and sadder, lose weight and lose interest in your work. You used to be the first of us here in the morning. Now you're arriving late. I'm sorry but you look a wreck. You've lost all pride in your appearance. That's not you. I've always thought how lucky I was to have two such glamorous female partners. I used to brag about it when I met my GP chums. Not any more. I wasn't born yesterday Clare. I know that something drastic is going on in your life.'

'I'm just a bit tired. That's all. I've not been sleeping well,' Clare tried her stock reply.

'There's more, Clare, I'm afraid. A patient came to see me this morning. She'd seen you yesterday. She wasn't dissatisfied with what you'd done but she was concerned by your lack of interest. She told me that you kept looking at your watch and chewing your fingers. She's seen you many times before and knows you well.'

Clare thought rapidly.

'I expect it was just a difficult surgery.'

John flashed her a quick look and continued.

'Two days ago, we received a letter of complaint about you from a Ms Felicity Lester, following a consultation in which, and I quote, you were 'rude, flippant and downright uncaring.' I know that we occasionally get complaints from patients but they are rarely about the doctor's demeanour.'

'Oh!' Clare clasped her hand to her mouth in horror. Her mouth was so dry she could barely speak.

John paused.

'I'll let you have a copy of the letter then you can draught your reply. Elliot has already acknowledged the complaint, so you can take a bit of time to think what you would like to say. Personally I would suggest that your letter takes a very apologetic tone and does not try to make up a lot of excuses. Offer to see her and talk to her if she would like, you know the sort of thing.'

Clare nodded dumbly.

'I'm finding this incredibly hard, Clare. There is something else. Before I tell you about it, I must assure you that, while I am deeply disappointed in you, I am still your friend and will do whatever I can to help you.'

Clare by now was shaking all over.

'A letter arrived at the surgery. It was addressed to the senior partner but, as it was not marked personal, it was opened, as usual by the receptionists and handed to Elliott, who passed it on to me. It's from an ex-patient called Rebecca Howarth.'

Clare let out an involuntary whimper.

'Her letter starts off well enough. She compliments us on our practice, in particular Ellie, who was apparently a great help to her in her hour of need. At this point I was rather basking in a warm glow but then I went on to read certain things which I found both distasteful and upsetting. Need I go on?'

Clare shook her head and gazed at her knees covered in her crumpled back trousers which had, she incongruously noticed a stain on the left thigh which was probably wine.

'Take my advice,' John continued. 'Have a couple of weeks off.'

'I can't go off sick,' sniffed Clare. 'I've things to do at work.'

Nothing,' John insisted emphatically, 'that we cannot do for you. Just because we're doctors, it doesn't mean that we are invincible and exempt from illnesses. Currently you do not appear fit to practise. Go away from here, sort out your problems and yourself. Give me a ring at home next week and tell me how you're getting on.'

Clare just looked at him.

'Would it be a help if I rang David and explained why I've sent you home?'

Hurriedly, Clare refused.

'Off you go.'

She stood up.

'Oh, Elliot has the copies of those letters that I promised you. Collect them before you leave, please. For goodness sake, go and have some sleep. You look washed out.'

Clare, speechless, managed a small squeak.

John softened.

'Clare, I'm still your friend. I want to help. I'm being stern with you because I know that someone has to try to save you from yourself. You can't work in this state, you know that. You'd be outraged if you came across a doctor working like this, wouldn't you?'

He got up and went to her and wrapped his arms round her, feeling her little more than skin and bone. She laid her head on his rough sports jacket, her tears drenching his neatly ironed checked shirt which smelt of a mixture of soap powder, dog and after shave. He held her gently while her sobs reverberated through both their bodies.

'Could I see Ellie?' requested Clare, blowing her nose.

'Of course you can. I'm sending you home to take some time off, not dismissing you from your job. You stay here. I'll go upstairs and send her down. Look after yourself Clare. I hope very much that you will look vastly improved when I next see you.'

Left alone, Clare rushed to the washbasin and retched. She had never before had to listen to such humiliation. The remaining, barely glowing embers of her self-esteem were now completely extinguished. That was how Ellie found her, bent over, gripping the edges of the basin with either hand, trying to take deep breaths through her nose. Ellie rushed over and put her arm around her.

'Come on Clare, come and sit down before you fall down.'

Clare allowed her to lead her back to the chair. Ellie supplied her with more tissues and also dampened some of the paper hand towel so that Clare could wipe her face.

'Have you heard what's happened now?' she moaned.

'Yes, more or less. I think John's right. You're not fit to work at the moment. I'd hoped that it would help but I was wrong. I'm sorry.'

She rubbed Clare's back.

'None of this is your fault,' Clare reassured her. 'It's all my own doing. Every last bit of it.'

She took a few moments to wipe her eyes and nose.

'And now John knows. Oh God, Elliot does as well. I've let everyone down, haven't I?'

'You couldn't let us down if you tried,' Ellie murmured comfortingly. 'Hey, that looks better now you've cleaned your face up a bit.'

Clare managed a stunted laugh.

'I can't imagine I look anything like human.'

'No, you don't but that's not what I said,' Ellie took the opportunity to try to make her laugh more.

'What's everyone going to think?'

'None the worse of you, for certain. The staff will be told that you're not well and so will the patients. John and I will have a word with Ed. What's more important is that you go home and start getting better. Look, I'll come over this evening. I'll bring Lydia and Virginia again with me. They've been so worried about you since the other day when they saw you. They need to be reassured. So that presents the ideal opportunity for you to go and do some shopping and then tidy up at home. If you do those two things you'll really feel that you've done something positive, which in itself will make you feel better. Come on, write a list. You need lots of things from basics to luxuries. Those are particularly important because, from this moment forward, you are going to put yourself first. So, spoil and pamper yourself! OK?'

The tone in Ellie's voice made it quite clear that this was a rhetorical comment.

'Get started while I go and fetch you a drink and something to eat. This is your turning point Clare. You are on the way up again.'

'I don't think I could get any lower,' agreed Clare.

'Good, because now you can keep telling yourself that you're getting better.'

If only Ellie was with me all the time, I'd be able to cope, thought Clare, reaching for a pen and piece of notepad from John's desk and starting to write.

Ellie was back in no time and presented Clare with a glass of fresh orange juice and some oatcakes.

'I thought a plain biscuit was the best idea,' she said. 'Now, how are you getting on?'

It took Clare almost half an hour to string her thoughts together into sufficiently logical sequences to be able to compile her list, even with Ellie's continual help and encouragement.

'What about toilet rolls? Don't forget that Virginia's favourite is flapjack and anything covered with chocolate will be a hit with Lydia.'

Clare obediently added to her list.

'A lovely bath oil, so that you can soak for a long time this afternoon. Have a look in the book section. You might be able to pick up a few paperbacks and then have a really good read to look forward to. Something for your tea? You've got to start eating regularly. Talking of which, have a drink of your juice and an oatcake.'

Clare did as she was told.

'Flowers!' Ellie decided. 'They'll brighten you up.'

Eventually, Ellie was satisfied with Clare's consumption of all the juice and the best part of two biscuits, plus a comprehensive list of items needed to restore Clare's house into a home. With the promise of Ellie and the twins visiting later, Clare went back to her surgery and sadly collected her belongings, before making her way down the corridor to the practice manager's office.

Elliot saw her standing in the doorway and motioned for her to come in.

'Ah, Clare, have a seat.'

'Elliot,' started Clare, 'I really don't know what to say.'

Elliot waved his hand at her.

'Clare, my dear. I suggest you say nothing. We are all united in our desire for you to get better as soon as you can. I've got those letters here for you in this envelope. There was another letter for you this morning, marked personal, so I've popped that in there too.'

'Thank you,' Clare took the large brown envelope from him. 'Everyone's been so kind to me. I don't deserve it, you know.'

'Clare, to misquote a well known phrase, "this practice needs you." With hindsight, I wish that I'd never agreed to you covering for Ellie. I should have got a locum in. So I do feel personally responsible for some of this. But you're a strong, confident person Clare and before you know it, you'll be back here, seeing patients and working as efficiently as you always have done, maybe even better. Some good will come out of this chaos, believe me.'

He held out his hand and Clare shook it. His firm grasp gave her a tiny seed of hope that he might be right. He considerately walked her across the waiting area and past the receptionists who were, as it happened, all busy with the telephone or waiting patients. Outside, he held her car door open for her and closed it carefully behind her, waving her off as she reversed out of her parking space. As she drove away, she passed Sam's car, returning to work but avoided looking at the driver.

The supermarket was pleasantly empty. Clare, still feeling the effect of Ellie's inspiration, disengaged a trolley and unfolded her list. It was not quite a fortnight since she had been in there but they had had the temerity to move everything round and Clare found bread where she expected fresh vegetables and plastic plates and mugs in the household cleaner section. Exasperated, she wandered up and down the aisles aimlessly. She managed to find flapjack and chocolate chip muffins in the bakery but breakfast cereal continued to elude her. Passing tinned soups for the third time, Clare spotted the toiletries and cheered, made a bee line for them. Triumphantly, she chose the most expensive bath bubbles and proudly selected a new nail polish, on impulse. Dawdling by the loofahs and pumice stones, conveniently placed near verruca remedies, Clare remembered that she needed more paracetamol and made her way to the medicines. She paid the pharmacist for her purchase and as she took her change, dropped part of it into the goods on display on the counter. Apologising for upsetting the display, she moved some boxes to one side in order to retrieve her two pound coins. Her eyes were drawn to the content of the boxes, highly sensitive pregnancy testing kits. Impulsively she picked one up and looked at it.

'I'll take this, please,' she motioned to the assistant.

'I'm going to post it to David, with a letter suggesting that we go and start IVF as soon as possible,' she told herself as she pushed her trolley off towards the checkout. 'If he sees this, he'll know that I'm serious about it.'

Impatiently she queued to pay, eager now to get home and carry out her decision. She crammed her shopping into various carriers, lugged them to the car and heaved them into the boot. Turning into her drive rather too quickly as usual, she came to a halt almost touching the garage door. She opened the boot and in two trips managed to transfer all the bags into the kitchen. Leaving them to one side, she extracted the pregnancy test from her handbag and put it on the table. Sickened, she saw that her purse was missing and deduced that she must have left it in the supermarket.

'Damn,' she cursed out loud.

By the telephone in the study she unearthed the directory and rang the shop who, thankfully, confirmed that her purse had been handed in and was waiting for her, if she would like to report to customer services. Rushing, Clare fled out of the house and drove as quickly as she could to reclaim it. Having lied about road works earlier in the day, she now became a victim of them and had a considerable delay at temporary traffic lights in both directions. Breathing heavily she let herself into the house again and went first to find notepaper and a large envelope and then back to the kitchen table to write her letter.

She stopped, aware of some subtle change but unable to pinpoint it. Some of the shopping had been put away, the bags neatly folded and placed in a pile. Only one person she knew did that, David.

A whirlwind tour of the house proved that she was still alone. Some more of David's clothes seemed to have disappeared. How long had he been there for? Had he just come for his clothes?

Spirits tumbling from their previous high, Clare ambled back to the kitchen and noticed a letter propped up against the pregnancy test box.

"Dear Clare,

"I needed some more clothes. I was also going to suggest that we meet, on some neutral ground to talk. But I found this and can only assume the worst. I got your messages – all fifty three of them. Please don't send any more for a while. I'll be in touch. David.

"PS – I put your frozen stuff in the freezer for you."

'Oh no, no, no!' cried Clare, the volume of her voice increasing with each expletive before she burst into tears.

She felt as though she had just been thrown from a great height. All the optimism, all the positive thoughts, all the hope hurtled into the distance at a frightening rate of acceleration. Back where she started the day, there was nothing to look forward to; everything was bad, black, and hopeless. Now there was no reason to try to make things better. Leaving the shopping in the bags, not caring if anything needed to be in the fridge, she sloped back into the lounge and crept under the duvet. The curtains were still drawn enough to make the room dismally dark, time indeterminate which was just how she liked it. At least she could just fester there, not think about work, and be on her own, feeling the decay seep into her very being.

Clare switched on the television and escaped into the fantasy world of an American forensic scientist where, after several predictable twists, truth inevitably won the day.

Recklessly dismissive of the day, Clare made strong black coffee and poured herself a glass of wine. Drinking the latter down in two gulps, she took the bottle back with her. Oscillating violently she alternately hated David and wanted him so badly she thought she would burst. More wine did not improve the situation and she sobbed unreservedly at an advert featuring two kittens, one of which had more to eat than the other.

Chapter Twenty Three

Clare must have dozed off because she woke a little later, thirsty and with a headache. She had no idea what time it was but found, after checking on the television that it was late afternoon. She stretched out under her duvet and then recoiled into a ball as the events of the day came back to taunt her. Cold and shivery, she wandered into the kitchen to make a hot drink. As she stirred it, Clare noticed the envelope she had brought from Elliot's office and picked it up, looking at it apprehensively. She took it back with her and ensconced herself under the covers again, sipping at her tea. The envelope sat menacingly on the table in front of her, tempting her to open it and read the contents. Part of her longed to, the rest of her was too afraid. Ellie and the twins were due soon so Clare decided to wait and open it while they were there. Ellie's presence would make Clare feel brave enough to read the damning contents and Ellie, as ever would be a tower of support and good advice.

Content with her decision, or perhaps merely appeased because she had devised an excuse to postpone looking at the letters, Clare sat back to have her drink. It felt comforting as it slipped down her throat and the heat from the mug breathed some warmth into her mottled, thin fingers as they protruded from the baggy sleeves of her jumper. Well aware that she had promised Ellie that she would tidy up before her arrival, Clare reluctantly went back to start putting the shopping away. She was quite surprised at the number of carrier bags on the table as she really could not recall buying that much. Regardless, she put tins and packets in cupboards, fruit in a bowl and dairy produce in the fridge. Reaching out for the penultimate bag, she pulled it towards her and looked inside. The contents were like a cornucopia of pharmaceutical items –boxes of tablets, inhalers, half used tubes and tubs of creams, a sticky bottle of laxative medicine and some suppositories. Baffled, Clare pulled the other bag over and discovered disposable gloves, dressings and bandages and lastly

237

insulin. Suddenly recognising the latter, Clare remembered Mrs Sparrow asking her to dispose of her husband's unused drugs and how she had just dumped them in the boot of her car. Carefully, she put everything back in the bags and left them by the kitchen door, for her to take back to the pharmacy the next time she went out.

Turning to the sink, Clare fetched dirty mugs from the lounge, plus her wine glass and washed and dried them all, feeling very virtuous. She wiped down the worktops, draining board and washing up bowl. Using one of the clean plates she arranged flapjacks and chocolate chip muffins thereon and placed this on the now empty table so that Lydia and Virginia could tuck in as soon as they arrived. Thinking that the muffins did look quite appetising, Clare ate a few mouthfuls of one, then another, enjoying the sweetness, the light texture and the richness of the solid pieces of chocolate. Almost immediately, she broke out in a sweat, felt faint and her stomach reacted violently causing a precipitate rush to the cloakroom where she vomited most of them back and had to kneel on her heels in front of the toilet, as if in some bizarre act of adulation until the violent contractions of her guts subsided.

'Oh I feel dreadful,' Clare sobbed, not daring to move from her genuflective state for fear of further vomiting. But as the intensity of the nausea started to subside, she gingerly stood up, moving in slow motion to splash water onto her face and rinse her mouth out. Keeping her head down she carefully avoided looking in the mirror, unable to face the image that would look back at her if she did.

With a deep breath she tried to summon up some of the determination she had not to let Ellie down and Clare ventured back into the lounge. She surveyed the scene before her with despair and more than a little shame. Hardly knowing where to start, she shook out the duvet and then folded it, fairly neatly, leaving it on the settee with the intention of taking it back up to the bedroom the next time she went.

Fatigued after this simple task, Clare found herself unable to decide what to do next, whether to dust, tidy or vacuum. Frustrated by her failure to make even a simple decision such as that, she gave up and sat down and flicked lethargically through the television channels.

The telephone rang, making her jump and Clare was tempted to ignore it and let the answer machine pick up any message. But, as she still had a microscopic flicker of hope that it might be David, she went to answer it.

'Hello Clare, it's Ellie. Are you alright?'

'Hi Ellie. I guess so.'

'Have you been shopping?'

'Yes but I left my purse in the supermarket and had to go back for it.'

'Well done about the shopping. You did really well. Look, I'm really sorry, but we're not going to be able to come round after all.'

Clare felt rejected.

'The girls have gone to a party at a friend's and Ian's desperate to take me to look at the new pony he's thinking of buying. We did think we might go out for a meal later; you'd be welcome to join us.'

'Oh,' the disappointment in Clare's voice was undisguised.

'I'm really sorry,' repeated Ellie.

'Not to worry,' Clare tried to sound bright and convincing.

'Would you like to come with us? I said I'd ring Ian when I'd spoken to you.'

'No thanks.'

'Would you like to come over tomorrow and stay the night?' Ellie suggested, trying to inspire some enthusiasm in her friend.

'Maybe.'

'Clare, you sound very down and flat. Has something happened?'

'Not really.'

'Tell me, I know there's something,' Ellie persisted.

'I just hoped that you'd read Becca's letter with me. But it can wait,' Clare whispered, feeling pathetic.

'We can do that this weekend, I promise. It's probably not a good idea to do it today as you've had a difficult time. You'll do better after a good night's sleep.'

'Whatever.'

'What else is wrong?' interrogated Ellie, perceptively.

'Oh, it's nothing.'

'Clare,' Ellie was getting impatient, 'you are making this really hard going.'

There was a long silence in which the only indication Ellie had that Clare was still on the other end of the line was the sound of her catching her breath.

'David came round,' she finally announced.

'That sounds like a good thing, surely,' Ellie said, emphatically.

'It might have been,' began Clare, going on to explain about the pregnancy test.

'Oh dear,' Ellie commiserated.

'Ellie, every single time I try to do something to repair all the damage, I just end up making things even worse. I'm so fed up; I really don't know why I bother any more.'

Ellie could hear Clare starting to cry.

'Please don't talk like that, Clare.' There was a stern edge to Ellie's voice. 'Write to David now and explain. He just jumped to all the wrong conclusions. He'll probably laugh when he reads what he's done. Do it now and then go and post it this evening.'

'But I don't know where he is.'

'Send it to the hospital. He'll get it on Monday then, possibly even tomorrow, if he goes in at the weekend. You'll feel better if you write to him.'

'I doubt it,' Clare replied negatively.

'Please do it,' Ellie urged her.

'I'll think about it,' Clare said finally.

Ellie spent several more minutes trying to cheer Clare up but met with little success. Clare even refused to commit to the offer of an overnight stay at Ellie's. Feeling exasperated, Ellie promised to ring first thing in the morning, stressing that they would all be very pleased if Clare were to come and visit. After various fond remarks, aimed to make Clare feel wanted and cared about, Ellie rang off. Seconds later she picked up the telephone again and tapped in a number.

Deflated, Clare sighed deeply and dramatically, wondering what to do. Any enthusiasm she had had for tidying up had evaporated and been replaced by apathy. The weekend loomed ahead promising nothing apart from frightening loneliness. She did not want to go and stay at Ellie's again, feeling that they had only invited her out of pity, that Ellie was merely trying to make up for letting her down this evening. She suspected that they hadn't wanted her to join them for a meal at all but were too polite not to ask her. In fact as her thoughts ricocheted from side to side down the path of self destruction, she imagined that Ellie's excuse for this evening was a complete fabrication, devised so that she could avoid spending any more time with her worthless and miserable colleague. Hadn't Ellie said something about the twins being upset last time they saw Clare? Doubtless then, their mother would not want to expose them further to such a loathsome person as Clare. She, Clare, could see them now, in her mind, all sitting round their kitchen table, relieved at having extricated themselves from the burden of visiting.

Returning to the settee, Clare sat and reached for the open bottle of wine that still stood on the table before her and drank from it. Despite the protestations from her stomach, she continued to take mouthfuls, pausing only to force each swallow. Her eye fell on the envelope from the surgery. She picked it up and opened it, hands trembling. Inside were two letters and one unopened envelope. Steeling herself, ineffectively, she read the first letter which was from Felicity Lester. On thick, expensive notepaper, it was meticulously typed, succinct and signed with a flamboyant signature at the bottom. Her heart raced in response to the adrenalin coursing round her arteries as words like 'appalled,' 'blatantly rude and hostile,' 'unprofessional' and 'uncaring' leapt out at her from the contents. She had seldom felt so ashamed in her entire life. Putting this to one side, Clare moved on to the letter from Becca. Much as she did not want to read it, there was some irresistible compulsion making her do it. In contrast to the first letter, it was long; over four sides of A4 paper, handwritten in large, round, almost childish script but the contents were far from the muddled and unreasoned ravings of a troubled individual with mental health problems. Carefully constructed and very well written, she had begun, as John had said, with praise for the surgery and gratitude for Ellie. What followed though was a horribly accurate account of what had happened before finishing off with a tirade of abuse about Clare, including further comments about her unprofessional behaviour. The more she read, the more distraught Clare became. She was shaking violently all over, as if freezing. Grabbing the duvet from next to her, she roughly pulled it around her. She could not believe what she had just read, yet at the same time she knew that Becca's comments were true and justified. If only she had had the opportunity to talk to Becca before she left Lambdale, then this letter could have been averted, leaving work blissfully ignorant of her deplorable behaviour. Memories of that evening reared up in her thoughts like wild and angry stallions. She screwed her eyes up tight and put her hands over her ears but nothing would make them go away. More wine was consumed, she turned the volume on the television up loud and tried to concentrate on a soap but there were louder voices in her head, mocking, derisory, accusatory.

'Stop, please stop,' she screamed.

Somehow, she calmed down a little, enough to get her tears under control and listen to the inanities on the television and there she stayed, barely moving for what seemed like hours. The bottle of wine was finished but she had fetched a replacement, waddling across the room to the sideboard, not caring whether it was white or red, wearing her duvet like a voluminous cloak. Programmes finished, others started but they all merged into one as far as Clare was concerned.

It was dark outside and in, save for the eerie shimmering from the television. Stiff and achey, Clare uncurled and stretched out her legs to lie down on the settee. In doing so she knocked off one of the cushions which in turn, sent her letters floating to the floor. She picked them up, glancing at them and feeling a new surge of pain. There amongst them was the third letter, still sealed in its envelope. She peeled this open and not wanting to see the contents tried to squint inside to read the address of the sender. This required assuming an uncomfortable and twisted position in order to let enough illumination from the television allow her to see 'Jarvis, Jarvis and Catten.'

Hurriedly, Clare slapped the envelope shut and literally threw it across the room where it disappeared into the blackness behind one of the armchairs. Having two letters of complaint already was more than enough and a letter from a local firm of solicitors was more than likely to herald another.

'I can't take any more of this,' Clare cried angrily, withdrawing into her cocoon again and pulling it up over her head. Stilted laughter poured into the room. To Clare it seemed they were laughing at her and she ferreted around until she found the remote control and switched off the volume. That was a definite improvement but the light continued to annoy her so with one further finger movement, she plunged the room into darkness.

Half dozing, half awake, her thoughts persisted in spiralling downwards, becoming increasingly tortuous and black. She felt like an animal in a tiny cage, being teased and tormented by demons poking their fingers through the bars at her. She had no strength to fight back or stick up for herself. The more she tried to, the demons became larger and the cage smaller. In her mind she went over and over and over the things that had happened since the beginning of August, so much so that she could barely remember the time before that when she thought that everything was perfect. Though of course it couldn't have been because if it had, then none of this would have occurred and she would be sitting with David either on that very settee or maybe in a restaurant or pub, smiling, sharing confidences, making plans, holding hands.

I need to sleep, Clare thought. I am just so tired I can't think straight.

She summoned up some energy and went to the toilet, stopping in the kitchen on the way back to get a glass of water, her mouth rancid from no food and too much wine. The fluorescent lighting hurt her eyes at first and as she became accustomed to it inevitably her attention was caught by the pregnancy test, sitting smugly on the table unaware of the trouble it had caused. Clare realised that she had not written to David to explain but knew that she could not do it now. Perhaps in the morning but then again, perhaps not. What, after all, was the point?

Clare tried to imagine what it would have been like if they had had a family. Without a doubt David would have been a brilliant father. Fun but firm, always having time for his children, totally involved in their upbringing, teaching them everything he knew but encouraging them to be individuals. She would have been the doting mother, too soft, giving in to them, never wanting to upset them or see them unhappy.

Automatically she concluded that this would be another area in which she would have been a disaster which was only to be expected really as she had failed in her marriage and now at work.

Idly, she read the back of the box, thinking in passing how incredible it was that a woman could find out whether she was pregnant or not so soon after missing a period. Which was when an idea came into her head that was too harrowing to consider?

Irrationally, she tried to think it through. For days now she had had no appetite. Recurrent nausea and lethargy governed her waking moments. She had vomited twice that day. Her last period was when? She couldn't remember and since she had given up on the prospect of conceiving spontaneously with David, she had stopped writing any dates down in her diary.

'I can't be,' she breathed. 'But what if I am? It has to be Sam's. There is no other possibility, even though David and I did.....'

Clare pummelled both her breasts and convinced herself that they felt quite tender. Not only that but she could feel the sickness returning and worrying twinges in her lower abdomen. Her body sagged in hopelessness, drained by the perpetual motion of her mind.

Now at the nadir of her gloom, she was unable to see any atom of hope whatsoever. If, as she suspected, she was pregnant with Sam's child, there was no possible way that David would come back to her. He had his pride and although he had enormous powers of forgiveness, this would be too much for him, as it would indeed for anyone. To contemplate living on her own and bringing up a baby, conceived in such a moment of madness was an anathema to Clare. Her work would suffer; what little hope she had of re-establishing good relationships with people like John, Faye and Elliot would fizzle out completely so she would have to resign, before she was asked to leave, move away, and look for somewhere to live and for a job. If the baby looked like its father, she would be reminded on a daily basis of her misdemeanours and how she had ruined so many peoples' lives.

Clare looked around her at the chic fitted kitchen that she had chosen, David acquiescing to her every whim, oblivious of cost. It was the same throughout the house, he had always been so patient and understanding over her design ideas, never being disparaging or critical but merely commenting that if it made Clare happy then it did the same for him.

'I don't deserve any of this,' Clare spoke out loud. 'I have let everyone down. I have lost the person I love more than I have ever loved anyone before. I am so stupid that I have upset my partners by my sleazy behaviour which, if it becomes more widely known will paint both me and the practice in a very bad light. Because of my crass thoughtlessness and weak-will, I have sent Becca to the brink of madness and now even Ellie, who I thought was my ally, does not want to come round and see me. They all hate me and I deserve it. I am so tired, I haven't the strength to fight this any more. There is no way that things will ever get better and what's more I don't know if I can summon up the energy to care.

'I must sleep, I'm so so tired.'

Repeatedly saying these words, as though it was some sort of mantra, Clare hoped that perhaps they would exert some sort of hypnotic effect on her. Despondent that she felt no sign of even slight drowsiness appearing, Clare resolved that she must try any solution to help herself achieve the state of oblivion which she so yearned for. Determinedly, she went through to the study and rummaged through her doctor's bag, looking for some sleeping tablets. There were none left. Incensed, she looked for tranquilisers as a second best; they might at least, if she took enough, relax her enough to initiate sleep and then hopefully some blessed rest would follow. Again, there were none left. She remembered giving her last one to an acutely anxious patient in the throes of a panic attack two days previously. Having made a note to remind her to restock her bag, so much had happened that she had completely forgotten about it.

Disconsolately, she headed back to the kitchen, catching sight of the bags of unused drugs from Mr Sparrow. Surely there was bound to be something in there that she could take.

Clare picked up the two carriers and tipped out the contents onto the table. Blood pressure pills, diuretics, breathing pills, laxatives; she carefully read labels and arranged them in piles once they had been dismissed. Bandages, wipes, inhalers, none of these were any good. Becoming more frantic as she searched, convinced that someone with so many pathologies must be on sedatives of one sort or another, Clare frustrated, angrily pushed aside open packets of dressings as they spilled out onto the table. All that remained was Mr Sparrow's insulin. Two types, long and short acting, lay in front of her. As soon as she saw it, Clare knew what she had to do. It would guarantee sleep, peace of mind and escape. What more could she ask for?

Mind made up, it was a surprisingly calm Clare who went back to the study, opened up her doctor's bag for the last time and extracted the small box of equipment that she used for taking blood samples. Taking this, she went, via the kitchen, where she picked up the insulin, to her place of security on the settee. She switched the television back on and turned the volume to a whisper. There was a film on, she had no idea what it was about but there was a lot of sunshine, smiling faces and happy children milling in and out of a garden which was full of flowers and butterflies. It was just where she would love to be.

Clare opened the small Tupperware box and found exactly what she was looking for. She opened the packaging containing a syringe and attached a needle to it. With self-control that seemed the antithesis of all her indecision, Clare placed a tourniquet around her left arm, above the elbow. She plunged the needle into the cartridge of insulin and drew up the contents into her syringe.

Palpating the vein in the crook of her elbow, Clare glanced around her, at the home she loved so much. It was sullied by the letters of complaint, including the unread one which she just knew was more bad news.

Clare closed her eyes briefly and breathed deeply, in through her nose and out through her mouth. At least I'll be asleep soon, she thought. She allowed pictures of her favourite patients to dance in front of her eyes, led by Prudence Kerfoot who was saying,

'If only you'd come to see me doctor.......;

Ellie replaced her suggesting

'You must come and stay with us this weekend.....'

Ellie's face became blurred and then metamorphosed into John, looking disappointed, side by side with Elliot who was trying to be nice. But they turned away and Clare could hear them talking about her, discussing how they could ask her to leave the practice.

Then there was David, arriving at the house, finding the pregnancy test, shaking his head and leaving, while Sam was looking on, laughing, drinking champagne, reaching out to touch her.

Clare positioned the needle point over her vein and then coolly punctured the skin and entered the vein. Drawing back, clouds of blood ballooned into the barrel of the syringe, confirming that the site was correct.

'I'll be asleep soon,' Clare told herself and slowly, without the tiniest sign of a tremor, injected the contents of the syringe into herself.

246

She laughed for the first time in so long as she carefully replaced the protective cover over the needle. Cuddling down, she pulled the duvet up to her chin and concentrated on the television. Feeling colder and trembling, she drew her knees up to her chest as sweat broke out on her face and consciousness started to fade away, her last vision being that of David standing over her, then kneeling beside her and holding her tight.

Chapter Twenty Four

Irritated, Clare felt something annoying her left arm and tried to brush it away.

'Calm down, dear,' said a pleasant and melodic voice, 'that's your drip. It's helping you get better.'

Clare tried to open her eyes but the lids were heavy and did not want to obey her request. Reluctantly they did and she looked from side to side, confused. With no idea where she was, she tried to make sense of her surroundings. She realised that she was in bed, but not her own bed as the sheets were crisp, white and slightly rough, as opposed to her soft Egyptian cotton in various shades of blue. There was a bed side table which, even in her confusion, she recognised as standard National Health Service issue, with the ubiquitous paper bag stuck to the side of it with tape to collect rubbish. Looking upwards and to the left, there was a large bag of intravenous fluid which, if she followed the path of the giving set, seemed to be running into her. Turning her head slightly to her right, Clare was greeted by a smiling face, evidently a nurse, who was taking her pulse.

'Hello, Clare. How are you feeling?' the nurse asked solicitously.

'I've the most dreadful headache,' Clare heard herself reply.

'Would you like something for it?'

Clare's head nodded.

'Where am I?' she asked.

'On Patterdale ward.'

'In hospital?' Clare was incredulous.

'Yes, sweetheart. You've been very ill, but you're getting better all the time now.'

The nurse, who had the most reassuringly caring features beamed at her.

'I don't remember anything,' Clare stated, honestly.

'In the circumstances, that's probably all for the best. Now, I'm going to get you a drink and something for that headache of yours. Then I want you to go back to sleep and rest. We'll talk some more when you wake up, ok?'

Clare nodded and watched the nurse departing from her room, her figure neat and business like in her dark blue uniform. Turning her head to her other side, Clare saw bright blue sky out of the window in her room. She closed her eyes, only to open them again as the nurse came bustling back in.

'Look what's arrived for you!' she exclaimed and Clare saw that she was almost invisible behind the hugest bunch of flowers she had ever seen.

'Gosh,' Clare agreed, wondering why she deserved them and who had sent them.

'Here, take these painkillers. I just need to check your pulse and blood pressure while I'm here. Can I have an arm please?'

Clare obliged, all the time looking at the flowers, which had been put on the table at the foot of her bed. She felt the cuff of the sphygmomanometer tighten around her arm and then deflate.

'Mmm, a little low but I'll keep an eye on it. Here's some water, have your tablets and then close your eyes again.'

Dutifully, Clare swallowed the tablets plus some extra water and a small glass of juice that the nurse had produced from somewhere. Feeling deliciously soporific, she gratefully surrendered and drifted off into the most peaceful sleep she had had for weeks.

When she woke, she felt better, more alert, her headache clearing. Taking care of the drip in her arm, she pulled herself up a little onto the pillows, which turned out to be harder than she expected as she discovered electrocardiogram leads burrowing under the bedclothes and her nightdress to attach onto her chest. She reached out for a glass of water and sipped it, trying to remember what had happened.

'Well, you're looking a lot better,' commented the nurse, who appeared at the door to perform some more routine observations on Clare. 'Has that headache gone?'

'More or less, thank you,' Clare smiled.

'Do you fancy something to eat?'

'No, not at the moment. A cup of tea would be lovely though.'

'Let me just check your drip and one or two other things and then I'll get you one.' The nurse, who introduced herself as Jenny, filled in various charts at the bottom of Clare's bed, left the room and returned in no time with a mug of tea.

Clare received it gratefully.

'What happened, Jenny?' she asked.

Jenny came and sat on the bed beside her.

'You gave yourself some insulin, dear. You must have been so very unhappy. Fortunately someone found you and rang for an ambulance.'

'Oh,' gasped Clare, putting her hand over her mouth.

'Dr Stephenson will be in later to see you. She'll help you fill in all the gaps. She's been very worried about you. Well, we all have – the nurses, your family and friends.'

Clare felt embarrassed and rather ashamed.

'Who are those flowers from?' she changed the subject.

'Here's a little card with them,' replied Jenny, leaning over to reach it and handing it over for Clare to read.

'They're from everyone at work. How kind of them.'

'People care an awful lot about you, Clare,' mused Jenny, rearranging some of the blooms which looked as if they might topple out of the vase.

'I feel I've let them all down, so badly though,' mumbled Clare.

'Nonsense,' Jenny was brisk in her response. 'What you've got to do is concentrate on getting better. A few days and you'll be able to go home. Keep looking forward to that.'

Jenny stood up and straightened the bedclothes which were rumpled from where she had been sitting.

'I'll be back shortly,' she promised.

Clare relaxed back into the pillows and tried to piece together the sequence of events that led up to her current position. Some facts came back to her, mostly unsavoury, the rest remained elusive. A flurry of activity entering her room made her look up.

'Clare,' cried Ellie, her arms full of magazines, books and a basket of fruit. She deposited them all at the bottom of the bed and rushed to hug her friend.

'Careful,' Clare laughed as she almost became disengaged from her drip.

'How are you? I came yesterday but they wouldn't let you have any visitors.'

'I'm feeling almost normal, thanks. Thank you for all these things, Ellie and for the flowers that work sent.'

'We wanted you to know that we were all thinking of you and missing you,' Ellie told her. 'I've got some cards here somewhere amongst this lot. One's from work. Everyone's signed it. The others are from Lydia and Virginia and Smudge. It's not everyday that you get a card from a pony!'

'I'm quite overcome.'

Clare opened a giant, vividly yellow envelope and produced an equally huge get well card. Inside were lovely messages written by everyone at work, from the senior partner to the cleaners. She took some time to read them, laughing softly as she did so. More seriously she scanned through them again.

'I see Sam hasn't signed this,' she observed.

'No, agreed Ellie, 'he hasn't. But I've some good news on that front. Matt Smillie rang about him. I took the call as I was the only one in the building at the time. Doug Smedley is keen to take Sam for his final three months, so I told him it was an excellent idea. He'll be leaving at the end of the month.'

'Thank goodness,' Clare was more relieved than she could imagine.

'Clare,' Ellie began, suddenly serious, 'I just wanted to say how sorry I am that I didn't come and see you last Friday evening, after I'd promised I would. I feel responsible. If I'd been there for you, then perhaps this wouldn't have happened. I had no idea that you were feeling so depressed.'

'It's not your fault, Ellie. Please don't feel bad. Was it you who found me? Apparently someone did.'

Ellie took Clare's hand and grinned at her.

'No, that was David.'

'David?'

Ellie nodded vigorously.

'How did he know?'

'I rang him after I spoke to you. I couldn't bear it any longer. I had to explain to him about the pregnancy test at the very least. He promised me he would go round and see you straight away.'

One of Clare's lost memories was restored with a sickening jolt.

'But Ellie, I think I might actually be pregnant,' Clare told her.

'No you're not. I've spoken to Dr Stephenson to try to help her as much as I could. They've done a pregnancy test and an ultrasound scan –they're both negative.'

Clare went white with happiness and relief.

'I was so sure,' she shrugged.

'You were desperately low, Clare. You couldn't think sensibly. All you could see was things going wrong and getting worse.'

'That's true enough,' nodded Clare. Then, 'have you seen David?'

'Yes,' affirmed Ellie.

How is he?'

'Worried about you,' Ellie informed her.

'Is he angry with me?' Clare worried.

'He's been by your side since he found you. The nurses sent him home to shower and change his clothes. I expect he'll be back soon.'

'I feel nervous about seeing him,' Clare admitted.

'You'll be fine. Here, do you want to brush your hair?' Ellie produced the necessary from her bag.

'Thanks. Ugh, it needs washing, urgently!' Clare could feel her hair sticking to the side of her head.

'That sounds more like you!' Ellie chuckled.

They sat and talked for a while longer. Ellie chatted about her family who had all promised to visit just as soon as she was ready for such an onslaught. Carefully steering clear of anything relating to work, she told Clare about the new pony, Jester, a dun gelding, reputedly unflappable, who was due to arrive very soon. The twins were ecstatic and so excited that they couldn't sleep and were consequently driving their parents to distraction.

'I'd better go, Clare. The nurse said I wasn't to tire you. It's wonderful to see you looking and sounding more like the real you. I'll come back tomorrow.'

Ellie leant over and kissed Clare on the cheek before crossing the room, turning and blowing her a further kiss. Clare waved back, the giving set of her drip wriggling in unison.

Alone again, Clare opened the cards from the twins and of course, the one from Smudge, which included details of the pending new pony. Their cards were all hand made, covered with drawings of galloping horses, being ridden by girls with extremely long hair. Clare balanced them, albeit precariously, on her bedside locker. She re-read the messages inside the card from the surgery, humbled by the words, having had no idea that she was so popular.

Sliding down as best she could, she was delighted to fall asleep easily. After so many weeks of insomnia and early morning waking, this proclivity for sleep was luxurious. The dreams were still bizarre and energetic but they were different in that she seemed to be able to recognise them for what they were and not be distressed by them. She woke to the sound of cutlery rattling together and the first thing she saw was a new nurse, putting a tray on her table.

'Hello Clare, you've had another good sleep. I've brought you some tea.'

'Thank you, stuttered Clare, still a bit groggy.

Under a metal lid, which reminded her of school dinners, Clare found two sausages, a scoop of mashed potato and some baked beans. For dessert there were two cream crackers, a piece of bright orange cheese and a melting pat of butter, all squashed together in Clingfilm. A banana completed her feast. To her surprise, the sausages were very good and before long, the plate was virtually clean. She buttered her biscuits and attempted to cut the cheese with her blunt knife. Ending up with chunks of disparate sizes, she then arranged them as best she could on top of the biscuits and ate them leaning over the plate, not wanting to have a bed full of crumbs.

Full, she put the banana to one side, planning to eat it later and wondered if she could get out of bed to go to the toilet. Still attached to medically equipment, this was going to be tricky, so she rang her bell and waited for some help. A young male nurse popped his head round the door.

'I'm sorry,' apologised Clare, 'but I'm desperate to go to the toilet.'

'Just coming,' he promised.

He duly returned with the ward sister, who competently unhooked Clare from the ecg machine and instructed her how to push the drip stand with her left hand. Horrified at how wobbly her legs felt, Clare was immeasurably glad to have the help of two nurses. Bladder empty, which afforded considerable relief, Clare felt exhausted by the short walk back to her room. She stopped at the door, breathing heavily, gazing at the floor.

'Oh look, you've a visitor,' the male nurse tried to encourage her to keep going.

'I'm so weak,' observed Clare before she looked up and gasped.

David was sitting on the chair by the bed. He looked pale and tired. At the sight of Clare, he jumped up and came over to help, relieving the ward sister as he guided his wife back to her bed.

As soon as she was settled again, he picked up her hand and kissed it.

'Hello Clare.'

Clare could not speak. Tears poured down her cheeks. She was unsure whether they were tears of sadness or joy, either way; there was nothing she could do to stop them.

'I've missed you so much, Clare,' David spoke softly. 'Please don't cry.'

'I'm so sorry David,' she sobbed.

'I know, so am I. Try not to get too upset.'

Clare gulped and blew her nose.

'It's been so awful without you,' she went on.

'Let's try to put it all in the past.' Clare felt she had never heard a voice as soothing as David's.

'But so much has happened,' persisted Clare.

'Ellie's told me all about it. I don't need to know any more.'

'But…'

'I mean it. I know about Sam and the fact that he's leaving the practice. You need never see him again. Ellie also mentioned that you'd been upset by some letters at work. I found some them in the lounge at home. I read the ridiculously pompous one. Don't worry; we'll concoct a reply that will satisfy her. I did not read the long one from Becca. I felt that was private for you. When you're better I suggest that you reply to it and then leave things be. She'll be fine. She's a lovely girl who'd just been fooled into thinking that she was in love with that conceited, irresponsible guy, who enjoyed seeing you both turn into his victims.'

Unsure, Clare held out her hand to him and was amazed that, without any hesitation, he wrapped it up in both of his hands. Suddenly, with his help, she could see that there was a way out of the black hole she had fallen into.

'There was another letter as well, David. From some solicitors. I didn't dare read it. I was so sure that it was another complaint.'

David looked pensive.

'Oh yes,' he agreed. 'I've read that one. In fact I've actually brought it with me. I thought you should see it.'

Letting go Clare's hand he twisted round to where his jacket was hung over the back of his chair and fished a piece of paper out of the inside pocket.

'Here,' he offered it to Clare.

'I don't think I can, David,' she said doubtfully.

'Trust me,' he promised her, looking intently into her eyes. She gazed back before turning her head away and unfolding the letter.

David watched her as she read, seeing the fear seep away from her face as she progressed down the page, by which time he was smiling broadly.

'How about that!' he exclaimed.

'I'm speechless,' Clare declared. 'Prudence Kerfoot has left me one thousand pounds in her will.....'

'For being the best doctor that she could ever have hoped to have,' finished David.

'I don't think I was though, certainly not at the end,' Clare was full of misgivings.

'Clare, you did more for that woman than any other GP would have done. Accept this with grace – you deserve it.'

'I'm amazed,' Clare read the letter again to check.

David laughed and helped himself to a handful of grapes. They sat in silence, each lost in their own thoughts. Clare listened to him munching and considered the day's events, the flowers, the cards, Ellie and most important of all, David. It seemed so natural having him sitting next to her.

'Will you come home David?' she asked, tentatively.

'I think that would be for the best,' he replied nonchalantly. 'I've already taken my things back, if it's ok with you.'

Clare beamed.

'Of course it is. Do you think everything will ever go back to the way it was?'

David regarded her seriously.

'I certainly hope not.'

Clare felt panic start to rise in her throat until David continued.

'There was very definitely something wrong before. I think that, given time, you will recover completely and then, if we're blessed with good fortune, and there's absolutely no reason why we shouldn't be, you and I will go from strength to strength and end up happier than we have been for years.'

'That sounds good to me,' Clare remarked, contentedly.

'Let's keep our fingers crossed then.' David squeezed her hand.

They smiled conspiratorially at each other, just like they used to.

'Shall we go for IVF?' suggested Clare.

'Let's just take one step at a time.' David leaned across and very gently kissed her on the lips.

The End